Book One of t

M000013028

Crumbling Walls
By
Laura Strandt

Orange Publishing
Strasburg, PA

Thank You to those who made this possible...

My husband, Chris and daughter, Abby, who were always willing to be quiet while I wrote. I love you tons!

My mom and dad, Joe and Lois, who are truly awesome beyond all comprehension.

My cousin Dave Measel, who said if I didn't publish this book, it'd be a crime ... and then decided we might as well do it ourselves.

My first readers, who took a chance to read a pile of paper, which, by the end, had tire marks, food stains and smelled of gasoline:

My nieces Sarah and Ashley Mangrum, Dave Measel (Davy), my mom and my Aunt Carol, my mother-in-law, Marilyn Strandt, Sarah Rowse and Benny.

And finally, the people who helped us fund our little venture:

Chris, Joe and Lois, Marilyn, Ken, Kim, Marvin and Tracey, Bee, Kelly, Katherine, Jessica, Aunt Carol, Christina and Peter

Crumbling Walls

Orange Publishing

No part of this publication may be reproduced, stored in a retrieval system or transmitted in any form or by any means including electronic, mechanical, photocopying, recording or otherwise without the express written approval of the publisher. For information regarding permission please write to Orange Publishing, LLC, 102 Miller St, Strasburg, PA 17579.

Library of Congress Control Number: 2013930162

ISBN: 978-0-9887480-0-2 (paperback)
ISBN: 978-0-9887480-1-9 (eBook)

Printed in the U.S.A.
First Printing – January, 2013

About the Author

Laura's Version

I love books, plain and simple.

After devouring them for decades and telling stories to myself for years, I decided to take up the NaNoWriMo challenge in 2006 to try my hand at actually writing things down.

Dave, my cousin/best friend/partner in crime for the last 36 years, then spent our two-week vacation to the Grand Canyon reading it.

Fast forward to 2012. I still love books and thanks to NaNoWriMo, I have written six more (so far).

I'm a children's librarian by day (and some evenings) but by night (and lunch hour), I am a writer. It's totally the most perfect thing in the world: deadlines, writer's block and all, including Dave's hounding to change a paragraph, chapter or whole character personality because it's crap.

I wouldn't change a second of it and hope that you'll read my book over and over again, so, like many of my own books, it needs liberal amounts of duct tape to hold the cover on and the pages in.

Dave's Version

From a very early age, books and reading were very important to Laura Strandt. As a child she would sit up reading Little House on the Prairie with her mom before bed. During her adolescence years she discovered the joy and excitement that can be found in stories such as the *Chronicles of Narnia*, *Choose Your Own Adventure* series, and the *Dark is Rising* series. She was an early fan of the *Harry Potter* series before it became the world-wide phenomena that it is today. It was clear to everyone who knew her where she belonged and upon graduation from college she entered her career as a children's librarian.

While reading was a passion of hers from very early on, writing didn't start until later in life. Originally she wrote for fun on fan fiction websites for one of her favorite shows ever, *X-Files*. Here she discovered that not only did she enjoy writing, she was good at it. This would lead her to taking up the challenge presented by National Novel Writing Month (nanowrimo.com) in 2006. This effort would produce the earliest draft of what would become *Crumbling Walls*. The rest, as they say, is history.

Prologue

As she slowly pulled the door shut, the shaft of light from the top of the stairs shrank, until the only thing illuminated were the two fingers of his left hand.

The door clicked shut a moment later, plunging him into complete darkness and for the first time, showing her the light.

Chapter 1

He'd passed by the house at least twice a day for the past two weeks and, whenever she was there, he wished she would glance his way so he'd have an excuse to stop.

Being just 15, he didn't have the courage, gumption or enough of what some would call an approaching sense of self, to talk to her first.

Until now.

Because now he had a reason.

Oh, it was a crappy, concocted, 'set the chain of events in motion' kind of reason, but again, being 15, he thought it was pure gold.

He would pretend his tire was going flat.

It was simple. It was ideal. It was perfect … and also rather stupid.

In the quick and easy act of leaning forward to stare at the tire, he managed to over-balance, tip sideways, knock into the small picket fence surrounding the front yard and take out several small snapdragon plants.

This, of course, not only made her look up, but stand quickly, causing the pile of papers in her lap to scatter all over the porch.

He righted himself quickly, turned a lurid shade of red in embarrassment and said the first thing that popped in his brain, still managing to stick to his story, "Sorry about your flowers. I, um, I've got a flat tire."

After this, he just stood, wondering how odd it would be if he began banging his head on the concrete and wailing in sheer idiocy at his previous and hopefully last statement ever.

The girl, standing stock still on the porch steps, didn't come over, didn't open her mouth, didn't even seem to breathe. She simply stared until the boy thought it better for everyone if he just got the hell out of there and found a new bike route.

Giving a small, pathetic wave by way of apology for disturbing her, he turned and continued down the street, cursing himself when he remembered that the reason for him stopping in the first place was a broken bike. Yeah, he was damn sure he'd blown it before it had even begun.

●●●

Later that night, he sat at his family's dinner table long after his brothers had run off to various summer entertainments: bike-riding, evening jobs, video games. He sat so long that his mother came over and tried to pry out of him exactly why he'd been so quiet. But prying tonight would be fruitless. And soon, his mother just shook her head, ruffled his hair and asked if he'd like to join them in a game of Monopoly.

With a shake of his head, "No thanks. I've still gotta go cut the lawn. It's my turn."

"Well, maybe when you're done, see if Nate'll help with the trimming. If I recall, he owes you for taking out the trash last week."

Finally smiling, "Good thinkin'."

●●●

The next day, he found himself following his usual route. He wasn't sure why, but for some reason there he was, pedaling along, feeling an overwhelming nervousness and excitement mixed with a healthy dose of embarrassment.

He wanted to see her again. And he wasn't disappointed. As he approached the house, there she was, this time a book propped on her lap rather than the paper. She was looking right at him as he swallowed hard and put on the brakes.

"No papers today?" She shook her head and held up the book so he could see the title, "*Algebra for Dummies*, huh? Just some light summer reading?"

She shook her head again, although this time a voice followed, "Summer school." Now, normally, he'd have responded with something, but after hearing her voice, coupled with the piercing green eyes, he managed to forget exactly how to speak. He instead stood, staring openly at her until she finally, finally, finally, broke into a small smile, "You okay there?"

And he crashed back to Earth.

Shaking his head, "Um, yeah. Sorry. Didn't mean to stare."

"It's all right. Algebra pretty much makes me catatonic as well."

Returning the smile, "I'm Jack."

"Would you laugh if I said my name was Jill?"

"Probably."

"Just checking."

Slightly intrigued now, he hesitated before asking, "Your name isn't actually Jill though, is it?"

"No. I just wondered if you'd laugh."

Shaking his head, "So, you gonna make me guess? 'Cause we could be here for an awful long time?"

Setting her book on the porch, she walked towards him, "I imagine you might end up trying names like Bertha or Clementine and I just couldn't handle that so," holding out her hand, "I'm Emily." After shaking his hand in an oddly formal gesture, she excused herself quickly, "I hate to go but I've gotta get ready for work. I'm sorry."

"You have a job?"

She nodded her head, "Yeah. I work at Dragon Gardens, the Chinese place down on Main Street. I wash dishes, bus tables, anything really."

"Are you 16 then?"

"Nope."

Figuring one of her parents had signed some kind of work release, he moved on, "What about your Algebra?"

"That's for after I get home." Turning towards the house, she stopped and faced him again, "Why didn't you ever stop to say hello before?"

Feeling his face heating immediately in embarrassment, he couldn't believe the honest answer that dropped from his mouth, "I guess I was scared."

"Of me?"

The surprised curiosity in her voice made him relax a little, "No, of those vicious snapdragons you've got by the fence … grabby little things."

"Well, I'll hold them back next time I see you. Promise."

"Then I might just have to stop and say hi again."

"You'll probably find me trying to solve for X."

"I could probably help with that."

Nodding, "Maybe."

And with that, she disappeared around the back of the house after scooping up the other books from the porch.

And with that, Jack decided that Emily could very well be the most beautiful name in the world.

■■■

It took three more days of ride-bys before she was back outside on the porch. Slowing to a stop, he carefully avoided the replanted snapdragons, "Hey there."

"Hi."

"I haven't seen you for a few days. Are they trying to drown you in the egg-drop soup?"

She shook her head, "No, but this math is slowly beginning to kill me. You'd think it would sink in after awhile."

"Stuck, huh?"

"More like buried deep with no hope of resurrection." Shrugging, "But I'll get it eventually. I always do."

"You know, I know somebody who pretty much knows what X equals all the time. Maybe I could convince him to help you."

Emily, feeling just as nervous, if not more, took a bold step towards him off her porch, "You know a guy?"

"Last I checked he had an A or something like that."

"Would that be you?"

By now, she'd made it to the gate, girl on one side of the small picket fence, boy on the other.

"Am I that transparent?"

"Just a little bit, but I'll forgive you if you can tell me what a factorial is."

Jack, smiling, shook his head at her, "Oh lord, do we have some work to do."

She unlatched the gate so he could come in.

And they sat.

And learned.

And talked just a little bit.

All across the worn top of the rickety old table on the tiny porch.

And it was good.

●●●

An unspoken routine developed and by the end of the next week, Emily managed to get her first ever B on a math test.

"We should celebrate."

She looked at him, confused, "For a B?"

"Yeah. Are you kidding? Given what you didn't know two weeks ago, I'd say that B is a miracle."

This time, the look went from confused to bewildered to completely blank, "Well, thanks for the help. But I think I've got it from here."

Now it was Jack's turn to look taken aback, "What? You've still got another test and a final to take."

"I'll be fine."

Not sure what the hell had just happened, "Wait? I think I missed something here. What'd I do?"

"I refuse to let anyone call me stupid ever again. You did and now we're through." Turning to go, "Like I said, thanks for the help, but I've got it from here." Reaching out to stop her, the minute his hand touched her arm, she jerked away, "Get off me."

The anger behind those three words made him cringe back slightly and not wanting to do anything else to upset her, he walked away quietly.

■■■

It was an amazing thing, what happened next. Jack made it home and when he walked in, the house was quiet. Either the Earth had swallowed up the herd or they were all lying dead somewhere, victims of some stupid stunt involving catapults and flaming tennis balls.

Neither was true. All the younger ones were at the library for some afternoon programs and, of course, his older brother was at work.

That left him to find his mom, calmly sitting on the back porch, her feet up and a bowl of ice cream on her lap.

Without a word, he exited through the screen door and dropped down next to her. She finished the spoonful she was on and offered him the last little bit in the bowl, which he gladly slurped down.

"So, how's Jack today?"

"Jack is beginning to wonder what makes girls freak out?"

"Ahhh. 'Bout time you got around to her. I've been wondering how long you'd hold out before you cracked."

"You knew?"

"Are you joking? You've been surreptitiously digging into old Algebra books, you disappear every day between two o'clock and four o'clock and you've been wearing clean shirts."

"All that points to a girl?"

"Of course. That and, while I was driving to the store the other day, I saw you sitting on a porch with someone."

"I assume you didn't tell the rest of them?"

She shook her head, "I was kind of hoping you'd tell me first. It's nice to know something before the mob for once."

He grinned at her, then remembered, "But I think I'm finished anyway so it doesn't matter."

"Finished? It's only been a few weeks." Turning, she pulled her leg up next to her, "What happened?"

With a shrug, "She got a B on her test and I told her we should celebrate. She asked why we'd do that 'cause it was just a B.' I told her that with what she didn't know two weeks ago, a B was a miracle."

"Okay."

"Then she said something like 'I refuse to let anyone call me stupid again' and she walked away. I reached out to stop her and the minute my hand touched her, she panicked, said 'get off me' and went into her house."

"You didn't grab her did you?"

"No, I swear. I barely even felt her arm." Demonstrating, "I'm amazed she even knew I touched her."

Both turned towards the house as the commotion of four boys began to leak out of the open windows, "So much for quiet." Looking back at her son, "A piece of advice, something hurt her; from the sound of it, probably a lot of things. You've already walked away and I won't say a thing if you stay away, but …" with a tilt of her head, "maybe she needs a friend and I know you're good at that."

With a grin, she ruffled his hair and stood, heading into the chaos of the house while he sat back, his head on the cushion and his eyes closed, contemplating the complicated life of a 15-year-old boy.

●●●

The next day, Jack had to watch the younger kids so he didn't have a chance to find Emily but, as luck would have it, she found him.

They'd all just gotten back from an extremely long bike ride. After dropping their bikes on the driveway and collapsing in various piles on the front lawn, all was quiet.

That silence, however, was broken by a girl.

A girl with a voice that made Jack smile in spite of himself.

"You weren't kidding about all of you looking alike, were you?"

Scrambling to his feet, "Um, yeah. Mom likes to joke that at least we don't look like the mailman." He motioned for the other four to stand up, "These are my younger brothers." Pointing first to the tallest of them, "That's Dave, he's thirteen and a compulsive sock changer," moving down the line by height, "next is Nate, eleven and willing to sell any one of his brothers for a jar of crunchy peanut butter." Shifting his finger to the next boy, "Then we have Tucker, who's ten and the only left-handed, double jointed one in the bunch." After a quick demonstration by Tucker of his thumb bending backwards to touch his arm, to which Emily could not contain her combination wince and grin, Jack finally turned to the smallest boy, "And this is Sam. He's six, believes that any food dropped on the floor is fair game and that if he wishes hard enough, he truly will be able to fly one day."

Emily said hello to them and once the boys settled back on the ground, Jack nodded towards the book in her hand, "So, math being a bitch again?"

"Kind of. Think you could help a girl out?"

And that's how they ended up on a different porch on a different street, the same Jack and the same Emily, only this time, surrounded by talk of ninjas and Spider-Man and the occasional friendly arm-wrestling match between the younger boys.

Jack only joined in when his ample knowledge of the ninja was needed to settle several arguments.

Emily could only smile, realizing that maybe people weren't so bad after all.

...

Emily was gone before Mrs. Callaghan got home, but from the look on her son's face, it appeared that everything would be just fine and, grinning, she informed him that she would eventually have to meet this girl, for security purposes and all.

Chapter 2

Three weeks later, Emily found Jack sitting on her front porch, biting his nails. Now, normally, this was a disgusting habit to her, but given he was waiting to see just how well she had done on her newly graded final, she only smiled.

Standing up, "Well, how'd you do?"

"Geez Jack, do you really think I want to advertise my grade to the entire world?"

His face fell immediately, "I'm sorry ... I just ... I've been waiting here for almost an hour and I didn't ... sorry."

For the first time he heard her laugh outright as she held up the exam, "But I'll advertise to you my big, fat B+."

He had her in a hug before he realized what he was doing and to his thankful amazement, she didn't slug him. He then thought about letting go but realized she hadn't pulled away either, so he held her for a second longer before backing away, "You know we get to celebrate now, don't you?"

Just as surprised by her reaction to his hug, she took a step back and prayed he would mistake her blushing cheeks for a simple summer sunburn, "You mean by forgetting everything we just learned in hopes we'll never need it again?"

With a chuckle, "Nuh-uh. If I'm gonna keep helping you, I'm gonna need you to remember a few things. As for celebrating, I was thinking some ice cream at the Dairy Queen in town."

Her cheeks continued to burn, "You want to keep tutoring me?"

"Of course. I can't let all those good skills go to crap. Unless you don't want me to?"

"Are you joking? There's no other way I'll get through high school at this point. I was just too embarrassed to ask if you'd keep helping me."

Walking backwards away from her, "Then it's settled. I'll keep you mathematically inclined and you'll let me take you out for ice cream whenever you're free."

Not wanting him to leave, "Actually, I'm free now. Someone switched days with me."

He stopped so suddenly that his momentum made him stumble backwards, "You're not doing anything tonight?"

Shaking her head, "Nope. Free as a bird who knows entirely too much about X and Y."

Totally torn by what he should do, he finally stepped back, "I've gotta get home now, but how 'bout I come back after dinner around six-thirty? We can walk down there or I can give you a ride on my handy-dandy 12-speed?"

Looking over his shoulder at the beaten up bicycle, "I think walking'll be just fine."

"Cool." Turning before continuing to walk, "See you later."

"Bye."

■■■

Jack, out of breath, met her on the porch at 6:40. Apologizing for being late, "With eight people trying to eat at the same time, I'm amazed I got here so early."

"What happened?"

As they started down the sidewalk, "More like what didn't happen. Sam spilled his glass of juice all over Tucker. Tucker decided to retaliate by flinging a spoonful of mashed potatoes at him. Sam knew it was coming and ducked, which plastered Nate in the side of the face." By now she was grinning at him so he continued, "Nate shoved Sam's chair with his foot and broke one of the supports underneath, which caused the chair to collapse. Given my brother has this thing with tucking his napkin in his collar and under his plate to catch anything he drops, when he fell, he took the plate with him and you can just picture that."

Fighting back the laugh lodged in her throat, "Your mom must have wanted to kill everybody."

"Oh, that was just the beginning. When his chair went down, he knocked into Nate, who jumped over to get out of the way. And being the original napkin tucker, his plate went onto the floor and pretty much right on top of Sam."

Now she just let the laugh loose, "Did your parents explode?"

"No, but Tim, my older brother, nearly did. You could see him getting redder and his eyes rolling around. Sometimes I think he would have been happier as an only child."

"What about you? Ever wish you were an only?"

"No way. It'd be too boring. Anyways, the rest of us just kept on eating because, in all honesty, it's probably one of the less eventful meals we've had. Remind me to tell you about Thanksgiving sometime." With a shake of her head, they continued on in silence for a minute until Jack suddenly remembered, "Hey, got my class schedule today." Digging it out of his pocket, he handed it to her, "did I get any good teachers?"

Taking the crumpled piece of paper, "I keep forgetting you're new around here. Let's see."

...

By the time they'd ordered their ice cream and carried it to one of the picnic tables, she'd given him a detailed analysis of every teacher's quirks and qualms, "Most of them are pretty cool. Just watch out for Mr. Tannen. Avoid the first row if possible; he likes to spit when he talks."

Trying to keep ahead of his dripping cone and failing miserably, he smeared the chocolate drop across his schedule, "Tannen, spitter ... got it."

Quietly handing him a napkin to catch the line of chocolate running down his chin, "Do you always get this much ice cream everywhere?"

With an embarrassed nod of his head, "Sorry, it just gets away from me."

"S'okay. I'll just remember to get more napkins next time."

"So ... you think maybe you'll do this again with me?"

Answering with a smile, she caused him to completely miss his mouth with the next pass of his cone. Giving him another napkin, "Can't take you anywhere, can I?"

...

After the ice cream, "When do you have to be home?"

She shook her head, "I don't actually have a curfew."

"Really? So you can stay out as long as you want without getting in trouble?"

"Yeah, but I don't stay out late anyway. I usually have too much homework to get done after work."

"But still, not being ruled by a clock must be pretty cool. Mom likes everyone but me and Tim home by eight in the summer. I need to be home by ten unless I let Mom know in advance and Tim gets until one 'cause of his job."

"Well, she does it because she worries and it's a nice thing, having a mom worry about you." Getting up from the table, "But for now, I think I should take you to Grant Park."

Letting the subject of curfews drop, "Why?"

"'Cause they have the best swings."

"We're gonna swing after eating ice cream?"

"Sure, why not?"

"Do you mind looking at a puddle of brown puke?"

Wrinkling her face at him, "Okay, how 'bout you sit for a few minutes while I go on the best swings ever?"

...

They found the park mostly empty, only a few families here and there. The swings were completely open and Emily hopped on, pumping her legs immediately, "Sure you're not up for it?"

Leaning against one of the poles, he shook his head, "I think I'll just hang out over here for now."

And with that, he watched her swing, legs working back and forth, taking her higher and higher until finally she cracked, letting out an uncharacteristic girly giggle. Leaning back, the world tipped upside down and righted itself a moment later, causing another giggle to emerge.

Jack couldn't help but laugh himself, "Enjoying?"

She grinned again and pumped her legs harder, "I'm still trying to wrap the swing around the pole."

"You know that isn't possible, right?"

"Don't burst my bubble. Right now, anything is possible." Shaking his head, he watched for a few more minutes until she began to slow down and eventually stop. Still grinning, her hair a complete windblown mess of red tangles and with eyes shining, "Thank you."

"For what? You did all the work."

"For celebrating my B+ with me and letting me swing like an eight-year-old for as long as I wanted."

Taking a step closer to her, he held onto one of the now stilled chains, "I could watch you do that all night long."

She stared up at him a moment, her ecstatic smile wavering for barely a second before coming back full force, "You haven't even seen me work my magic on the jungle gym yet."

Realizing he was once again invading her space, he stepped back and gestured towards it, "Lead the way."

...

They returned to her porch a little after nine o'clock and grabbing the mail from the box, she settled on the porch steps, scooting over so Jack could sit next to her. The first envelope she pulled out was from the school. Handing it to him, "Want to open that?"

"Sure." Tearing into it, he pulled out her upcoming schedule and, setting it next to his, began comparing classes under the glow of the porch light. "Well, we've got two together, math and English. And from what I can figure, the same lunch."

She looked over at the schedule, "That's the good lunch, too. Some get first lunch and have to eat at ten-thirty."

"My old school did that. Eat lunch at ten in the morning and you're starving again by noon."

"I was stuck with ten-thirty last year, so I switched into an art class that ran around noon. Since you can eat in the art room and no one cares, I'd do homework when I was supposed to be at lunch, then eat during class. I told a few people about it and a whole pack of us switched."

"I'll have to keep that in mind." Leaving the schedules on the step behind him, he turned and leaned back on his elbows, "Although now, I think I have to get home."

Not making any move to get up, "Probably. It's almost ten."

And with that said, they sat quietly for another minute before Jack asked, "Do you think I could come over tomorrow again? Maybe we can take a break from math, play some cards or something? Go for a bike ride?"

Emily felt a small smile curl her lips, "I only know how to play War and I think a bike ride'd be fun. I could take you up to the school? Show you around?"

"Cool."

"Tomorrow then? I have to work at four, so maybe around one?"

Finally standing, "Definitely tomorrow and definitely one."

Grabbing his bike from where he'd parked it against the side of her house, he walked it to the gate, working hard to try to wipe the crazy grin off his face.

He didn't succeed.

Not by a long shot.

●●●

Before their ride the next afternoon, Emily spoke quietly to her obviously third-hand bike, "You are the best bike ever, you know that?"

Jack tilted his head in her direction, "Are you giving her a pep talk?"

"I firmly believe that if I don't, she'll fall apart when I'm the farthest from home."

With a laugh, "Well, call me if that happens. I'll come find you and fix her up in a flash."

"Thanks." Kind of enjoying the warm feeling in her chest from his comment, "Um, you ready to go?"

"Lead on." After their tour of the school grounds and a few other highlights, they were back on her front lawn, Jack teaching her how to play Rummy on the walkway between them. As he waited for her to organize her cards, "I meant to ask you the other day, where do your parents work? Do they work crazy hours or something?"

"Um, it's only my mom and she's a nurse up in York. Her hours are always changing."

"Is York close?"

"About a half-hour away."

Quickly laying her cards down, "Is this right?"

Immediately distracted by her completely wrong hand, "Nope. Here's what you need."

...

And so it went for the rest of the week and through the last weekend before school started. They played cards, rode bikes, swung on the swings, and every day, Jack showed up at the restaurant at 8 p.m. to walk her home.

The first time he showed up, Emily wasn't quite sure what to do with him. When she had walked out the back door to go home, she was startled to see him leaning on the wall. Staring at him for a moment, she raised an eyebrow at him and walked past, with him immediately taking stride next to her.

They were part way home before she finally cracked the silence, "You don't have to walk me home."

"I know."

And that was the extent of their conversation that night, with Jack leaving her at her gate and turning down the street to his own house with only a wave good-bye.

The next day, they spent the afternoon together and again, without warning, he was there when she finished her shift.

"You really don't have to walk me home."

"Do you mind that I do?"

With a shake of her head, "No."

And with that said, he quietly wound his fingers with hers and they walked home in silence.

Chapter 3

School began the following Tuesday and Jack, with Tim in tow, showed up at her front gate promptly at 7:30 a.m. wearing a smile, "Morning."

Tim immediately stuck out his hand, "Hi, I'm Tim and none of what Jack has ever told you about me is true."

She liked him immediately and as she shook his hand, "He's never said anything bad. Promise."

Cuffing his younger brother on the back of the head, "Then apparently I need to smack him around a bit more."

Jack punched him back lightly, "Shut up." Turning to Emily, "Ready to go?"

"Yup." Pointing over her shoulder towards her backpack, "I've got a blank notebook, two pencils and an intense dislike for math all ready to go."

Before Jack could reply back, Tim stopped suddenly and pulled a piece of paper out of his pocket. Handing it to her, "Do you know anything about these teachers? From what I hear, at least one is a spitter."

As Jack prodded his brother to get him moving again, she smiled before looking at the paper, "Yeah, your spitter is 3rd period and you've got a fast talker for 6th, but your 5th period's a multiple choicer and your 1st is a definitioner, so you got lucky there."

"A what?"

"Sorry. 5th period likes multiple choice tests and 1st period usually has a lot of definitions on her exams."

"Ahh, okay."

"Hey, you've got art class with me."

"Really?"

"Yeah, 4th period with Tassleman. That's advanced drawing. Jack never mentioned you drew."

Tim nodded, "Yeah, I seem to be able to do a few things with a pencil."

Jack, during their conversation, felt the incredible need to pull Emily over beside him, laying some caveman-like claim to her, letting Tim know loud and clear to back the hell off.

Tim caught his look and, taking an opportunity when Emily had to stop to re-tie her shoe, leaned into Jack, keeping his voice to a whisper, "Never fear, brother, she's all yours … unless, of course, you screw up royally, then who knows." Seeing Jack's glare intensify, he grinned, "Dude, I'm kidding, all right? I promise."

Knowing that idiot grin of Tim's too well, he relaxed some, nodding, "Thanks."

Just as she stood and they headed towards the main steps of the school, Tim nodded towards a girl quietly standing on the steps, studying a piece of paper "Hey, Emily, do you know her?"

"Yeah. Um, at least I know her name. Sarah Wheaton."

With a grin, "I think I'm gonna go play the lost new student routine."

Jack just shook his head in amusement, "Be nice."

"Always." Before he walked away, he thumped his brother on the back, "Good luck."

"Thanks."

Knocking Emily's backpack lightly with his knuckle, "See you in class."

■■■

Reams of kids streamed past and, without thinking, Emily took Jack's hand and guided him towards his locker on the other side of the building. "You're here and I think I'm," turning around once before pointing across the hall, "right over there." Jack nodded, his stomach jumping as it usually did the first day of school. Indicating her backpack, "I'm just gonna dump this off, then I'll get you to your first class." Staring for a second into his slightly pale face, "You okay?"

He nodded again, "Just nervous. I'll be fine once the day actually starts."

With a final squeeze to his hand, "Be back in a minute."

Jack turned to his locker and for the first time in his school career, got the lock open first try. Stashing his stuff and grabbing a pen, pencil and his notebook, he shut the locker again, only to be confronted by a tall boy with green spiked hair and a pierced eyebrow.

He was also mumbling to himself as he wrestled with his own locker, "Two more years, two more years." Jack guessed he stared a second too long because the boy suddenly looked over at him, "Problem?"

"No. Just wasn't sure if you were talking to me or not?"

The boy finally yanked the door open and heaved a saxophone case into the locker, slamming it shut with a satisfying bang, "Nope. Just cursing the world." As the door swung open of its own accord and the boy tried slamming it again, "And apparently the world wants some more."

At this point, Jack was pretty sure he should walk away, but Emily returned to his side quietly reaching out to shut the still stubborn locker door, "Dex, it's not the locker's fault."

"Girl, it's always the locker's fault."

"Boy went green."

"Girl like?"

She nodded, "Girl like." Turning to Jack, "I see you've found Dex."

"More like Dex found me."

Dex turned towards Emily, "I was bitching about my day and he got to listen in."

"How can you be complaining already? We've still got ten minutes until class starts."

"It's easy to complain when you find out that the girl you've been lusting over for two years has moved to Georgia."

"You finally scared her away, huh?"

"But I'll get over it … eventually … maybe … with the help of a good six days of very loud and obnoxious music listening." Pulling out his class schedule, he handed it to her, "So, what's your take?"

Jack interrupted, "Are you like the number one go-to about every teacher here?"

Dex slapped him on the back, "This girl is the authority on everything you or I will ever need to know. Except for math, but that's not her fault. Everyone needs to have something they suck at."

Rolling her eyes, Emily studied the schedule, "You've got both math and English with us, but you haven't got any easy test givers. Sorry."

Taking the schedule back, "Well, at least I'll have company for a couple of classes."

Turning on her heel and heading down the hall, both boys keeping to her sides, "Where's Gil?"

"We had a falling out this summer. He decided he likes to smoke weed and I decided he was an asshole. That and the fact that he got busted for the aforementioned weed and is now attending a nice little place I like to call private school."

"I'm sorry."

"S'okay, who needs him anyway?" Putting his arm over Emily's shoulder, which Jack noticed she didn't flinch away from, "I've got my girl and the new kid who hasn't figured out yet that I'm not exactly normal and who hopefully won't see that until after he discovers he likes me for me and not for my hair color."

Jack laughed, "Um, can I ask why green?"

"'Cause they were out of orange."

As they dropped Jack off at his first class, "Makes sense."

And with that, their junior year began.

■■■

By the time art class rolled around Tim was dragging a thousand books with him and he dropped them with a bang on the table next to Emily, "Mind if I share?"

"Nope. What's with all the stuff?"

"Locker lock's broken and apparently maintenance can't fix it until after school, so I get to haul all this crap with me until then."

Standing back up, "Come on. I'll let you use mine for now. You can't be carrying everything with you. You'll look like a freshman."

Gathering up his pile, "Thanks."

They made it back to class before the bell rang, given her locker was only a few feet down the hall. Settling back at the table, "So, how's Jack surviving?"

"He's doing okay. A little nervous this morning but then I turned him over to Dex and he should be completely corrupt by tonight."

"Dex?"

"Yeah, tall kid, green hair, pierced eyebrow."

"Cool name."

"Well, Dexter really didn't fit him so he shortened it. I'd say it was a good call."

"Oh yeah."

Just then the teacher walked in, "Pencils up, paper ready, draw." And she set a bowling pin, a Rubik's cube and a golf ball on the table in the middle of the room. "One catch, they can't be actual size. Bigger, smaller, I don't care, just not life-size." And with that, she walked back out.

Tim looked over at her confused, "What?"

With a grin, Emily stood to collect two boards and some paper for them. Clipping the paper on the plastic boards, she handed him one, "Do what the lady said."

"We just draw then. No teaching?"

"Not today. She did this last year too. First day out, she jumps in to see where everyone stands. We'll critique near the end of class and go from there."

Already digging up his favorite pencil, "Kick ass."

"Generally."

Everyone talked throughout the class. There were several room wide discussions of movies, vacations, classes and teachers as well as people getting up, moving around, looking for different angles, light sources, more comfortable chairs. By the time Ms. Tassleman got back and critiques began, Tim had decided this was by far the best class he'd been to yet.

Emily had turned slightly away from him and worked diligently throughout the hour. When her critique came up, Tim couldn't do anything but stare. He had thought he was good, but he could see now she would be very tough competition.

After the class had finished ripping her paper apart, as they had with everyone's, with extremely constructive criticism, it was his turn. Walking to the front of the class, he set his board against the chalkboard and stood beside it.

He wondered whether they'd be slightly easier on the new kid.

They weren't … although for the first time ever, he didn't feel like he was being attacked. Sure, they were directing their onslaught at his paper, but the things said were useful and he could immediately see how to make the picture better.

And Emily seemed to be the worst critic in the bunch.

He fell in love with her right then and there in that classroom. Not the whole 'sweaty palms, stammering, wanna hold your hand' kind of thing, but a genuine artist to artist 'I know you'll tell me the truth and I'll still like you in the morning' kind of thing.

After class, their drawings were collected and filed away in wide, slim slots in the walls, each person already having their names assigned.

"Everything gets saved from the semester and at the end, there's an art show for the best stuff. She also likes to see our progress when it comes time for grades."

Tim nodded, "Does she keep the homework too then?"

"Yeah. She says that she knows teenagers and their lockers and the work is far safer in her room than anywhere else." Spinning her lock, "So we can also drop our stuff off when we get here in the morning. You don't have to store it in your locker until class."

"Cool." Reaching over her head to get one of his notebooks and his lunch from the top shelf, "Can I have your combination so I can get in here for the rest of the day?"

Writing it on the underside of his notebook, "Just make sure it shuts."

"Will do." Having already turned to go, he stopped and came back, "Thanks."

"It's just a locker."

"I mean for the critique and the locker and being nice to Jack and being my friend."

She just smiled at him, "You're welcome."

...

Jack was already sitting by the time Emily made it to English and sliding into the seat behind him, "Where's Dex?"

"I left him with the principal, arguing the merits of his hair."

She smiled, "He'll win."

By now Jack had turned around in his seat, "How can he win against the principal? Isn't he basically law around here?"

"For the most part, but I've seen it happen. If you do it rationally, quietly and politely, he'll listen and decide from there." With a twinkle in her eye, "How do you think he got to wear the eyebrow ring?"

"He's done this before?"

She nodded, "Yup. And he'll do it again, too. It's only the first day." And true to form, Dex walked into class ten minutes later with a late pass and a grin. Emily leaned forward and whispered in Jack's ear, "Told you."

Now, a girl should know she should never whisper in a boy's ear during class. For starters, the message rarely gets through and if it does, it's immediately forgotten in the wake of the girl's breath tickling those small and extremely sensitive hairs.

Suffice it to say, Jack wasn't good for much for the next few minutes except for thinking of that beautiful girl stationed only one chair behind him.

···

Finally, they made it to lunch and were regaled with a word for word account of the hair argument. It was animated, done in several different voices and with some food involved to show proper positioning of the principal and Dex. After he'd finished replaying the discussion, Dex gleefully bit the head of the carrot principal off with his teeth, grinning hugely.

All in all, the day passed quickly, with the group heading to math together then splitting up for the final class.

···

Jack found Emily back at her locker after the final bell and watched as she dug out several books, jamming them into her backpack before moving out of the way so Tim, who had just came up, could get to his stuff.

"So little brother, how'd it go? Any fights? Detention? Hot teachers slipping you numbers?"

Jack just grinned, "No, but I'll bet you've hit on at least three girls and already sniffed out the best exit for ditching class."

Tim shrugged, "Just Sarah and she shut me down, but I'm pretty sure she wants me to keep trying. As for ditching, there're actually two exits that I can use to get to the parking lot unnoticed and if you're nice to me, I'll tell you which ones." Reaching over Emily's head as he had earlier in the day, "Thank God you're short," he dragged out a couple things, "and can I leave my stuff here, at least until tomorrow when the lock should be done?"

Emily nodded, "'Course."

"She's a keeper, Jack, don't screw it up." Smiling over at the slightly red-faced Jack, "Sorry to talk and run, but I've gotta get home and back to work by four. See you tonight."

"See ya."

Left alone once more, Jack asked if she was ready to go.

"Sure am." Starting down the hall, "You know, you don't have to walk me home."

Loving the mirrored conversation, "Do you mind if I do?"

"Never."

Twining fingers with her once again, "Perfect."

Dex chose then to come up behind them, "Do you know that my hair could very well be the new rage that drives women wild?"

"And how do you know this?"

"Some girl stared at me when I walked past her just now and it was one of those 'I think you should date me' stares as opposed to the 'you'll never date me' stares."

"Dex?"

"Yeah Em?"

"Are you sure it wasn't one of those 'he's got green hair' stares?"

"Potayto, potahto ... choose to see the world how you must." Speeding up, "Gotta go, duty calls. Catch you tomorrow."

Finally clearing the hallways and making it unscathed to the sidewalk, "Duty calls?"

"Yeah, Dex watches his nephew after school."

"He's an uncle?"

"You know what they say about all shapes and sizes."

•••

Given Dex's nephew and Emily's work schedule, the three took to spending their lunch hour in the library, eating stealthily while holding breakneck tutoring sessions for math because, as it turned out, Dex wasn't that great at the subject either.

"Dude, what the hell is all this? Why am I learning it? And who decided math teachers were allowed to be so sadistic and get paid for it?"

"Dude, shut up and do the problem."

Yes, Dex and Jack were definitely getting along just fine.

Suddenly the librarian was next to them and she set a carpet sweeper beside Dex's chair, "Dude, if you're gonna eat in here, at least clean up after yourself." With a smile, she pointed towards the sandwich sitting on his lap, "as for that, put it on the table and eat properly. You're not some green haired beast in the wild."

With a sheepish look, "But we can't eat in here."
"I'll bend the rules for you because you actually seem to be trying to learn something. Just don't let it get around or else this place'll go to the mice."

Dex grinned at her, "Thanks." With a last amused look, the woman walked away and Dex turned to Emily, "You womenfolk might not be so bad after all."

Chapter 4

A week or two later Jack deposited Emily at her front gate, but didn't leave as usual. "Can I ask a question?"

"Sure."

"It's still a few weeks away, but would you maybe like to go to Homecoming with me? I mean, I know it's a silly dance but ..."

Trailing off, he let the sentence hang there between them, shaded in nervousness, until Emily moved back towards him, standing closer than she normally would, "I'd love to, but I don't think I can."

"Oh. Okay."

"It's not that I don't want to go with you. I just don't have the money."

He nodded, trying not to show his disappointment, "It's okay. I just thought I'd ask."

Tilting her head slightly so she could look him in the eye, desperately wanting to alleviate his saddened look, "If I could find the money, I'd go ... in a heartbeat. But given I don't have a dress, tickets or anything else, I don't see a way around it."

"You can't ask your mom?"

She just shook her head, "I'm sorry."

He continued to stand there for a few moments, thinking fast, until a grin spread across his face, "Well, are you working that night?"

"I assume until eight, like usual."

"Okay, how 'bout I take you out for an extremely cheap dinner after work, then maybe I can take you to the really cheap dollar show and we can watch really bad movies for as long as we can stand it?"

Not sure if there was sarcasm hovering somewhere in there, "Huh?"

Taking her hand and playing with the fingers, "I just want to spend the night out with you without worrying about school or anything else but having fun. And since I'm still unemployed, cheap is all I can really afford at the moment, too."

"I can pay for myself you know."

"Not on this date, girl. I'm going to give you the red carpet treatment for under 20 bucks."

Taken aback by his wording, "A date?"

His lips curled slightly at the edges, his eyes lighting up, "Well, we should probably go on one eventually. Might as well get it out of the way."

And with that, she moved closer and kissed him on the cheek, "How 'bout I get out of work at seven-thirty?"

...

In the interim before their date, Emily was assigned a project in art class; draw a classmate. With stipulations of course: use a medium not familiar to them, must be done outside the confines of the classroom, must not be posed and each person must work at least 3 hours.

Tim, of course, got the same project and given the two were friends, they chose to draw each other. Asking her after class, "When do you want to get this started?"

"I work until eight all week."

"What about the weekend?"

"I'm free Saturday morning and most of Sunday."

"Well, I have to work until seven-thirty Friday, so we could meet about eight-fifteen and start then, maybe?"

She nodded, "Your house?"

"Well, my house would probably be easiest. I can't imagine your mom would want you to have a guy at your place without her home." Her look of confusion made him smile, "Jack mentioned your mom works late."

"Oh, yeah. Forgot. Sorry."

"S'okay." As they made their way out of the classroom, Tim asked "So, any idea what you'll work in?"

"I've always wanted to try my hand at pen and ink but I think the size requirements will slow me down so I guess I'll see how I do in pastels. I rarely touch those. You?"

"I was thinking either charcoals or crayon."

"Crayon? As in Crayola?"

"Mmm-hmm. Never did a picture in those before."

She laughed outright at this, "I'm gonna be rendered in crayon. How cool is that?"

"Very."

...

That Friday night, Jack, for a change, which he pointed out to Emily, walked her back to his house instead of her own. "You seem awfully tired. I'm sure Tim'll understand if you don't want to do this now."

With another yawn, "Well, it's due next Monday and I'm drawing him tomorrow so this is all we've got. I'll be fine."

"Well, at least you don't have to deal with most of the posse tonight. Three of the four are at a camp out/birthday party kind of thing, so it's only Mom, Dad and Sam tonight."

"I don't know that I've ever managed to see you all together. I'm gonna begin to wonder if there really are that many of you or you just make them up for sympathy sake."

"No one could ever concoct these people out of thin air, trust me."

Finally making their way inside, Mrs. Callaghan came down the hall, wiping her hands on a dish towel, "Hi. You must be Emily. Nice to finally meet you."

Holding out her hand, "You too ma'am."

With a smile, she gave a firm handshake, "Please call me Elizabeth. Ma'am reminds me that I do indeed have six children running rampant in the world."

"Yes ma'am ... I mean, Elizabeth."

"Very good." Turning to Jack, "If either of you are hungry, the leftovers are in the fridge. Tim's in the living room, probably already finished and licking his plate hoping for more. Your dad and me'll be upstairs keeping Sam out of your hair."

And then she was gone, running up the stairs yelling, "If you started that movie without me, there's going to be tickling involved."

"I think I like your mom."

As Jack walked her into the kitchen, "Yeah, I think I do too."

...

Moving to the living room, she asked Tim, who was indeed nearly licking his plate, "So, where do you want me?"

"Anywhere I guess. What would you normally be doing if you weren't here?"

"Probably sitting on my couch, doing my homework."

"Then why don't you do that. You won't be moving too much and you can still get something done."

Jack immediately went to retrieve their book bags from the front hall, dumping them on the coffee table, "Might as well get some of my own stuff done."

As the pair dug up the proper books and settled in, Tim sat himself against the wall, a brand new box of 128 Crayola crayons on the floor beside him and a piece of laminated counter top on his lap, "Found it years ago in the garage. Perfect size for holding paper."

Before cracking her history book, "I've got an old slab of Formica I found in the trash one day. It's a bit awkward, but it'll do for now."

"Well, ignore me and try not to move too much, but talking's fine." Taking up his first crayon, "Here we go."

···

At first he was having some trouble with the picture, but about twenty minutes later, an odd thing happened.

Emily fell asleep.

She was sitting beside Jack and the combined warmth of him and the quiet of the house took its toll. First her eyes began to get heavier, then her head tilted to the side and finally, she leaned a little more, resting her head on Jack's shoulder. From there, she was out in a matter of seconds.

Tim finally saw his picture. Whispering to Jack, "Don't wake her up."

Jack, in his own glorious heaven at the moment, "Are you kidding? I'm not going to breathe if I can help it."

Giving his brother a grin, Tim moved to a new sheet of paper and began working quickly and confidently.

He worked diligently for the next two hours while she slept peacefully on his brother's arm. Jack, in turn, took his own nap, head resting gently on hers.

Eventually, Tim's hand cramped up and his neck screamed for movement. Sitting back, he studied his paper with extreme satisfaction, only looking up when Jack asked quietly, "Can I see it?"

"Nope. Not until after class. You know nobody sees my stuff early."

"Like that's ever gonna stop me from asking."

"I'm just gonna run this upstairs." Gathering up the worn down crayons, "Think we should wake her up?"

Pushing a fallen piece of hair from her cheek, "I hate to, but I probably should." Gently tapping her cheek, "Emily? Hey, Em, time to wake up."

Tim left him to the task and went to stash his supplies upstairs. Coming back into the living room, he found Emily squinting at his brother in confusion, "Jack?"

"Yeah?"

"Did I fall asleep?"

As she sat up, he was able to shift, get off the couch and finally stretch his arm out, "For a couple of hours actually. It's about ten-thirty."

She sat bolt upright, "What about Tim's picture? Why didn't you wake me up?"

Tim picked up one of his stray crayons, "I'm all done. Well, mostly done. I'll do the finishing touches tomorrow or Sunday."

"I'm sorry. I didn't mean to fall asleep." Letting off a yawn that nearly split her head in two, "The picture's okay though?"

Tim nodded as he slipped his coat on, "More than okay, trust me."

Jack grinned at him, "You going out?"

"Yeah. I called Sarah while I was upstairs to let her know I was done. I'm gonna go get her and maybe see a late movie."

Emily looked at him with interest, "Sarah Wheaton? When did that happen?"

Heading out of the living room, "'Bout two minutes ago. She finally said yes."

Emily shook her head with a smile, "How long's he been working on her?"

"Since our first day."

"Wow, most guys would have given up by now."

"You've gotta know Tim though. He's a persistent pain in the ass when he wants to be."

"Are there any Callaghan's who aren't persistent?"

"Not that I know of." Moving to stand in front of her, "So, we have a few choices. We can do some more homework, I can walk you home or we can watch a movie or some TV?"

"What do you want to do?"

"Well, I don't want to do any homework and I definitely don't want you to go home, so how 'bout we dig us up a movie and make some popcorn?"

Hoping he would decide that, she kept her happiness in check, "Works for me."

"Then why don't you find us something to watch while I get the food and tell Ma and Dad we're staying here for awhile."

Looking around dumbly, "And I would look for movies where?"

"The door on the side of the TV." After he left, she got up and opened the correct door. She was immediately engrossed in reading titles and examining covers. Jack came back about five minutes later, a large bowl of popcorn in his hands, "What're we watching?"

"I have no idea. I'm still in shock at how many you have."

Sitting the bowl down, then dropping next to her, "Are you reading each one?"

With a nod, "Yeah. How else will I know what they're about?"

"You mean you haven't seen any of these?"

Emily shook her head, slightly embarrassed at this point, "I don't have a TV or a DVD player."

Now Jack was just shocked, "Are you serious?"

After shrugging, she changed the subject, "Which one will I enjoy?"

Knowing when to follow a topic change, he went along, "Well, do you like being scared but in a sciency, serial killer kind of way?"

"I have no idea."

Pulling out a box from the bottom of the shelves, "I think it may be time to introduce you to a little something we like to call the best scary show on TV. Or, at least used to be on TV." Holding up a DVD, "The X-Files."

"Am I going to wake up screaming?"

"Hope not, but if you do, call me up and I'll come chase away the monsters." Finally standing and turning off the living room light, "I may be forced to show up in my pajamas and beat them away with a Mag-Lite, but I'll be there nonetheless."

As both settled down on the couch in the now partially lit room, the bowl of popcorn between them, "Thanks."

With a grin, he hit the play button, "Welcome."

•••

Jack walked her to her front door for the first time that evening. Usually it was a garden gate drop off, but given it was after dark, he followed her to the door.

"So, when are you gonna show me some more of those?"

Jack laughed, "Hooked after one episode. That's gotta be a record."

"What can I say? I love a good bowl of free popcorn."

Sliding his fingers into hers, "You're coming back over tomorrow morning right?"

"Yup. Eight o'clock ... Tim has to be at work by noon so that'll give me plenty of time."

"Then I'll see you tomorrow."

At this point, he should have left the porch, but he didn't and Emily should have made him go, but she didn't. Instead they stood there, just holding hands for a minute or two until Emily asked, "Was I okay while I was asleep?"

Seeing the worry suddenly cloud her face, "What do you mean?"

"Did I, um, say anything or do anything while I was asleep?"

"You mean during your nap? No, why? Do you sleep walk or something?"

As a flood of relief washed over her, "Something like that."

He wanted to ask more, but opted not to, "I should really go."

"Yeah, probably." But instead of turning, she came closer and kissed him once again on the cheek, "I'll see you in the morning."

...

The next morning she arrived bright and early, beat-up tackle box in tow and board under her arm. Tim answered, rubbing his head and yawning, "Come on in. Let me just brush my teeth and we can start."

Emily was then left to awkwardly stand in the front hall, alone and wondering if she should just wait or head into the living room. She also wondered where Jack might be, but Tim came back from the bathroom by then, "Well, where would you like me?"

"I guess I'll ask you what you asked me. What would you be doing right now if I wasn't here?"

"Given that my manager called and asked if I could work tomorrow, I'd probably be working on finishing up my picture of you."

"Then go get it and I'll draw you drawing."

Tim's face lit up, "Cool. Kill two birds with one stone kind of thing. Back in a second."

Retrieving the picture from his room, they were soon both settled on the floor, Emily hunkered on the old sheet she'd brought with her to control the pastel vs. carpet issue while Tim sat on the floor, his board propped up on a pile of old books.

So intent on the task at hand were they that neither heard Jack shuffle into the kitchen. He even stood in the archway for several minutes watching the pair of them work, wondering if he should bother them at all. Opting not to, he instead grabbed a banana and an apple and went back to his room.

Tim soon finished his drawing, but given Emily seemed to be going strong, he quietly switched to a new piece of paper. With his favorite nub of a pencil he began a series of rough sketches of her, particularly her expressions, which changed with every passing moment. Her arched eyebrow, her furrowed forehead and the best one, in his opinion, her darting tongue. In moments of total concentration, it sneaked its way out of the corner of her mouth, the tip of it wiggling as she chewed, lost in her pastel world. He had to keep from smiling about it, but once, he slipped, just as she looked up at him, "Why are you smiling?"

"What? A guy needs a reason to smile now?"

"My tongue was hanging out, wasn't it?"

Grinning even wider, "How does that thing not dry out, flapping there all the time?"

"It does, at times." Sticking it out further in his direction, "Now go back to your picture. I've only got another half-hour to finish this."

Already planning on drawing her at least another dozen times, he settled back against the couch, "Yes, ma'am."

...

The magic of the quiet living room was broken around eleven o'clock when the rest of the boys came home, tumbling through the door with shouts and yells.

Barely seconds before the boys reached them, Emily managed to save her picture from the onslaught of feet by holding the board above her head. Tim mirrored her action after slipping all his drawings into the pad of paper and shutting them in safely.

Tim called over the din, "Whoa guys. Precious homework here. Watch it."

The boys slowed down, finally realizing Emily was grinning in the corner, old board held high, "Sorry Emily."

"S'okay. Just watch the supplies, please."

The kids looked down and gingerly stepped away from the sheet, "Where're Mom and Dad?"

Tim shrugged, "Not sure. I know they left early this morning with Sam. I think they were going grocery shopping or something."

"Well, we're gonna go to the park, okay? We'll be back by three. Dave's got a watch."

Waving them away, "Just be careful. And hey, take something to eat with you. I know Mom just bought a huge box of granola bars."

Already heading back out of the room, "Okay."

Once the room had returned to its original state of peace and quiet, "You all right over there?"

She smiled, "Yeah. Just kind of shell-shocked, I guess you'd say."

"Yeah, it tends to happen to new people."

Jack's voice drifted from the kitchen, "This was nothing compared to what a meal looks like." Coming into the living room, "Speaking of which, anybody hungry for lunch?"

Her stomach growled her answer, "A little."

"Then come on in. I was gonna cook some Mac and Cheese. You want any, Tim?"

Looking at his watch, "No, but thanks. I've gotta go get ready for work." Trying to look around Emily's shoulder as he walked by, "Do I get a peek?"

"Nope. Grand unveiling in class."

"You are so not fun."

"Do I get to see yours?"

Stuffing his hands in his pockets, he left the room whistling, "See you Monday in class."

...

While they were eating their way through their lunch, "Um, Jack?"

"Yeah?" as a noodle hung from his chin.

Reaching over and tapping it so it fell back in the bowl, "Why didn't you come down while Tim and I were working?"

"I actually did, but both of you looked so serious and focused I wasn't about to interrupt, so I went back upstairs and did some homework. Once the others got home though, I figured you wouldn't be able to concentrate anymore, so I came down."

"For a second there, I thought you had forgotten I was here."

"Forget you? Are you kidding?" Without stopping himself, "I haven't forgotten about you for a minute since I faked that flat tire."

Well, that little secret jumped right out in the open didn't it?

And Emily couldn't help the smile that spread from ear to ear, "I knew there wasn't anything wrong with that tire."

"How?"

""Cause you rode right away on it without ever checking it again."

Looking rather sheepish, "Well, it was the only way I could think of to stop in front of the house."

"You could just as easily have quit pedaling and said hello instead of taking out half a flat of snapdragons in the process."

Collecting their now empty bowls and putting them in the dishwasher, "My idea seemed better at the time."

She just shook her head, "Well, next time you want to talk to a girl, just say hi. Works surprisingly well."

He was going to reply with something suave and cool, but was interrupted by the front door opening and Sam rushing headlong into the bathroom. His parents came into the kitchen a moment later … and for the first time, Emily laid eyes on Jack's dad.

It was all she could do to keep the macaroni in her stomach.

…

Jack saw her cringe and pale immediately. Luckily, his parents hit the fridge looking for lunch after Mr. Callaghan shook her hand, so Jack called a quick good-bye and mumbled something about walking Emily home. He then steered her towards the front door, grabbing her supplies as he passed them.

Once on the porch with the door safely pulled shut behind them, "Are you okay?"

By now, Emily had come back to reality and, though covered in a thin sheen of sweat, seemed calmer, "Yeah, I just don't think the food is sitting very well."

Almost positive she was lying, he chose to let it slide, walking home next to her slowly and delivering her at the front gate as usual. "You're really sure you're all right? You seemed fine until my parents walked in."

With a nod, "Maybe I just woke up too early or didn't get enough sleep last night."

"If you say so." Leaning forward, he kissed her forehead, "Call me if you need anything, okay?"

"I'll be fine."

"Then I'll see you tomorrow or Monday okay? I have to go to some family picnic at Dad's work tomorrow and I don't know when I'll be back."

Remembering him mentioning it, "Okay. Have fun."

Still more than a little worried about her, "I'll try."

...

He didn't mention anything about what happened to anyone. After a day of thinking about it, he had nearly managed to convince himself it really was the whole food, getting up early, staying out late combo.

Chapter 5

On Monday morning, Tim made it to class just in time for the bell and slid into the chair beside her, "One of these days, the mob at senior rail is gonna make me late."

"You're a senior."

"Doesn't mean they don't need to get the hell away from me. And I still don't understand why the seniors need some place to hang out during school. Just use the hall like normal people."

With a shrug, "Who knows? Apparently it's been tradition for decades and who's gonna mess with tradition?"

"Still annoys the piss out of me."

Class started then, so Tim's rant ended early as they both turned towards the talking teacher, "So, everybody ready to do the unveiling?"

Their pictures were already sitting in a pile on the front table and, two by two, she picked them up, propped them against the chalkboard, turned and stepped back to let the critiquing begin.

Most were good, some were better than good, but then, "I decided to save these two for last. Honest opinions folks. Don't hold back."

Turning the last two, the class stared in silence until, "Damn, couldn't either of you at least fake some inconsistencies so the rest of us don't look like simplistic freaks who accidentally landed in an art class through a scheduling mishap?" Tim turned a beet-red color as he took a quick glance at his heckler. It turned out to be Jim wearing a big grin, "Just kidding, man."

Ms. Tassleman looked over the class with a small smile, "Anything?"

It was then the questions started to flow until just before the end of class, "Tim, did you add yourself in later?"

"Huh?"

"How are you in the picture with Emily?"

He grinned, "That's not me. It's my brother, Jack. All us kids look the same."

Jim, with his usual timing, "Damn, no kidding."

The bell rang and everybody but Emily stood, gathering their things. She in turn just sat, staring at the pictures still leaning on the wall.

"Hey, you okay?"

She hadn't said much during class, answering the questions she was asked quickly and quietly. Even now, she was still answering in a daze, "Yeah, I'm fine."

"Then why do you look like the pod people got you?"

Not even hearing the comment, "Do I really look like that?"

Tim looked from her to the picture and back to her in confusion, "What do you mean?"

Grabbing her bag, she moved to stand in front of the picture of herself, "Do I really look like that?"

On the paper, there sat a girl, eyes shut, head leaning against Jack's shoulder. The lips were slightly apart and one small strand of stray hair had fallen across her face. Her hand was lying against Jack's thigh and Jack himself was asleep as well, his fingers entwined ever so slightly with hers.

For lack of a better word, she looked beautiful and peaceful and completely content with the world.

When Tim didn't answer, she asked again quietly, "Is that how you see me?"

"It's how everybody sees you, Em. Don't you ever look in the mirror?"

With a shake of her head to clear the fog, she turned towards the door, "But that's not what I see." Not wanting her to walk away yet, he reached out to grab her elbow and stop her. With that motion, Emily came crashing back to the real world and jerked her arm back, "I'm gonna be late."

Ms. Tassleman came back through the door just as Emily was leaving and nearly knocked into her. Looking confused, she spotted Tim still in the room, "Need anything?"

He stayed by the pictures, "Can I ask you something?"

Coming to stand next to him, "Sure."

"Do you think it looks like Emily?"

"Are you kidding? It's a near dead ringer. Why?"

"She just asked if she really looked like that and I told her yeah. Then she said 'that's not what I see'. I just wanted to make sure I was seeing her the way everybody else did."

Ms. Tassleman stood staring at the two pictures for a moment before responding, "You have to remember, she's 15. Most girls at that age see themselves as ugly, unattractive and probably hideous individuals. Maybe you're the first person to show her she really is beautiful." He shrugged his response, still contemplating and she continued, "I'll also say this. I've had her in classes for three years now and I have never, ever seen her so relaxed. She's usually guarded and wound tight but here, well, it's just nice to know that she can take a break."

He nodded, "She had me worried for a minute."

Patting him on the arm, "That just means you're her friend and that's a very good thing."

They stared a few more seconds at the side by side images, then, "I hate to ask, but do you think I could get a pass to my next class? The bell rang like five minutes ago."

With a smile, "Of course."

...

The rest of the week passed quietly, Jack still having a stray thought every now and then about what had happened with Emily the previous Saturday, but by Wednesday, those thoughts were crowded out by their upcoming Friday night date.

He showed up on time and, ringing her doorbell, it occurred to him he had never had to do that before. Usually she was waiting outside already, either leaning on the porch post or sitting on the steps. Feeling suddenly rather grown up, he stood a little straighter and made sure the flowers in his hands weren't falling out of their tie. But, as usual, when the door opened, he forgot the world completely.

Now, usually boys get bowled over by the appearance of their dates in gorgeous dresses and heels, their hair done perfectly, make-up flawless and jewelry sparkling. Jack was done completely in by Emily opening the door dressed in a pair of jeans, her black boots, remarkably scuff free for the first time ever, and a simple burgundy sweater that nearly matched her hair.

Holding out the flowers to her, he opened his mouth like a fish a few times before the words came, "Hi."

She took them with a smile, "Hi." Aiming those sparkling green eyes of hers at him, "Let me just run these upstairs." Back next to him before he could get his brain working again, she pulled her coat on, "Thanks for the flowers. They smell wonderful."

Since it was a date, he decided he'd better get in as much hand holding as possible and sliding his fingers into hers, "Hungry?"

"Starving, but I've only got ten dollars on me, so we're gonna have to go real cheap."

Waving his wallet in the air for a second, "Dad took pity on my allowance and slipped me another 20, so tonight, everything's on me."

"I said I could pay for myself Jack."

"I know you can. And I recall saying that I wasn't going to let you, not tonight." And with a smile that made her melt, "But I might let you buy the popcorn … maybe … if you're nice to me."

"Define nice."

Squeezing her thumb, "Right now."

...

Dinner was eaten at an extraordinary place called Fred's Diner. And, unlike most girls Jack had heard Tim and other guys talk about, Emily ate like a horse. Yes, there was salad involved, but also a hot dog, fries, a chocolate shake and Opa cheese.

As he watched her pack all this into her remarkably small body, "Are you sure they feed you at home?"

Looking across her plate at him, she wiggled her eyebrows, "I offered to pay, remember?"

He laughed, "Eat some more if you must. We're still working on my dad's cash."

After slurping the last of her ice cream, she sat back and stared around the mostly empty diner, "Is it wrong I kind of like it in here without all the people?"

"It's a lot quieter if nothing else. Nice not to have some three-year-old bouncing on the booth behind me."

"We could just stay here all night if you'd like?"

Pulling out his wallet, "No way. You're not getting out of buying me that industrial size tub of popcorn."

···

Making it to the dollar show by nine, they found two movies starting at the same time, both of which Jack wanted to see. "Which sounds better to you?"

Emily, to be honest, had never heard of either one and told him this. He then explained a bit of each plot, and asked again, "Which one would you prefer?"

"Well, what time do you have to be home tonight? We could always just stay for both?" Pointing to the schedule, "We could watch this one, then head right into the other theater to catch the replay of the other."

"I love how your mind works." Pulling out his phone after paying for the first round of tickets, he called his mom, "Is it okay if I'm probably not back until around one or so? There're two movies playing that we want to see." After listening for a second, "Yeah, I'll make sure she gets home safe, promise. I'll even wait until she locks the door."

Hanging up a minute later, he turned to her, "I honestly think she could care less about me, but she was all about making sure you were gonna get home okay."

"You know she loves you."

"Oh, I know. I'm just amused, that's all." Motioning ahead of him and holding the door, "After you."

···

Movies watched and popcorn consumed, they found themselves back on her porch a little before one o'clock on Saturday morning. "I think we may actually be out later than some of the people at the dance."

"And we did it cheaper and in more comfortable clothes."

Jack took a step closer to her, "That reminds me, did I tell you just how beautiful you look tonight?"

Wanting so badly to stand that close to him, her panic still overtook her, and she stepped back, "No you didn't."

Fighting the urge to follow, he stayed where he was, "Well, you look absolutely perfect tonight and I'm not just saying that 'cause you bought me junk food."

With a smile, "But if it helped, I may buy you some more."

"Then would it be alright if I asked you out next Friday? Maybe we can watch a few more X-Files or something?"

Hoping the darkness would keep him from noticing her blanch, "At your house?"

"Well, that is where we keep the TV. The kids'll probably watch with us if that's okay?"

She breathed out slowly, "Your parents won't mind?"

"Nah. Dad's out of town anyway and Mom'll watch with us, too."

The world suddenly righted itself again, "Your mom watches?"

"Who do you think showed us our first episodes?"

...

Fridays in Jack's living room became the norm for Emily. She enjoyed having the younger boys around her and Elizabeth made it even more fun by really getting into the episodes, turning off all the lights and grabbing her children at just the right scary moment to make them yelp in terrified glee. Mr. Callaghan never joined them though, choosing instead to read upstairs.

Elizabeth said he didn't get much time to get through his books, but Jack just laughed, "Come on, Mom. You know the show gives him the willies."

She gave her son a serious-eyed stare, "Just make sure not to rib him about it, okay?"

"'Course. I'm not that evil."

Emily was about to ask what exactly gave him the willies, but Jack gave her a look that plainly said, 'I'll tell you later.'

One night, after everyone had trooped upstairs for bed and Jack was about to walk Emily home, she stopped him while still on the couch, "What scares your dad?"

Jack could only shrug, "Not really sure. He watched the first few episodes, but once Skinner showed up, he stopped watching. Said he'd rather read. I guess maybe the guy who plays him reminds him of somebody. I asked once and he just told me the show was a little too disgusting for him."

Mr. Callaghan's voice drifted in from the kitchen, "Are you telling lies about me again, boy?"

Calling back to him, "Of course I am. What else are dads there for?"

He came into the living room, cup of tea in his hand and looked at Emily, "Don't listen to a word he says. I'm perfect and it just kills him."

This was the first time since the kitchen, weeks ago, that Emily had actually seen Jack's dad. On Fridays, he was usually at work until after they had started the shows and he always yelled hello from the front hall, going immediately upstairs. Now he was approximately six feet from them and Emily felt as if she had a vice wrapped around her throat. Air wouldn't move into her lungs and she thought they were going to explode. He looked just like he did in her nightmares and forcing herself with every ounce of strength, she sat stock still, nodding in the proper places but never looking him in the eye.

Finally, he left and Emily stood quickly, "I should probably get going."

"Let me just find my shoes and I'll walk you home."

She couldn't get out of the house fast enough but, once again, the fresh, crisp air outside brought her back down to reality and the concrete fact that she would not be sleeping that night.

Chapter 6

Tim's birthday fell on October 16 and Jack's on the 19th, so they always had a joint birthday party. Well, more like the immediate family got out the confetti and poppers and plenty of silly string and had a very loud and entertaining celebration for the pair, which didn't really deviate much from a normal family dinner but at least this time there was cake … and presents.

Anyway, this year's party took place on the 19th and Jack had asked Emily to come celebrate with them. She accepted gladly, never one to pass up cake or an evening with the family, but she also had an ulterior motive … it was her birthday as well.

She just opted not to mention it to anyone.

Waking up the morning of the 19th, she stared up at the cracked ceiling, grinning to herself. Today, she was 16. Honest-to-goodness 16.

She had made it to her 16th birthday, scarred, but still kicking.

She also wondered if he was somewhere knowing it was her birthday as well. She hoped he wasn't. She hoped that if he was indeed still alive, he'd forgotten all about her.

But of course, she buried the possibility of his being alive at all deep down in the hidden parts of her brain.

She was 16 today and she felt as if she could conquer the world.

But first, of course, she had to conquer another day at school

···

The party that night was indeed loud and more fun than Emily had had in a long time. She stayed on the other side of the table from Will and, seeming to sense her wariness, he respected the space. She helped devour the giant chocolate cake and her fair share of the ice cream and when they all sang 'Happy Birthday' she joined in, completely off-key, adding her own name silently and smiling all the while.

Eventually, after gifts and cleanup, most everyone disappeared to bed, except for Tim, who was taking Sarah to the movies. Sooner than Jack would have liked, it was quarter to midnight. Turning off the final credits of their second 'X-Files' episode of the evening, "I guess I ought to get you home, huh?"

Emily shrugged, not wanting to go just yet, "Maybe. But I want you to do something for me first, okay?"

"Sure. Anything."

She'd been debating this all day, but decided to plow forward anyway, "Shut your eyes first."

Doing as instructed, he felt her lean forward and shivered at her breath grazing his ear as she whispered, "Can you wish me a happy birthday?"

It took a second for what she said to register, but when it did, he sat back and opened his eyes, "What?"

Biting her lip, "It's actually my birthday, too. At 11:56 tonight to be exact."

"What?!? Why didn't you tell anybody?"

"Shhh. You don't want to wake the whole house, do you?"

Bringing his voice down a few notches, "Why didn't you say anything?"

"Because I just ... didn't."

He quickly looked at his watch, "Well, why did you wait until there's 12 minutes left of it before telling me?"

"I wasn't going to tell you at all at first, but then I realized," taking a deep breath before continuing, "I really wanted someone to wish me a Happy Birthday 'cause it's been the best one I've ever had."

Cocking his head to one side, he shook it slightly as if to clear a few lingering cobwebs, "Well, since you did tell me that means I've got, what, 11 minutes now, to celebrate it with you." Standing up, "Come here."

After pulling her into the kitchen, he lit the candles from a few hours previous on the stove, then stuck them in the last remains of the cake. It was a rather sad looking birthday cake, but Emily thought it the most beautiful thing in the world. As he presented the plate to her, he whisper-sang 'Happy Birthday' and made her blow out the candles, demanding she make a wish on each one before putting out the flame.

Then, together, they finished the cake and each had a glass of milk while they sat on the couch. Her eyes were already shining when he looked at his watch, "I've still got five minutes. Hang on a second, I'll be back."

Racing upstairs as quietly as possible, he came back down a minute later, clearly holding something behind his back. Making her shut her eyes much as she had done to him minutes earlier, he laid something on her lap. "Okay, you can look. I didn't have time to wrap it, but I blame that solely on you and your inability to inform me of your birthday."

On her lap were new copies of the battered and horrible-looking books he'd seen her reading and re-reading over the last few months. Looking up at him, "Where did ... when?"

Going rather sheepish on her, "Well, I've been buying 'em for the last month. I've seen the duct taped ones you read and rubber band together, so I thought I'd collect a few for you, let you actually read a book without pages missing. I was gonna give 'em to you for Christmas, but since it's your birthday, why wait?"

Quickly moving the books from her lap, she slid forward and wrapped her arms around him, smiling through her tears, "This is the best birthday I've ever had." Hugging him tight, "And given it's the only birthday I've ever had, I don't know how to thank you."

Pulling back from her, "What do you mean it's the only birthday you've ever had?"

Heart twisting in her chest, "My mom, um, she doesn't really do birthdays. Never has."

With a quizzical look, "Are these your first birthday gifts, too?"

Now more than a little embarrassed, she stood, "I should be getting home. Mind walking me?"

Once again, he obeyed the subject shift, "Never. Just let me find my shoes and get a bag for you."

"Jack?"

"Yeah?"

"Could you not tell anybody for a little while, okay?"

With a quick nod, he turned, hopefully fast enough not to notice her face crumple for a second, tears rushing to the surface then being blinked back.

···

He finally made it back to his room a little before one and had just gotten in bed when Tim walked in from his date with Sarah. Seeing Jack with his eyes open and CD player resting on his chest, he tapped his brother on the foot, "What're you doing up?"

"Just thinkin' about a girl."

"Ahh, I see."

Jack gestured at the clock between their beds, "And why were you out so late?"

"G'night brother."

Still not closing his eyes, "'Night."

•••

The following Tuesday, Jack showed up to walk Emily home from work with a grin spreading from ear to ear. Eyeing him in amusement, "Um, I'm gonna take a stab in the dark here, but I think you might be just a little happy about something."

His smile got bigger as he held something up the size of a credit card, "I got my license today. I can actually drive myself around." By then, Jack was doing a little hopping dance around her, "Not that I have a car or anything, but if my mother needs a gallon of milk, I am so gonna be able to go get it for her." Genuinely happy for him, she also prayed silently that he wouldn't ask the inevitable next question, which he did only moments later, "When do you go get yours?"

Her heart sank a little, but trying to keep her voice light, "My mom wants me to wait a year before I get it. She doesn't have much time to take me out and we couldn't afford to get me a car anyways. I'm good with my bike, though, so it's fine."

Beginning to think her mother was somewhat annoying, but keeping his mouth shut about that, he instead took her hand, "Biking is good, but walking let's me hold your hand, so I say we keep walking until it gets too cold, then we'll go from there."

Emily pulled him to a halt, "Wait. You're gonna keep coming to get me, even in the winter?"

"Sure. I'll just have to remember to wear my boots and bring my fat scarf."

Smiling at the fat scarf, she then tilted her head, "Even through a foot of snow and nose freezing winds and do you have any idea how cold a winter can be here?"

"Um, I'm from Chicago. I'm pretty sure this winter will be a cake walk in comparison to that. And if the weather is that bad, my mom will tell me to take the car anyway because she won't let me let you freeze. So, I'll come here and stuff you inside even though you'll be protesting that it's really not THAT cold and then I'll just reach across and hold your hand that way, even though I'll probably also have my fat mittens on."

Squeezing his fingers, she started walking again, her face pinking slightly at the thought of his fighting snow and wind chills to hold her hand, "Um, what's with the fat scarf and mittens? Why are they fat? Or did you used to weigh four hundred pounds and they're just all stretched out now?"

Jack chuckled, "I used to be skinnier than this, actually. They're fat because it's a scarf my grandma knitted with three strings of yarn or something, so that makes it thick already, then she lined it with flannel, then fleece, and made it almost six feet long so it wraps around at least three times. Then she made me extra fat mittens to match." With a look of amusement at her, he shrugged, "My grandma really, really loves me."

"Are they warm, I hope?"

"Toastier than a trip to Florida in July."

"You better really, really love your grandma back."

"Totally do and yes, I tell her every week when she calls or when I email her."

Zipping her coat up further against the chilly wind, "Although, right about now, I could go for a fat scarf."

"I'll email Grandma and see what I can do."

Chapter 7

October passed, November flew by and December began.

December was a fairly big deal at school. Especially for the art kids, who had spent all semester working their hardest. They were all hoping to be rewarded by being part of the Christmas art exhibition, held alongside the Christmas concert.

Finally, the best items were chosen and, given both Tim and Emily's abilities, each had multiple items hanging, including their portraits of each other.

The day of the show, Tim asked her while they waited for the teacher to begin class, "So, is your mom coming tonight?"

"No, she has to work."

"Then did you want to hitch a ride with us? I think the whole family's coming."

She nodded, "Jack already asked. I'm gonna be at your place around six or so."

"Cool. I guess Mom wants to stay for the concert, too."

"It'll be good. Dex has a solo and he's fabulous. The things that boy can do with that sax are beyond me."

"He mentioned it last time he was over. Something about eight minutes of mind-blowing perfection."

"Yeah, that would be about it." With a grin, "You wouldn't know it to look at him, but he's already got a music scholarship waiting for him once he graduates."

"Really?"

She nodded, "Just listen to him tonight and you'll hear why."

"It's frightening what you learn about people sometimes."

"Just don't let it get around about the scholarship. He doesn't want to jinx it."

Nodding, "No problem."

···

Later that night, they all piled into two cars to get to the school. They were used to arriving early at places to find seats all together and, once they'd staked out a whole row for themselves and spread their coats around, Tim lead them en masse to Ms. Tassleman, who was hovering nearby.

"So these must be your parents, I expect?"

"Yes, ma'am. My mom, Elizabeth, and my dad, Will."

Shaking hands with both of them, "Glad to finally meet you both." Looking the rest of the boys over with a smile, she turned to Tim for a moment, "You weren't kidding about the resemblance."

"Blame my mom."

They all laughed at this and Ms. Tassleman led them over to the free-standing boards brandishing art projects from most of her classes. "Tim's are intermixed with Emily's. They complement each other so perfectly I didn't dare separate them. They're both, by far, the best students I've had in years."

She continued to talk for another few minutes before excusing herself as more families walked into the cafeteria.

"Tim, I must say, I've never had a teacher gush about you. It would be almost embarrassing if it weren't so wonderful."

He blushed at her, "Geez Mom, you'd think all my teachers thought I was the devil's spawn and made it a point to tell you that every chance they got."

She just squeezed her son's arm as she turned to Emily, "And you, Miss Emily, are just as outstanding." Turning towards the picture of her son, "I wish I had some of that talent."

"Sometimes I wish I was just as good in some of my other classes."

Without thought, Elizabeth slipped her arm around Emily's shoulders and gave her a squeeze, "It's not all about grades."

Tears came rushing to her eyes and with every fiber of her being, she fought to keep them from falling. To her relief, she succeeded, mostly because of the distraction of Tucker and Nate knocking over a chair.

Tim hissed at his mother through clenched teeth, fairly embarrassed by his family at this point, especially with his favorite teacher nearby, "Could they be any more annoying?"

"Probably." Elizabeth started over towards the pair already righting the chair and looking sheepish, "Would you like me to ask them to be?"

Jack noticed him rolling his eyes and kicked him lightly in the foot, "Dude, they already fixed it and nobody cares."

"One time. That's all I asked for. One time without them doing something obnoxious."

Jack went on to say something else, but Emily didn't hear what, given she'd used the distraction to move away from the group. Needing a few moments to calm herself down, she studied the other displays until Ms. Tassleman showed up at her elbow, "Mom working again?"

She nodded, "Yeah."

"I'm sorry. Maybe she'll be able to make it next year."

Not able to look her favorite teacher in the eye, she remained focused on the work in front of her, "Maybe."

■■■

Everyone was settled in their seats a few minutes before the concert began. Even Sam, who was a notorious fidgeter from what Jack had mentioned, had promised to sit still.

It helped, of course, that both Jack and Tim had threatened him with bodily harm if he did anything bad and promised ice cream if he was good.

Emily, seated next to Jack, who was next to Tim, leaned over, "Can I get in on some of that ice cream action?"

"Do you promise not to sing along or scream for the next hour?"

"I think so, if properly motivated."

Tim grinned past his brother at her, "Two scoops?"

"Deal."

■■■

Most of the concert was fun. There was a sing-a-long, which Sam, after getting the okay from Tim, belted out along with the rest of the crowd. Then more holiday favorites, during which Sam did nothing more than hum, which, for this particular six-year-old, was truly amazing.

He nearly lost the ice cream promised him, however, when Dex walked to the center of the stage. Sam stood and called out over the silent audience, "Hi Dex!"

With a wide grin and a Santa hat perched atop his newly dyed neon green hair, "Hey Sam. Be sure to clap for me when I'm finished, okay?"

"'Kay Dex."

And once the audience stopped chuckling, Dex began to play.

Who knew such a strange looking, pierced individual could create such a feeling with a chunk of brass.

He played through "Oh Holy Night" then slipped into "White Christmas" and finally melted his way into "Silent Night". Once he was done, everyone just sat mesmerized for a few moments until Sam, God love him, climbed up on his seat and started clapping his little hands off.

After that, the rest of the crowd woke up and began thundering the applause while Dex just stood there, enjoying the one moment of the year no one thought of him as 'that nut case with the hair issues.'

...

Afterwards, Dex brought his parents and sister over to the Callaghan's. "Mrs., Mr. Callaghan, this is my mom, Cindy, and my dad, Jim, my sister, Annie, and her son, Caleb."

Everyone shook hands, "Nice to finally meet you."

Cindy smiled, "Glad to finally meet the woman who's been saving me on food bills. I really should offer to help with your groceries."

"Having to feed six already, you don't even notice another mouth or two around the table."

They all stood around talking until Dex's mom looked at her watch, "Honey, we've gotta go." Shaking hands again with Jack's parents, "It was wonderful to meet you."

"You too. Hope to see you again soon."

Elizabeth turned to Will, "We ought to go, too. It's getting late."

Will tossed his keys to Tim, "Don't be too late."

Sarah, who had been standing next to Tim for the last few minutes after saying good-bye to her own parents, "We won't. I've gotta work early tomorrow morning, so I can't be out very late anyhow."

"Well, have fun and be careful."

While everyone was getting their coats on, Tim motioned Jack and Emily over, "Hey, me and Sarah were gonna go over and get something to eat at Fred's. Do you two and maybe Dex want to come?" Smiling in Emily's direction, "I owe you ice cream if I recall."

She nodded, "Sure, I'm always in for free ice cream."

Jack nodded as well and ran back over to his dad, then to Dex, who was about to leave. Returning a minute later, "All set."

Having managed to stay on the opposite side of the crowd from Jack's dad the entire night and, now, knowing that she wouldn't have to be in a car with him as well just made the upcoming ice cream all the more appealing to Emily.

•••

Settled in a back booth of the extremely busy diner, Sarah and Emily eyed each other shyly, never really having had a conversation before and neither really knowing where to begin. Luckily, the minute both groaned in unison when Tim ordered strawberry, chocolate and caramel topping for his sundae, they grinned at each other and from there, the conversation flowed easily.

•••

On the other side of town, Elizabeth got the older boys into their pajamas while Will hauled the sleeping Sam straight from the car to his bed.

Settling down on the couch next to his wife after everyone was quiet, "She doesn't like me."

"Who?"

"Emily."

"Why do you think that?"

"Every time I catch her eye, which is extremely seldom by the way, there's this fear there and I can feel the panic rolling off of her."

Knowing she should tell her husband that he was wrong, that Emily just didn't know him, she couldn't lie to him either, "I've seen it, too." As she rested her head on his shoulder, "There's so much there, I don't even know how to begin to figure her out."

"Have you ever met her mother?"

"No. She seems to be working all the time. Emily's mentioned she has a really crazy schedule that changes constantly. It's why she couldn't make it tonight."

Will chewed on the inside of his cheek for a moment, "Does she ever talk about her life or anything?"

"She's 16, honey. What 16-year-old do you know that sits down and discusses her family with her boyfriend's mother?"

With a sudden glimmer in his eye, "Speaking of which, are they going out or not? I can't tell and it's really beginning to bug me."

She laughed at her husband, "At this point, I don't know if they even know what's going on, but I like her, so I hope she stays around for awhile. Both for Jack's sake and for Tim's."

"Tim?"

"Yeah. Did you take a good look at his things tonight? They've gotten much better since he started school here. It's either the teacher or Emily who's pushing him, maybe both, but if he keeps this up, he could possibly use it to get into college."

Will sat back, putting his feet up on the coffee table, "How did this happen? In Chicago, Tim was dating three different girls, breaking curfew and God knows what else that I don't want to think about and now he's got Sarah, who's aiming for valedictorian, and he's getting decent grades again." Now settling his head against the back of the couch, "Then Jack finds Emily and the musical prodigy and he seems happier than he's been in a long time." Knocking his knuckles into his wife's knee lightly, "Which reminds me, I found him talking to Claire the other day."

This raised a surprised set of eyebrows, "Really? She finally apologized?"

"I don't know about that, but they were on the phone for a good half-hour and he came away smiling."

Elizabeth grinned, "Good. I'm glad they finally worked it out. I was talking to Jenny yesterday, she didn't say anything about Claire and Jack, but she did tell me that there's talk at Bob's work about a promotion or possibly relocating."

"Where to?"

"Either York or Pittsburgh."

Will grinned, "I'm going to hope for York. Jack would be thrilled to have Claire back."

Snuggling down into his arms while he switched on the news, "It'd be nice to have Jenny around again, too." Squeezing her husband's hand, "But we can't say anything to anyone yet. There's a good chance it won't happen."

"I know, but it's a nice thought."

···

Tim dropped Dex off first, then left Emily and Jack at her house, "I'll be home in a little while."

Tim just nodded, "You'll probably make it home before me anyway, but okay."

Standing under the clear sky, he waited until Tim had driven off before turning to Emily, "Do I have to go home?"

It had to be the sweetest and most heart-breaking thing she'd ever heard. Fighting back the tears and the secrets that suddenly threatened to spill over, she nodded, "I don't want you to, but I think you have to."

Hoping the disappointment wasn't too visible on his face, "Then can I ask another question?"

She nodded, "'Course."

"Do you think you might ever possibly sometime in the future maybe want to kinda be my girlfriend?"

In complete seriousness she answered back, "I think that sometime in the future, I would very well love to be your girlfriend."

"Do you think you'll ever let me kiss you?"

Reaching up to run her finger down his cheek, then her thumb across his lips, "I wish I could let you kiss me now."

As her hand left his face, he caught it and bought her fingers back to his mouth, kissing each of the tips, "Make sure you tell me the minute I can." With a final squeeze of her hand, he turned her towards her door, "I'll see you in the morning."

···

The nightmares began that night. She wasn't sure if they were brought on by Will, by Jack and her anger at not being able to get closer to him or things were just finally beginning to surface, but, regardless, she watched the world wake up from her comfortable spot on the couch, where she'd been wide-awake since 1:30 a.m.

Chapter 8

Jack saw the sleepless night plainly on her face the next morning, "You okay?"

Nodding and yawning at the same time, "Yeah, just couldn't sleep last night."

"All night?"

"I slept for about an hour, maybe a little more, but that's it."

Hiking her book bag over his shoulder, "You should have called. I'd have talked to you until you fell asleep from sheer boredom."

Too tired to catch herself, "I can't call you."

Half-joking with her, "What? Your mom keep track of when you use the phone?"

Still not really hearing her own words, "I can only afford a land line with local calling and your cell phone number's out of the area."

Attributing her answer to exhaustion, he still filed the statement away in the back of his mind unconsciously, "Ahh, well, next time you can't sleep, just imagine the boring conversation you could be having with me. Should work the same way."

"I don't think you could ever bore me enough to put me to sleep."

"But it would be fun to talk to you all night."

She could only bump shoulders with him, "Well, as much as I'd love to talk to you, I'd much prefer that tonight, I hit the pillow and don't move until tomorrow morning."

"Well, if for nothing else, winter break starts in a couple of weeks. You can always catch up then."

As they continued trekking towards school, she stared ahead, unfocused and exhausted, "Maybe we'll get a snow day in here somewhere and we'll all be forced to stay home and nap all day long."

"You're making my mouth water, woman. Stop it."

...

She did sleep like a log that night. For a whole two hours. Then, once again, she watched the neighborhood wake up through the front window while curled on the couch, pad of paper on her lap and pencils strewn everywhere.

She especially did not enjoy when this seemed to become the routine.

The one very dim, very sad bright side to the whole situation that she grasped onto during this two week bout of insomnia was that she had been keeping ahead on her homework. She couldn't stay focused during tests to save her life, but her homework had never been more thorough.

Dex walked head-on into Emily's loosening grasp of composure the day before Christmas break began and once he got over the surrealness of her reaction, he caught Jack in the hall between classes, "Is Emily okay?"

"I think so, why?"

"Well, I had to ask her the same question three times in a row before she answered and then she got real snarly with me for asking it and I don't mean her just telling me no, but getting honest-to-God bitchy with me. It was just about some of her notes, nothing major."

Aiming a look of sympathy towards his friend, "She hasn't been sleeping much lately."

"Huh. Well, thought I'd better ask. I'll just set her shit meter a little higher for now."

"Shit meter?"

"Yeah, how much shit I can take from her before I get annoyed. She's usually got hers set astronomically high for me which is why I thought I'd better ask if something was wrong."

Stopping next to their lockers, "Something's keeping her awake, but either she hasn't figured it out or she has and can't figure out what to do about it."

Grabbing the book for his last class, Dex slammed the locker, "Well, let me know if you find out anything else."

"Sure."

As Jack and Dex headed to Spanish class, Emily was trying to keep herself awake while she waited for history class to begin. Her head kept bobbing and for the first time ever, she seriously debated slipping back out of class and heading home.

She immediately banished the thought, however, because the teacher came in just then and began to pass out the exam papers for the test she had studied a good four hours for the previous night. It looked completely foreign to her. It had to be in English but for the life of her, she couldn't figure out what the questions were asking.

Her brain felt cloudy and realizing anything she had learned the night before was gone, she took a few deep breaths. She figured she had two choices. Try to force some information from her empty mind or put her head down and take a nap. Neither one seemed doable at the moment so she chose a third option. Standing up, she gave her unfilled pages to the teacher and walked out the door.

Everyone looked up at her in unison as she opened the classroom door and left.

Mr. Castle told them to keep working as he hurried out behind her, "Emily?"

Turning back around, she looked at him standing in the doorway, keeping one eye on his test-takers and the other on her, "Yeah?"

"What are you doing?"

"I'm leaving, sir." At this point, she just wanted to lie down and didn't care what she had to say, as long as she could just shut her eyes, "I can't answer anything on that test so I might as well go home."

"You can't just leave."

"It's last period. You always let us go as soon as we're done with the test as long as we're quiet about it."

He couldn't believe he was having this conversation with one of his best students and, by now, a few teachers' heads were also popping into the hall to see what had happened, "But you didn't even try."

With an almost maniacal chuckle, "I looked at those questions and I can't answer them."

Knowing he ought to be making her come back inside, he realized she had him. She could choose not to take the test, fail and leave, given he did let them go as soon as they were done. He also knew a call to her mother would go unanswered, so all he could do was shrug and wave her off, "I still wish you'd change your mind."

Already turning and continuing down the hall, "Have a good holiday."

...

Jack had just finished giving his presentation in Spanish when he caught sight of her walking past the door. Knowing full well she should be taking a test right now, he waited until the teacher finished her critique of him before asking, "Can I use the bathroom?"

Nodding at him and believing it was just stage jitters sending him to the bathroom, she handed him the pass. Giving Dex a look as he left, Jack headed quickly down the hall, stopping only long enough to shove a few books in his backpack and grab his coat. Leaving the pass hanging on Dex's locker, he raced after her, catching up in the parking lot, "Emily? Hey, Em? What're you doing?"

When she turned to him, he caught his breath. He'd just seen her last class, but somehow, she looked even more beat, her face was pale as a sheet and eyes glassy, the lids heavy in exhaustion.

Taking a second to focus in on him, "I just want to go home, Jack."

"Aren't you supposed to be in history? Taking a test?"

She repeated herself, "I just want to go home. Can you take me home?"

Instantly weighing his options of detention vs. doing as asked, he put his arm around her waist, "Come on."

•••

She dug in her pocket fruitlessly for the key to the front door before nearly crying as she realized, "It's still in my locker."

"Do you have a spare laying around anywhere?"

Nodding, she really did begin to cry at this point, "Jack, I'm so tired."

"Then tell me where it is and I'll get it."

After he'd opened her hidden lock box and let them in, he helped her up the stairs to the second floor loft, "I didn't realize you lived upstairs."

"It's cheaper than an apartment because of just the one room."

She aimed for the corner of the large room where a single mattress lay on the floor, an old comforter and several blankets neatly covering it. To his surprise, she also began shedding clothes as she went. By the time she crawled under the blankets, she had only a long-sleeve thermal shirt and a pair of faded blue long-john pants on.

Jack watched until she got under the covers. He was about to sneak back out when she called to him in a small voice, "Jack?"

Walking over to the bed, "Yeah?"

"Can you keep him away?"

His forehead crinkled in confusion, "Who?"

"Him."

By now he knelt down next to her, straining to hear her whispers, "I don't know what you mean? Him who?"

The tears were rolling again, this time hard and fast, "Can you keep him away from here Jack? Please? Please keep him away."

Still having absolutely no idea what she was talking about, he immediately pulled off his coat and lay down next to her, gathering her and her covers up in his arms, "I'll keep him away, Em, I promise. I'll stay as long as you need me to."

Burying her head in his chest, she sobbed quietly for a few minutes until, at last, she slept. He held her for another half-hour or so until finally, gently, slowly, wiggling out from next to her. Sitting on the floor by the bed in case she woke up, he surveyed the room, until suddenly, he realized what had been bothering him since the second he followed her through the door.

She had said it was cheaper than a regular apartment because it was only one room. There was only one kitchen chair at the small table; there was only the one single mattress where they were. The bookshelves were homemade of bricks and boards, the kind that kids make in their closets and the kind that one makes when they can't afford real shelves. The walls had old milk crates lining them, holding a sparse amount of clothes and a few other possessions while the cracked and extremely wobbly coffee table held piles of pictures, library books, charcoal and pencil nubs.

He stood, moving painfully slow so as not to make a sound, and headed to the kitchen. Feeling nosy, he looked in the cupboards anyway. They were full of Raman noodles, pasta, spaghetti sauce, macaroni and cheese, canned vegetables and fruit, extremely off-brand cereal and plenty of pretzels. The fridge and freezer held lots of hot dogs, cheap hamburger and from the looks of it, enough eggs and blocks of cheese to feed an army.

Already knowing what he'd find, he checked the small bathroom anyways. One toothbrush, one towel and one bar of soap.

Coming back to the main room, he sat down once again next to Emily, gently moving the hair from her forehead while he pulled his phone from his pocket and dialed, "Dex?"

"Hey man, what the hell happened?"

"Did you call my house looking for me or talk to Tim at all?"

"No. I figured I'd wait until you called. It had to be something important or else you wouldn't have just up and left class. When I returned the pass, I also told Schettle that you had been puking in the bathroom, so she's not busting you for skipping out early."

He breathed a sigh of relief, "Thanks. Um, can I ask you a favor?"

"Probably."

"Can I use you as cover tonight? I've gotta stay here, but Mom'll crack if I tell her where I am."

"You at Em's?"

"Yeah. The no sleep thing kinda finally got to her. From what I can tell, she walked out of her exam and ..." Trailing off because he wasn't sure what Dex might know, "Well, she's here now, asleep and I think she's sick, but no one's with her and I hate to leave her alone."

Dex, asking cautiously, "Do you know when her mom's getting home?"

Answering honestly, "I have absolutely no idea."

"All right. Well, consider yourself sleeping on my floor tonight. If your mom calls, I'll cover."

"Thanks, man. I hate to do this, but I don't see any other way around it."

"Just let me know if anything changes. We don't need our stories to be different if somebody corners me." About to hang up, he suddenly remembered, "Oh, and can you tell Em I grabbed all her books for her. Figured she'd need them over break. I can drop them off whenever."

"Yup, I'll tell her and thanks again. Talk to you later."

···

Next he called his mom, "Hey, it's me."

"Hi there. I was expecting you after school. Something happen?"

Taking a deep breath, "I'm at Dex's. Is it alright if I stay the night? I came by after school and I figure since it's now winter break, it might be okay?"

"That's fine. I was just about to call and yell at you so nice timing." Both Sam and Nate were trying to talk to her at this point, "Sorry, honey, I gotta go. Have fun and don't forget, you start at the diner tomorrow morning, nine o'clock."

"I won't forget and thanks."

"Have a good time."

Hanging up, he continued to watch Emily's eyes move erratically under her closed lids. She was dreaming of something and he hoped with all his might that they were good dreams.

···

A few hours later, Jack finally had to raid her cupboards for something to eat. He cooked several hot dogs over the flame of her stove and supplemented with a couple of granola bars and a few handfuls of pretzels. Washing it all down with a large glass of water, he turned on the small lamp by the couch and, closing the curtains, he perused her bookshelves. Seeing several old favorites of his alongside the new books he'd bought her, he pulled one off and began reading, glancing over at her every so often to make sure she was all right.

About an hour after that, he was pulled from his book by the sounds of her moaning. Quickly by her side, he watched her hands begin moving and her feet kicking the covers. Her clenched fists began swinging at the air and, before he could get out of the way, one connected with his face, plowing him right in the eye. She woke up instantly once her fist caught him and, panicking, she tried to stand, immediately falling because of the tangle of sheets wrapped around her feet.

Catching her and ignoring the throbbing of his face, "Hey, slow down."

Fresh tears began falling as soon as she looked at herself, his eye and the slow trickle of blood from his nose. Dropping back on the bed, she curled her knees up to her chest and shut her eyes, "I'm sorry. For everything. I should have just told you to go home."

He had her in his arms by then and, cradling her face, he kissed the tears from her cheeks. Following the trail to her mouth, he let his lips brush hers before hugging her again, "Why didn't you tell me?"

Shaking her head into his chest, "Not right now, okay?"

And with a nod, he eased her back down on the mattress and held her close as they both drifted off to sleep.

■■■

He woke up when she moved to get off the bed. Watching her shuffle to the bathroom, he sat up rubbing his eyes, forgetting momentarily that he'd been punched just a few hours before. After swearing silently, he waited until the pain subsided then, checking his watch, found it was almost midnight.

She came back from the bathroom a minute later, pulling an afghan from one of the crates and wrapping it around herself, "You should probably go home."

"I'm fine."

After turning on the hall light and crouching in front of him, she touched the crust of dried blood near his nose and his already dark purple eye, telling him again, "You need to go home. Your mom's probably worried."

"I called her and told her I was at Dex's for the night. Then I called Dex to ask him to cover for me. I'm good."

For the third time, "I don't want you to lie for me. Go home Jack. I'll be fine, I promise."

Remaining where he was, "How long have you been on your own?"

She brushed her fingers across his cheek, "This needs to stay between us."

He nodded, "I know."

Pulling the blanket closer around her, "There's not much to tell. I've been by myself since I was 13. I got myself this far, decided to stay, eventually found this place and here I am."

Still stuck on, "13?"

"It was either this or social services. Which would you have chosen?"

"But Em, 13?" Scooting closer, "What happened to you?" The minute the question left his lips, he knew he shouldn't have asked and retracted it immediately, "Sorry, I didn't mean to ask." Realizing he might not want to know what would be bad enough to force a 13-year-old to choose independence over family, he apologized again, "I'm … I'm sorry."

Her eyes closed slightly, the weight of her response bearing down on her, "I couldn't tell you right now, even if you demanded an answer." Taking a deep breath in, trying to force her muscles to relax some, "All I can say is it was enough to make me realize that, right now, I live in total paradise."

Even through the exhaustion that crept back across her face, he could clearly see her fear and reaching out to wrap his fingers around hers, "I won't tell anyone. I promise."

"I know you won't."

With that, she got a look on her face that mirrored his mom's, stating clearly this line of discussion was closed for the moment. Knowing he couldn't fight that look, he moved on, "Just for future arguments sake, I'm still staying tonight so you might as well stop trying to get rid of me." With a small smile, "So, you awake now or ready to go back to sleep?"

She yawned her reply and crawling over him, slid back under the covers. Jack moved to sleep on the couch but she caught his arm, "You can stay here if you want. I've slept on that couch and it's horrific."

Not sure if this was such a good idea, "I've slept in some horrific places before. I think it'll be okay."

"Please? Except for the whole hitting you thing, I haven't slept this good in months."

Seeing the terror of nightmares looming on her face, he nodded, "Okay. Move over though 'cause I need more than a foot of space here."

Pulling off the long sleeve thermal he was wearing, he revealed his Grinch t-shirt, which made her laugh, "Grinch?"

"Hey now, don't be messing with the Grinch. Best Dr. Seuss character ever." After jumping up to turn off the lights, he made his way back to the bed guided only by the glow of the nightlights on the wall, "Do you have an alarm?"

Nodding, "Yeah. What time do you need to leave?"

"I start my job tomorrow ... today ... whatever ... at nine and I should go home and shower first."

"Will six-thirty be okay?" Once he nodded, she settled in on her back next to him, waiting a minute before she spoke, "I'm sorry. I don't mean to cause so much trouble."

Shifting, he placed his head beside hers and whispered in her ear, "I just wish you'd have let me know sooner."

"You shouldn't even know now."

"But I do and that's a good thing. Trust me."

Emily rolled her head in his direction, asking quietly, "Did you tell Dex anything?"

"No. I just said I didn't know when your mom would be home. I wasn't sure what he knew, so I played dumb basically."

Whispering a 'thank you' in his direction, she curled on her side facing the wall, "G'night."

"G'night."

···

He woke up on his own at six. It had been a fairly rough night after they had lain down. She hadn't woken back up, but she remained twitchy beside him, hands flexing and jaw grinding, occasionally whimpering before settling down for a few minutes.

If this was the best she'd slept in weeks, no wonder she was beyond exhausted. He lay watching her finally peaceful face for a few minutes before slipping out of bed and going to the bathroom. Then, after silently getting his shoes and coat on, he leaned over, "Hey Em, I've gotta go."

Stirring at the sound of his voice, "Hmm?"

"I gotta get going. You gonna be alright?"

She finally opened her eyes as she nodded, "Do you think we can just forget that yesterday ever happened?"

Kissing her forehead, "I don't really think that's an option."

"Well, I'm going to dwell in the land of denial for a while so if you'd like to join me, just knock."

With a laugh, "At least I now know where the key is."

Giving him his first real smile in days, "You can come in any time."

Chapter 9

His first day of bussing tables and washing dishes was draining and, given the previous night he'd had, Emily took one look at him after he stopped by and sent him home to bed.

The next day went easier and he wasn't as tired, so, stopping by her house, he invited her over for dinner and some movies.

As she stood in her doorway, "I don't know that I can look your mom in the eye yet. I wish you hadn't had to lie to her."

"Em, what's done is done. My guilt vanished when I walked in the door yesterday morning and she looked at me and, without even commenting on the black eye, said, and I'm not kidding, 'Oh, I forgot you were gone'."

She laughed at this, "I guess I could come over for a little while."

"Cool." Stepping inside out of the blowing wind, "I have got to get me a car or I'm gonna freeze."

"Well, come up and get warm for a few minutes while I find my coat and hat."

Shivering a little, "And scarf and gloves and boots and ski masks ..."

"Just shut up and come upstairs."

Following her, "You know, in the six months I've known you, this is the first time you've actually invited me in."

She didn't reply until they reached the top of the steps, "Jack?"

"Yeah?"

"Would you like to come in and see my house?"

He gave her a slow grin, "I think I would love to."

...

They got back to Jack's a little before six and could smell the wonderful aroma of stew before Jack even unlocked the door, "Mom, I'm home and I've bought another stomach with me."

Coming into the hall, she smiled warmly at Emily, "Brought your appetite with you too, I hope?"

She nodded shyly and quietly slid out of her coat, hanging it on one of the many hooks next to the door. Jack touched her arm, "Be back down in a minute. Gotta change."

After he thundered up the stairs, Elizabeth beckoned her into the kitchen, "Well, the boys are in the living room causing general mayhem, so you're welcome to join them or maybe you'd like to hang out here with me?"

Listening to the din coming from the other room and eyeing the stack of dishes in the sink, "Do you need any help in here? I wash a mean dish."

Gladly holding out the dish towel, "Mostly I think I'd just like a girl to talk to. I've been trapped in the house with six boys for three days straight. I need some outside information. Any outside information."

Emily smiled, "Well, what would you like to know?"

"Let's start with the standard, read any good books lately?"

...

Jack made it back downstairs about ten minutes later, having decided to shower. Sliding into the kitchen on the socks he'd stolen from Tim's drawer, he nearly knocked Emily, who was trying to figure out which cupboards held which dishes, over. Catching her before she hit the ground, he held her for a second longer than normal before letting go and pointing out the proper cabinet.

This was not at all lost on Elizabeth, who contained her grin quite admirably, but, as she would embarrassingly admit to her husband later that night, she was doing all kinds of happy dancing in her head.

But back to the kitchen. Jack set the table and wrangled the rest of the boys to gather up any and all condiments, napkins and drinks that were still needed. Once everyone was around the table, "Where's Dad? Shouldn't he be home by now?"

With a twinkle in her eye, she glanced over Sam's head, "He's out doing some shopping."

"Ahhh, well, do you want me to make him a plate for the oven or no?"

Shaking her head, "No. I'll warm him up something when he gets here."

Emily looked slightly confused, so Jack leaned over and whispered, "Mom can't really go Christmas shopping with Sam because of Santa, so Dad must have had to finish up tonight."

Understanding finally, she whispered back, "What about the other kids?"

"They already know about Santa, but are under strict orders not to ruin it."

Her eyes glazed for a second, then returned to reality, "I think I would love to be Sam."

Reaching over, he squeezed her hand under the table before beginning to serve out the steaming stew to the boys' upheld bowls, "All right gentlemen, it's ladies first so you're gonna have to hang on a minute."

...

After dinner and clean-up, which Jack did with the ordered assistance of Dave and Nate, a nervous-looking Sam came up to Emily, "Emily?"

Kneeling down in front of him, "Yeah?"

"Do you want to color with me?"

Jack, who was standing behind him, went to open his mouth, but Emily shook her head at him then took Sam by the hand, "I'd love to color with you."

Sam's face lit up and he led her importantly into the big back room, "I have lots of crayons."

Emily glanced over her shoulder at Jack and grinned, "See ya."

He just shook his head in her direction with a smile and turned around, running directly into his mom, "Oops. Sorry."

"You're just running into everyone today aren't you?"

"Well, you know, I've never been one for gracefulness when falling is available."

"Very true." Glancing around the corner to where all the kids were, "Are you and Emily doing anything right now?"

He shook his head, "Sam's got her coloring. Why?"

"Well, I was wondering if you'd help me upstairs with a few things. Sam refused to leave me alone today, so I couldn't get anything done."

"Yeah, just let me go tell Em and then I'll come up."

"Thanks, honey."

Whispering his intentions to her, she glanced at Sam, who was watching her adoringly, "Me and Sam here'll be just fine, won't we?" Sam could only nod, completely happy that his favorite girl in the world was coloring Transformer pictures with him. Looking back to Jack, "I'll find you if I need anything."

■■■

After telling the rest of the boys not to kill each other, he headed upstairs.

"So, what're we doing?"

"I mostly need you to climb up into the attic for me and get the gifts out."

Knowing his mom's intense fear of enclosed spaces, "No problem. I'm not gonna see my stuff, am I?"

She smiled, "No, Santa is out buying your 'stuff' as we speak."

"Geez, Mom, nothing like waiting until the last minute."

"Hey, I can call your dad up and tell him to return everything?"

"So, where's that access panel again?"

■■■

Jack was back downstairs long before they were done coloring. He watched both from the archway, much as he had when Emily was drawing Tim, and he marveled at them both. Normally Sam's version of 'coloring' was to color as fast as he could while still trying to stay in the lines. But now, he was methodically and thoughtfully coloring one of a stack of robot images in front of him, emulating Emily's careful hand.

All he wanted to do was kiss her.

But since that wasn't possible at the moment, he instead stood watching, holding position against the wall until Tim walked in behind him, having just gotten home from work. Looking over his little brother's shoulder, he spoke low, "So, when are you finally gonna tell her?"

In an equally low voice, "I don't know if she'll let me."

■■■

Borrowing a car, he drove her home around ten that night and, given that he'd been repeating Tim's question over and over in his head for the past two hours, he was rather distracted, not hearing Emily until the third time she asked, "Hey, you in there?"

Jerking his head, he woke up, "Yeah, sorry. What did you say again?"

"I just wanted to know if you were okay. You didn't say much after you came back downstairs and you've been quiet the whole way here."

Hoping he wouldn't freak her out with his blunt asking, "Do you think I could hug you?"

"You've hugged me before."

Knowing he was stammering, "I … I know but that was before everything. I just … I didn't … I don't want to scare you or offend you or something."

Reaching for his hand, she led him up to her door and, once they were safely inside, she turned, holding her arms out to him, "Hug please."

As he hung his head, both from embarrassment and amusement, he slid his arms around her. He loved the feel of her head on his chest and, hugging her close, he wished he never had to leave.

Chapter 10

Elizabeth had invited Emily over for both Christmas Eve and Christmas Day. After talking to Jack, Emily had opted for Christmas Day. Mostly because she had the chance to work a full shift on Christmas Eve and, in her situation, such an opportunity was not to be turned down.

So she worked her tail off for nine hours, then went home and collapsed, sleeping soundly for the first time in months.

And that was her Christmas Eve.

Meanwhile, at the Callaghan house, chaos reigned as everyone did last minute gift wrapping and dessert making and tree decorating and general baking. Jack, as usual, had the duty of cookie maker. Somehow, he made the best cookies. He had little flairs he'd added to the recipes, which he always swore were secret and highly classified ingredients and would never reveal.

The one hitch was that Tim had to work as well, closing up the store at six, which still gave him plenty of time to get home and do his own catching up on things. As he drove home, he passed the restaurant where Emily worked and, as usual, he glanced at it and, for a second, swore he saw her through the big glass windows. He was so sure of this he circled the block and came to a stop in front of the building. Sitting idle for a minute, he caught sight of her again and there was no mistaking it this time.

...

Once Tim got home and ate dinner, he stole two of his brother's still warm Christmas cookies and took him by the elbow, "Can I talk to you for a minute?"

Since he was just starting to wash the dishes and all the cookies were out of the oven, he nodded and dried his hands. Following Tim into the front room, "What's up?"

Keeping his voice low, "Did Emily say she was working today?"

"No. She's at home with her mom." The odd look on Tim's face made Jack inwardly panic, "Why?"

"I just saw her at Dragon's on my way home."

"Maybe she got called in to cover or something. There's still plenty of time to be home tonight."

Tim studied his brother for a moment, "You're getting better at lying, you know that?"

"Who's lying?"

"I'm pretty sure you are and by default, that means Emily is, too." Finally detecting a bit of worry in Jack's eye, "All right. I won't say anything, but you better watch it. Lies have a way of coming back to bite you in the ass."

Jack nodded, knowing he was beaten, "Thanks."

Clapping him on the back, he bit into one of the cookies, "Also, don't tell Mom, but you make way better cookies than her."

He grinned at his big brother, "I guess we all have our secrets, huh?"

"You can say whatever you like little brother, as long as you keep a steady supply of cookies coming my way."

"I've been cooking 'em all day. We have enough to outlast even you."

Shoving the second in his mouth, "Then by all means, let's go get some more."

•••

Emily was up bright and early Christmas morning to open her gifts. Granted, she had actually purchased them herself weeks ago, wrapped them, then made herself wait until Christmas morning to open them. She'd given herself a whole stack of used books she had found at the library book sale almost two months earlier and, given she'd been wanting to read them since, she was almost giddy unwrapping them.

She also knew that it was silly, but given she'd never had her own Christmas morning when she was younger, she felt justified in giving herself one now. And so she sat, happy and content to read her new things and wait until ten o'clock, when Elizabeth had asked her to come over for Christmas breakfast.

Bundled up against the blowing cold, she left the house a few minutes before arriving on the porch and knocking right on time. Jack pulled the door open and hauling her inside, gave her an enormous hug, "Merry Christmas."

Laughing at the greeting, she wiggled out of her coat and scarf, "Merry Christmas back."

She could hear the commotion spilling out of the kitchen and walking in kind of shyly, she was confronted with the entire Callaghan clan in full holiday mode, which she'd never experienced before and suddenly, she felt inexplicably small.

Standing for a moment beside the stove, Jack leaned into her ear, "Intimidating lot aren't we?"

"Well, it is my first holiday."

"We'll try to make it as painless as possible."

After another round of 'Merry Christmas's', they all settled down to eat through stacks of pancakes that just kept appearing on their plates, along with piles of bacon and rivers of orange juice.

Emily finally had to throw in the towel after her second helping of everything, "Okay, I don't think I've ever eaten that much before."

With a glimmer in his eye, Dave leaned over towards her, "You ain't seen nothin' yet. Wait until dinner; it could very well kill you."

In mock horror, "I have to eat again?"

...

Sam was antsy all through breakfast and by the time the kitchen was cleaned up, he was positively crazy, "Can we see the tree yet? Please?"

"Almost, Sam. Promise. Just let your dad get the fire going then we'll go in."

Confused, Emily turned to Jack, "Why hasn't he seen the tree yet?"

"Nobody has. We always wait until after church and breakfast." Shrugging, "I think they started it because we sat better through church if they could threaten that Santa could still take everything away."

"Blackmail on Christmas. Nice."

Elizabeth overheard this and laughed, "With six boys, you try any and all means of keeping them quiet."

Finally, everybody was let into the living room and the Christmas insanity began. The gifts under the tree weren't wrapped. There were just designated piles that each of the boys seemed to know were theirs. Tim and Jack's were on either end of the tree and, working inward around the semi-circle, Sam and Tucker's piles were in the center.

Emily wasn't exactly sure what to do at this point, but when Jack motioned for her to sit next to him, she did, only to find a small pile of gifts that no one had yet claimed.

Jack, just sat grinning at her until she had to ask, "What?"

"Aren't you gonna look through your stuff?"

Confusion flooded her face and she asked again, "What?"

Picking up the pile, he set in on her lap, "Merry Christmas."

Staring down at the gifts, she then looked from Jack to Elizabeth and finally to Will, all of whom were grinning at her. She managed to only let one tear escape down her cheek before she joined in the fun.

She'd gotten a sweater, a set of new, whole and perfectly toned charcoals, one of the books she'd told Elizabeth about a few weeks ago, a pair of thick wool socks, a hat and a new pair of mittens, wool lined and warm.

She was honestly at a loss for words at the moment and all she could muster was a near-whispered thank you as she hugged her items close and couldn't stop smiling.

Once she came down from her happy fog, she noticed a few gift trends that made her smile. Each boy got a sweater, a pair of wool socks and either a hat or mittens. Those seemed to be the staples of the pile and other things were added to it.

Jack didn't notice at first but one of his socks was rigid and Emily leaned over, "What's in the sock?"

Puzzled, he finally realized something was hidden in the sock. Pulling it out, he let out a manly, low octave squeal of delight. At least that's what he claimed it was later on when his brothers began a good two days of merciless teasing about the sound.

It was an iPod. A glorious, sleek, black, gleaming thing of beauty and it was all his. Stumbling over both Emily and Dave, he dove for his parents, "Thank you, thank you, thank you."

Will knocked him gently on the back, "Careful with that now. You can't imagine the trouble Santa went through to find a black one."

Cradling it, "Santa is so awesome, you have no idea."

Coming back to sit beside Emily, he showed her his other things, then sat back to watch the rest of the family jumping up, trying things on, causing general Christmassy craziness. He also worked his hand into hers and squeezed gently before giving her a kiss on the cheek, "Merry Christmas." Laying her head on his shoulder, "Merry Christmas."

A few minutes later, the gifts everyone had gotten for each other and their parents were opened. Emily took in everything, happy to hang back and watch Christmas continue to unfold before her. These were the homemade gifts, the little toys and the fabulously bad, yet completely thrilled to get, B-grade monster movies from the $5 bins at Wal-Mart. These were what the boys knew their brothers would love and they all did, yelling thanks and tossing wrapping paper at each other. There were also grandparent gifts, one of which seemed to land on Emily's lap, "Um, I think someone threw something at me that's not mine."

Jack talked around the lollipop in his mouth, "You ought to read the tags on things tossed at you."

His smile made her eyebrows wrinkle in confusion but, turning the soft package over, she did indeed see her name written in neat, even, what could only be grandmother script, "Is this really for me?"

"Yes!" Poking at the seams of the paper, "Now would you open it, please?" Sliding her finger under the tape, she soon revealed her very own fat scarf, in blues, purples and blacks, double folded, then folded again, which, when she stood and held it up, puddled on the floor at her feet. Even Jack was impressed, "Holy hell, that thing's taller than you are."

Immediately wrapping it around her neck, then again, then again, she let the ends dangle to her waist, "And warmer than Florida in July."

"Grandma totally outdid herself this time."

Elizabeth had to laugh, "Yes, she did. Jack told her you're always cold and the only thing she asked was how tall you were." Examining the tasseled edges, "She mentioned it was her longest yet. Now I believe her."

Hugging her scarf to her, she then hugged Jack, who had stood up beside her, "I thought you were kidding when you said you were gonna ask her to make me one."

"Are you glad I did?"

"Completely." She then gave him a quick kiss, just grazing the corner of his mouth, "I'll need to tell her thank you."

Dazed by her mouth, he stumbled through a, "She'll call … I mean, we'll call in a little while … well, Mom will call and we'll talk to her … all of us, not just me and you … although, we probably could call her tonight or you could email her or … 'cause she emails and --"

Emily stopped him with a finger to his lips and aiming a lip curl in his direction, "I'll thank her as soon as I can."

He still couldn't stop watching her lips and talking through her finger, "You should totally kiss me again sometime."

Turning a vibrant shade of scarlet, she sat back down on the floor, pulling at his hand until he followed. Once settled, she quietly told him, "I just might do that."

···

Once the insanity had calmed down a bit, Will stood up and called for quiet. All six boys turned at once, wondering just what was going on and watched in collective confusion as Elizabeth brought out one more large box and several smaller ones, "This one's from us as kind of a thank you for not giving us much grief for moving you half-way across the country and for being generally good kids." Stepping back from the box, "Just be careful with it."

They watched the younger boys pounce on the box and the cheering began when finally some of the paper had been pulled off, with Dave's voice carrying over the other, "Are you kidding?"

Jack peered over somebody's shoulder and then looked at his dad, "Holy crap."

On the floor, finally unwrapped, lay a Playstation3 and several games.

Emily had never seen a group of boys so quiet, all staring at a box on the floor. Tapping Jack on the back, "Um, what is it, exactly?" And with that, the silence broke and the boys all stood, mobbed their parents and everyone ended up in a heap on the floor, giggling and squirming.
Jack extricated himself first and sat back down beside her, "It's a Playstation. We've all been hinting for months that we wanted one."

Elizabeth leaned forward, "More like begged mercilessly at every opportunity."

"So this is a good gift then, I take it," her eyes twinkling at him as he turned to answer her with only a huge grin and a slow nod.

...

Clean up took quite awhile, with Emily pitching in until she saw Elizabeth head into the kitchen. Leaving her precious pile of gifts on the carpet, she followed. "Elizabeth?"

Turning around from the oven where she was checking the turkey, "Yes?"

"Thank you. You didn't have to get me anything. Just being asked over was more than enough."

"It wasn't us, it was Santa." Tilting her head a little, she studied Emily for a second, "And you're welcome."

Emily just stood there, praying her quivering lip would go unnoticed, but, of course, it didn't. Elizabeth put her hand on Emily's back, "Come here for a minute," and gently led her into the front room, "are you okay?" Not trusting herself to talk, she just nodded, but Elizabeth wasn't letting her go just yet, "Because you know, if you need to talk about something and your mom's not around, you can always find me. I may be surrounded by boys, but I think I can figure out a few girl things if you give me a shot."

She was so close to pouring her heart out that she actually had to bite her tongue to keep it all in. Swallowing hard, "I'll remember that."

Elizabeth felt the inexplicable urge to take the girl in her arms and hug her for a good two hours. She could almost hear her silently pleading to talk, "I've got a few minutes now."

Emily's face crumpled for a second and Elizabeth watched her wall begin to crack. She also watched her harden up again a second later. Blinking back her tears, Emily squared her shoulders, "I'm fine, but thanks."

Not pushing further, she motioned back towards the kitchen, "Well then, ever make a fruit salad?"

Shaking her head, "Nope. But I'm a fast learner."

"Okay then." Resting her arm briefly on Emily's shoulders, "Ready to face the masses?"

"Yup."

"Then after you."

Once back in the kitchen, "If you wouldn't mind running down to the basement, you'll find all the fruit cocktail and other things down there, right at the bottom of the stairs on the left."

Without a thought, she opened the door to the basement and froze solid. She held onto the doorknob in a vice-like grip and sweat began pouring down her face and back. Over and over in her head, her voice kept screaming, "Shut the door! Shut the door!"

So she did. She managed to get enough air in her lungs, then up to her brain to command her fingers to let go of the doorknob. Then she simply backed up and shut the door. Turning to Elizabeth, "Is there a bathroom upstairs?"

Elizabeth nodded, "Yeah. Top of the stairs on the right."

In a frighteningly calm voice she barely recognized, "I'll be back in a minute."

Since Jack had just finished getting orders to bring up something else from the basement, Elizabeth tacked on some more ingredients to the list and called after Emily, "I'll just have Jack grab everything for you."

Still talking in that odd, detached voice, "Okay."

•••

Her breakfast stayed in her stomach until thankfully she had the door shut and her head over the toilet. When she had finally finished, she sat back against the wall, calming down. Rinsing her mouth well and opening the window to let in the frigidly fresh air for a few minutes, she stood in front of the mirror and, for the first time, hated herself.

There were eight people who actually cared about her.

And she was lying to every last one of them.

It was enough to have her back kneeling on the cold tile but, by now, her stomach was empty and there were nothing but dry heaves.

Dry heaves and tears.

Cleaning up as best she could, she knew her eyes were red, but hopefully no one would look too closely. Blowing her nose for a final time, she shut the window, dug deep and opened the door.

•••

Back in the kitchen, she began mixing all the ingredients as directed by Elizabeth and, soon, something resembling a fruit salad emerged.

By the time she had finished this and managed to avoid looking anyone in the eye in the last ten minutes, the younger boys came tearing into the kitchen, "Mom? Can we go outside? It's snowing hard and it's sticking."

Elizabeth, surprised by the talk of snow, moved to look out the kitchen window, which had the curtains drawn against any draft. Seeing the blinding blizzard raging outside, "When did that start?"

Emily answered from the sink, "It was just starting when I was walking over here. I didn't know it had gotten bad though."

With the boys hopping and jumping around her in excitement, she chuckled, "Yes, go. Just don't freeze or fight okay?"

In a chorus of "okays" the boys ran away to dig up boots and other snow accessories.

Elizabeth caught sight of Emily's red eyes and still slightly blotchy cheeks, "Hey, why don't you round up Jack and go play?"

"Outside?"

Tossing the dishcloth at her, "Yes, that's generally where the snow's kept."

Gesturing towards the counter, "But don't you need more help?"

"That's what I've got Will for. Playing in the snow is something that shouldn't be missed."

And all of a sudden, Emily felt wonderful and free, "You don't mind?"

"Not at all. You can borrow my boots if you'd like and I've got an old coat on the hook in the garage. Jack'll show you." Giving her a grin, "Jack? Get in here and take your girlfriend out to play."

Jack popped his head around the corner, "What?"

"I said stop what you're doing and take your girlfriend out to play in the snow."

He turned a scarlet shade from ear to ear, "Mom?!?!?"

She just pointed towards the door, "Get out. That's an order."

■■■

The seven of them trooped inside an hour and a half later, Tim having joined late in the game, but still getting in a few good snowballs and several Sam tosses into the drifts that were building up.

Shedding piles of wet clothes, everybody began tossing things in the dryer and the younger ones, given they had forgotten about the singular girl amongst them, were down to their long underwear before remembering Emily.

Immediately, there was a lot of yelling and laughing and poking and chasing each other upstairs to get away from 'the girl'.

Jack and Tim, however, remained clothed while they stuffed the dryer full of discarded items. Once the machine got started, the three of them made their way back to the kitchen where Will was standing in a daze, "What in the world just happened?"

Tim laughed, "First, they realized Emily was a girl. Then they remembered they were in their underwear."

Finally understanding, Will laughed, "Oh lord." Looking over at Emily, "We may need you to come over more often, just to acclimate this bunch to another female."

Given she couldn't help herself, she gave Will his first smile ever, "I'd like that."

He returned it with his normal, quiet smile, "We'd like that, too." Clapping his hands together, "But first, you should probably find some dry clothes or else you're all gonna catch pneumonia and the last thing we need is three more runny noses."

Jack took her by the sleeve, "Come on. I'll find you something to wear upstairs."

Following him up, he went into the room he shared with Tim at the end of the hall. Digging in his drawer, he pulled out a pair of jeans and tossed them to her, "Think these'll fit or will they be too big?"

Opening them up, "As long as I can borrow a belt, they'll be fine."

"Okay, well, you can change in the bathroom or in my mom and dad's room if you like. It's at the other end."

Nodding, she turned and ran smack into Tim, "Oops, sorry."

"S'okay. Rarely do I run into a girl in my room. Kinda nice actually."

Jack came up to him and dragged him into the room, "Get in here, idiot."

···

Even as she was changing, Emily could hear the wind beginning to slam the side of the house. It whistled around the eaves and the low howling made her shiver. Gathering up her soaked pants and socks, she headed down to the living room to put on her new socks and see if she could actually warm up her toes.

She felt strange enough walking around in Jack's pants, but to make matters worse, they were still falling down even with the belt on the tightest setting. Elizabeth laughed when she saw her, "Nice pants."

Turning slightly red, she just hitched them up a little and sat on one of the kitchen chairs to pull the socks on, "At least they're dry."

"Very true." Picking up her small, damp pile of clothes, "I'll just put these on top of the dryer for the next load."

"Thanks."

The rest of the boys had gathered back in the large living room. Will was wrestling with the back of the TV, attempting to hook up the PlayStation while the others began their thorough examination of the games.

Jack found her there, sitting quietly and watching from her vantage point slightly hidden by an arm chair. Crooking his finger, he beckoned her over, "Want to come back upstairs with me for awhile? See if we can get some of my CDs transferred."

Nodding, she stood and nearly lost her pants in the process, "I think I need another hole in this belt."

With a grin, he held up another belt, a braided one this time, "I found this in the back of Tim's closet. It'll work better than the one you have on."

Grateful, she quickly switched belts, relieved that it did indeed work much better. Once her jeans were secure on her hips, he took her hand, stopping by the chair Elizabeth was lounging in, "Did you need us for anything right now?"

"Not at the moment. Why, what's up?"

"We were just gonna go up and see what I can do with some of my CDs."

"That's fine. I'll call if I need you for anything." Sitting up, "And Emily, are you sure your mom can't join us for dinner? Maybe she'll be getting out early because of the weather?"

It killed her a little to have to lie, especially after everyone had been so nice to her all day, but she shook her head, "Bad weather usually means they'll keep her longer, but thank you for thinking of her."

Settling back into her chair, "Well, at least you got to spend last night together."

With that, Tim and Jack shot each other a look that, thankfully, both their mom and Emily missed. Tim cocked his head sideways for a second, then gave a slight shrug, returning to the game controller as he tried to keep his racecar on the track.

Heading upstairs, Jack sat down at the computer he and Tim shared (which they had pooled birthday, Christmas and allowance money to buy) and began installing software. Motioning to the boxes that were peeking out from under his bed, "Want to find a few things to put on here so we can try it out? Our CDs are under there."

Settling on the floor, she pulled out the boxes and was confronted with row after row of CDs, "All these are yours?"

"Well, mine and Tim's. We pretty much have a community collection going on. Whenever we buy one, it goes in the box and we both share and if it gets lost, whoever lost it buys it again, after asking, of course, because it may be one we don't really want anymore anyway or we'd prefer something else."

"You two have your own little democracy set up in here, don't you?"

With a grin, he turned back towards the computer, "Well, when you've shared a room with somebody since you were two, you kinda have to."

She began examining the contents of the boxes and it became glaringly obvious that she was about as current with her musical tastes as she was with movies, "Would you call me pathetic if I told you I haven't heard of 90% of these people?"

Hitting one final key, he came over next to her, "More like woefully underexposed. Sounds better than pathetic."

Bumping shoulders with him, "Thanks a lot."

"Hey, you asked."

After digging for a minute, he handed her a small stack, "These are some of my all time favorites. Now let's see if we can make that beautiful little machine bend to my will."

···

Succeed they did, and soon the iPod was charging in the wall, contents waiting for its owner.

Jack turned around to tell her it would be an hour or so until it was charged and found her half-asleep leaning on the bed. With a smile bordering on sappy sweet, he crouched next to her, "You can lay down you know? My sheets are clean and that comforter is the warmest thing you'll ever sleep under."

Emily shook herself awake and scrambling off the floor, stretched, "That's okay. I just need to move around for a minute and I'll be fine."

"You really can take a nap though."

For the first time, she reached for him, sliding her arms around his waist and resting her head on his chest, "I'd prefer a hug if you don't mind."

Never one to turn down touching her, "That's one thing I'll never mind doing." And so they stood in the center of his room, surrounded by CD cases, listening to the wind howling around the roof and enjoying the warmth of each other.

After a few minutes, "We should probably go back downstairs or Mom's gonna send a posse looking for us."

Making no effort to move, "Yeah, probably."

He held her for another few minutes until finally they heard the rumble of feet pounding on the downstairs hall. Kissing the top of her head, "Here they come."

They had time to break apart and start putting the CDs away when Sam and Tucker slid into the room, "Mom says to come down and peel some potatoes."

"All right. Tell her we'll be down in a second." And as the boys thundered back downstairs, "They have got to be the loudest people ever, but they do give advanced warning."

Making their way into the kitchen, "How many potatoes do you want done?"

"They're all in the sink. Peel away boy."

He just grinned at her and shook his head as his mom took Emily by the arm and led her over to the cranberries on the stove, handing her a spoon, "Now, you keep stirring until all the berries have popped open and it's kind of jelly-y looking."

"That's a real technical term you've got there, Mom."

She calmly took the spoon back from Emily and hit him lightly on the arm, then she gave the spoon back to Emily, "Okay with the technical terms?"

Taking the spoon, "Sure am."

Then she turned to Tim, who was leaning against the railing, "And you, oldest son and favorite, can you set the table and see if you can dig up the good silverware from your grandma? I think it's in the basement somewhere."

As Tim walked by, sneaking a cranberry from Emily's pot, "I'm always the favorite when she needs me to dig for something."

Flicking him with the towel, "And Jack's my favorite when I need cookies. It's just the way things happen."

As he opened the door to go downstairs, "Then I guess I'll take it. Be back up in about two months or so."

Jack leaned over to her, "Dad's kind of a packrat. Who knows what's down there."

She just continued to do her assigned duty, trying to think about anything but that basement stairway.

...

Dinner was a veritable feast. Food spread for miles across the table and carried over onto the kitchen counter. Emily had honestly never seen so much food in one place before except at the restaurant, but then, a spread of rice, bean sprouts, Sweet and Sour chicken and Moo Shu pork definitely did not hold the appeal that this table did.

Given her stomach had been emptied hours earlier, she was starving and kept pace with the rest of the boys until after she'd cleaned the plate a second time. Finally sitting back, "That's it. I just can't seem to get past the second plate."

Jack nudged her as he helped himself to yet another spoonful of cranberries, "You've gotta train for these kinds of things."

Elizabeth leaned over and patted her arm, "It's okay honey. I've been with them for years and I've never been able to keep up."

Exchanging a smile, Emily studied the rest of the table while at least three different conversations went on around her. It was only then that she realized Jack's dad was watching just like she was, smiling at his wife, helping his youngest cut his food, handing a dropped napkin to someone else. She watched him longer than she thought she could, but the panicked flutter that usually overtook her was barely registering.

That is, until he locked eyes with her, then she felt the wave rush through her, but also, for the first time, she didn't look away. She held the gaze and, swallowing hard, nodded at him.

He gave her barely a nod back, then expertly caught Tucker's glass before it spilled. But as he was doing it, she saw the barest hint of relief cross his face. She also had the sudden and passing thought that he might just understand what was in her head.

Chapter 11

After food and talking and laughing and several heated battles of Monopoly and Phase-10, Emily realized it was getting late and leaned over to Jack as he shuffled the cards, "I should probably get going. It's dark already."

He immediately handed the deck to Tim and stood, "All right. I'll get a bag for your stuff, then I'll drive you home."

Emily and everyone else stood and, after saying a multitude of thank-yous and good-byes, Elizabeth handed her a bag of leftovers, "Thank you for all your help today. We loved having you."

Elizabeth looked as if she were about to hug her, so Emily quickly reached for the food instead, "I loved being here."

Jack gave her her things then expertly wrapped her now dry, fat scarf securely around her neck. Once they were all bundled up, he opened the door, a blast of cold air and driving snow blowing into the house. Stepping onto the porch and pulling the door shut behind them, Jack looked around. The blizzard that they hadn't really been paying much attention to all day had apparently decided to dump a foot of snow on the city. The drifts were even higher and Jack could barely make out the cars sitting in the driveway five feet away, let alone the road they were supposed to drive on.

Muttering a 'son of a shit' to himself, Jack turned to her and, yelling through the whistling wind, "Feel like spending the night?" The cold had already set her teeth chattering, so she only nodded. Noticing the answer, he turned around and opened the door again.

No one had expected them to return so they were met with seven pairs of eyes staring in curiosity. After Jack had pulled his hat and scarf off, "Yeah, has anybody actually looked outside since we came in from playing?"

The younger boys immediately made a beeline for the windows and pulling back the drapes, "Oh wow!"

This brought the rest of them to look, "Dang."

"Yeah, I said something worse, but it's all the same in the end so, um, if it's okay, I thought maybe Emily could just stay here tonight?"

Elizabeth turned back toward Emily, "That's fine. Just call your mom and let her know where you are. I imagine she's not leaving the hospital any time soon anyway."

Emily nodded, "I will. Thanks."

After Emily went upstairs and pretended to get things squared away, she came down and joined back in the game playing, which lasted until around eight, when the traditional viewing of "A Christmas Story" took place.

By the time that was over, Sam was asleep, Tucker and Nate were nodding off and Dave looked completely unfocused and glassy-eyed. Will stood and announced, "All right. Time for bed guys. Come on."

Picking up Sam, the other three boys followed him upstairs, leaving Elizabeth to direct the rest, "Okay. Emily, the only spare bed we have is the couch but it's a really comfortable couch, if that's okay?"

With a nod, "That's perfect."

"Then Tim, if you could go find one of the extra comforters from the closet and a sheet to put on the cushions, that'd be great."

Tim was already standing, "Back in a flash."

Turning to Jack, "Then if you could find some pajamas for her and grab the extra pillow from your bed, we'll be all set."

With a silly grin, he raced upstairs after Tim and Elizabeth turned back to Emily, "The boys'll probably stay up for awhile but you have my permission to kick them out whenever you get tired."

Nodding, "Thank you for the couch and everything else today."

"Honey, you are more than welcome."

Emily set about cleaning up a little while she waited for the boys to return with their assignments. Once they did and after tucking in the sheet and unrolling the comforter, Emily changed in the bathroom.

She returned to the living room sporting a pair of blue plaid flannel pajama pants, the string tied tight because they were Jack's clothes once again. She was also swimming in the thermal shirt he'd given her as well, but she was warm and cozy and everything smelled like Jack, which she hadn't realized, until now, she really enjoyed.

Elizabeth said good-night to the three of them when Will came down a minute later, then they both returned upstairs.

Turning to Emily and Jack, Tim asked, "So, anyone up for a little three handed Euchre?"

And so they sat up until after midnight, teaching Emily the finer points of the card game, then proceeded to have the pants beat off of them by her. Tim, gracefully losing his third hand in a row, "Damn, does everyone in your family play like you 'cause I'm thinking of taking you to Vegas."

Emily shrugged in his direction, "Couldn't tell you. All I know is I'm having a lot of fun."

"Of course you are. You're winning." Still grinning at her, he dealt the next hand, "But I can feel the streak about to end."

And end it did, but only because Tim began yawning every few seconds and finally threw in the towel. "All right folks, I'm going to bed."

Emily was glad he gave up first because she was sleepy as well. She just didn't want to say anything.

Both boys said goodnight and left her in the quiet of the living room, the only sounds being the refrigerator humming in the next room and the snow and ice hitting the glass of the windows. Moving the doorwall curtain aside, she stood for a few minutes watching the snow swirl around the back porch before lying down, snuggling beneath the thick comforter she'd been given for the night.

Warm and toasty, she fell asleep easily, the smell of evergreen and Christmas dinner still permeating the house and making her feel, for the first time, like she was actually home.

···

Jack and Tim lay in the darkness upstairs for a few minutes, "Tim?"

"Yeah?"

"Do you love Sarah?"

Without hesitation, "Yeah."

"But are you in love with her?"

Still not hesitating, "Oh yeah. Have been since the day I saw her on the steps at school."

"Have you told her?"

"I told her on our second date. Didn't think there was any point in waiting."

Jack propped himself on his elbows and looked at him in surprise, "Your second date?"

"Sure."

"What'd she do?"

"She laughed at me, then kissed me." Turning the tables, he asked the same thing, "Do you love Em?"

"A lot."

"Have you told her?"

Thinking for a minute, he grinned, "I think I'll wait until our third date."

Tim's pillow hit him in the face, "You've known her for six or seven months, right? What's taking so long?"

Tossing it back to him, he smiled again and turned over, "We're taking it slow."

"Damn, any slower and you'll be going backwards."

"G'night Tim."

Rolling over himself, "Night Jack."

PART 2

Chapter 12

Will, cursing his internal clock the whole way downstairs, couldn't believe he'd woken up at 5:15 a.m. … who the hell wakes up at 5:15 on what he knew would be a snow day from work.

You'd think his mind would understand this and keep him asleep but no, his eyes popped open at exactly 5:15.

So here he was, wide awake and needing to use the bathroom. Sliding silently from next to his wife, he finished his business and then decided he might as well wander himself downstairs for a cup of tea and maybe the early news on TV.

Creeping down the stairs and into the kitchen, he heard a noise. It wasn't a loud noise, but it was not a usual early morning house sound. Stopping by the sink to listen, he realized someone was whimpering and moving around in the living room.

Taking a second, he suddenly remembered that Emily had slept on the couch. Peering around the corner of the wall, he saw her thrashing about, tossing and turning on the couch, a low, guttural crying sound coming from her throat. Thinking she had to be having a nightmare, Will came over in front of her and caught her hand before it knocked into him. If only he knew he was mirroring his son's actions from a week ago.

···

He was there again. He was there again and she begged and pleaded for him to leave her alone. She fought him, she swung at him, she yelled for help, but as usual, none came.

He wouldn't move, she couldn't breathe, she couldn't see, there was no sound save the pounding of blood in her ears.

He grabbed her wrist and pushing with all her might out of the nightmare, she opened her eyes …

… and he was still there …

… and she threw up …

···

Will wasn't even phased by suddenly being covered in projectile vomit because he knew, the instant she opened her eyes …

… he saw her world …

"Emily! Emily, it's Will. It's not who you think it is. I'm not him. I swear to you. I'm Jack's dad. Remember, you spent Christmas with us. It was snowing too hard for you to go home, so you slept on the couch. Emily!" He had her by the shoulders at this point, trying to make her see him for who he actually was, "Emily!"

And suddenly her eyes cleared, letting her focus in on him, "You're not him?"

Luckily he had had his robe on and most of the vomit had hit that, so pulling it off and tossing it in a heap onto the kitchen floor, he pulled her into a hug, "No, I'm not him." With that, she clung to him and began to sob uncontrollably into his shirt.

Doing the only thing possible at this point, he held her close and stroked her hair, rocking her back and forth as if she were any one of his children. Quieting eventually, she sat back slightly, only realizing then that he had been kneeling in front of her the whole time. Saying the first and only thing that popped in her head, "Your knees must be killing you."

He had to laugh at this, "They're fine. Promise."

Waves of embarrassment were rolling over her and, as she dropped her head in shame, he tilted it back up with a finger under her chin, "Don't be ashamed."

New tears made her eyes swim, "How can I not be?"

After taking a deep breath and holding it a second, "Because I spent years feeling embarrassed and ashamed and angry and scared and I realized that in the end, it wasn't my fault."

She stared at him for the longest time before she whispered, "I'm sorry."

"There's nothing to apologize for." Smiling at her, "You're safe here. And I promise, I'm not anything like him."

"But you don't know what he was like."

Silently, he turned around and pulled his shirt up to reveal the perfect outline of an iron burned into the middle of his back along with several other only slightly faded scars, "I know exactly what he was like." Sitting back on the beat-up coffee table, he leaned forward, elbows on knees, and studied her, "Does Jack know?"

"No."

"Okay. Then I'll keep a lid on this, all right?"

With a nod, she had to ask, "Do they know about you?"

"My wife does and so do Tim and Jack, but the rest of the kids don't." With a regretful smile, "I don't think any of them have really seen me without my shirt on."

"So, we've both got our secrets, huh?"

Tilting his head to one side, "Something tells me you've got more secrets in there than I can possibly imagine."

Her face crumpled for a second before straightening back out, "I wish I didn't."

Still looking at her intently, "Can I ask you something?"

Shrugging lightly, "Sure. You deserve at least one question after being on the receiving end of my stomach contents."

"Do I look like him? Is that why I scare you?"

"Yeah." Ducking her head and fiddling with the fringed edge of the afghan, "He had a mustache like you and his hair was a bit longer, like yours." Opening her mouth, she opted to chew her lip for a second before, "I know you're not him, but ..."

"S'okay. I know." Reaching out, he patted her on the knee before standing up, "Well, how about you go change and give me the clothes and I'll throw everything in the wash before anybody gets up?"

With a rueful smile, "I did kind of make a mess, didn't I?"

"There're six kids in this house. Believe me, I've been covered in worse."

...

Getting dressed in the bathroom, she put her own jeans back on and wrapped herself in her new sweater. Handing him the small pile, he tossed them, his robe, his own pajamas and the sheets from the couch in the washer. Turning it on, he looked at her, "Still tired or would you like a cup of tea with me?"

"Tea please."

"Will do. And back in the bathroom, under the sink, there are some spare toothbrushes if you'd like to use one."

"Is that your polite way of telling me to go brush my teeth?"

He just smiled and headed towards the kitchen sink as she returned to the bathroom.

...

Jack was the first of the family to stumble into the living room a little after seven, finding Will and Emily sitting across from each other at the coffee table in the now cleaned and aired room, playing what looked like high-stakes Scrabble. Long complex words covered the board, with only the occasional staple like 'dog' or 'cat' thrown in.

Elizabeth came next a few minutes later, followed by Nate. Each took a look at the board and settled in on the couch to watch, not saying a word.

Finally, Emily threw in the towel, "I'm sunk." Looking at the score sheet, "You also won in points."

Looking as well, "Not by too much though. That's a damn good game right there."

With a grin at him, "And I'll take a re-match any time you're ready."

After putting the board away, Will stood up, "Anyone hungry?"

This of course was met with a resounding yes and the smell of Will's waffles bought the rest of the clan downstairs.

Will disappeared upstairs while the boys washed the dishes. As Emily finished wiping the counter, she heard the boys begin hooting and hollering about something behind her. Turning around, she found a clean-shaven Will standing in the doorway, his hair also neatly trimmed and much shorter than it had been just a half-hour earlier.

Sam stood in front of his father, the only one not pointing and laughing at how strange he looked. Will picked him up, "What's wrong Sam? You okay?"

Never having seen his father without the mustache, he ran his fingers over Will's upper lip, then through his hair, "You're still Dad, right?"

Will smiled and kissed Sam on the forehead before putting him back down, "Yeah, Sam," now looking over at Emily, "I just thought I could use a bit of a change."

Emily could only offer her own private smile while the rest of the boys continued their jeering for a few more minutes.

...

Since the weather seemed to have calmed down, "I should probably be getting home. The snow's still deep but at least I can see where I'm going now."

Once all the good-byes and thank-yous had been said once again, Will pulled her aside quietly, "If you need anything, find me okay?"

The offer sent a happy, warm feeling through her and she smiled at him, "Thanks for this morning."

"You're very welcome and, remember, I still owe you a re-match."

"Don't worry. I won't forget."

And with that, her and Jack were gone.

Once the door shut, the rest of the house grew noisy again, but Will just stood at the door, watching them go. Elizabeth came back over to stand next to him, "You okay?"

Not really hearing his wife, he continued to stare out the window, "Be careful with her."

Taken completely aback with this statement, "What?"

Shaking his head to clear the fog, "Sorry. Forget it."

Knowing when to not question him further, she ruffled the newly cut hair on his head and hugged him from behind, "He'll call if they get stuck somewhere."

...

After slogging through foot deep snow because the car couldn't be freed and fighting the frigid wind, Jack was in desperate need of the hot drink

Emily offered him when they got to her place. Taking one look at his shivering form huddled over the heating vent, she almost laughed, "Give me your pants."

In mock shock, "Well, I never ..."

Holding out her hand, "I'll throw them in the dryer for you."

"And I'm supposed to wear what while this is happening?"

She looked around for a minute, then pulled the comforter off her bed, "Just wrap up in this."

With a look of 'that'll work', he hit the bathroom and returned a minute later, soaked pants and socks in hand. Handing them to her, "But where's the dryer?"

She opened a small closet door to reveal a stackable washer/dryer, "It came with the place and, for the most part, it's cheaper to do the laundry here than a laundry mat and a whole lot easier." Dumping his stuff in the dryer, she went and changed herself, putting her wet clothes in with his. Turning it on, "Well, it looks like you're stuck with me for at least a half-hour or so."

"Well, the clothes may not be dry by then and I'll just have to stay longer."

Seeing him standing there, goofy grin on his face, bundled in a patchwork comforter with his hair sticking in every direction, she realized something.

She realized she was comfortable with him.

And happy with him.

And safe with him.

And that she loved him.

This knowledge hit her like a brick and not knowing just what to do with it at the moment, she shivered, suddenly cold, "So, tea or hot chocolate?"

"Tea, if you've got some sugar I can put in."

Heading towards the stove, "Tea it is. Be ready in about five minutes."

With Emily occupied in the kitchen, Jack dropped down on the couch and began thumbing through the book he'd started the night he had stayed. Getting in a few more pages before she handed him his steaming cup, "Whatcha reading?"

"*Wrinkle in Time*. I started it when I stayed here that night and I've got about 20 pages left."

Feeling weird at the mention of that night, "Did you know there are about seven more books in the series?"

With interest, he glanced over at her bookshelves, "Do you have them?"

She got up, pulling off a stack of paperbacks, "They're not the greatest copies but they're readable."

Taking the stack from her, "That's all that matters. Do you mind if I borrow them?"

"No, go ahead. And if they fall apart, just use liberal amounts of duct tape and stick 'em back together."

"I'll remember that." Looking between his cup, the book in his hand and her, "Um, will you think I'm rude if I finish reading this now?"

"Not at all." Reaching for the book she'd gotten from under the Callaghan Christmas tree, "Enjoy."

■■■

He hit the ending of one book and, seeing Emily happily absorbed in hers, cracked open the second in the series. Eventually, both their cups were empty and the comforter was spread across their laps. Jack, yawning, "If you touch me with those cold toes one more time woman, so help me."

Emily also found herself yawning. She tried to stay awake, but soon the words were swimming around the page and she couldn't focus anymore. Putting the book down, "I don't know about you, but I need a nap."

Stretching his arms over his head, "I was just thinking that."

Feeling rather bold, she stood up, "Make you a deal?"

"Sure, why not? I'm feeling adventurous."

She went and pulled his pants out of the dryer, "How 'bout you put your pants on, we lay do …", another yawn broke her speech for a moment, then, "down and you play me something good on your iPod and we fall asleep?"

Reaching for his pants, he motioned for her to turn around while he stood to put them on, "Sounds perfect."

With difficulty, she contained her smile but Jack, being Jack, grinned from ear to ear at the simple prospect of being beside her, of maybe, just maybe, holding her and falling asleep feeling her breathe. Flopping on top of the blankets, she curled on her side and waited for him to grab his earphones and player from his coat pocket. Handing them to her, he hit the lights, plunging them into semi-darkness, given the snow caked on the windows and the dark clouds swirling outside.

Next he sat, spreading the comforter over them both and laying down, held up the player, "Any preferences?"

Already shutting her eyes and burying herself in one of the pillows, "Anything."

As he watched her put one of the earphones into her ear, he turned it on and scrolled down a bit, "I was up at five-thirty this morning putting the CDs on here. Dad woke me up when he went to the bathroom and I couldn't get back to sleep."

"Ahh, that would explain why you're tired."

Finding the playlist he'd made earlier, "You should be more tired than me. You were up playing Scrabble. Just thinking about it exhausts me."

With a soft smile on her lips, "Well, if we hadn't been awake then, we wouldn't be sleeping here now."

Scooting a little closer to her, he hit play and shut his eyes, "And I can't think of anywhere else I'd rather be."

The first thing that went through her mind was how relaxed and warm and cozy she felt.

The second thing that went through her mind was that there was a hand on her.

The third thought was that this hand was resting on her skin under her shirt.

The fourth thought was that this hand was attached to Jack, who was spooned up behind her.

The fifth thought was she could very easily get used to this.

And the sixth and final thought to pass through her mind in the three seconds she'd been awake was that if he moved his hand any further, he'd know.

This had her up like a shot which of course startled Jack. "What? What's wrong?"

Groping for the words in her head she knew had to be there, "Bathroom. Sorry."

Breathing a sigh of relief once she shut the door behind her, she actually did use the bathroom, then sat down on the edge of the tub, waiting for her heart to stop pounding. Once it did and her face stopped being so flaming red, she came back out and found him wide awake and sitting on the bed, "You all right?"

"Yeah, um, just woke up fast and had to go."

Wrapping his earphone wires around the iPod, "I should probably get going. It's after two. Mom and Dad might send out the search squad at this point."

"Oh god, I forgot about them."

With a sheepish grin, "So did I, but they didn't call me so they must think I'm still alive."

Going to the kitchen and grabbing a plastic bag, she put the books in it and tied it tight, "So they don't get wet on the walk home."

After getting up, he just stood there, "I really don't want to go."

He looked so pitiful and adorable, she couldn't help it. She walked towards him without a word and sliding her arms around his neck, kissed him. It was a quick kiss, a soft kiss and a perfect first kiss by Jack's standards and over too soon when Emily backed up a foot or so, "I'm sorry."

Jack, who was still off floating in his own part of heaven, came back to Earth with a, "Huh," and closing the distance between them, "sorry for what?"

Oddly, she wasn't able to keep her eyes off his lips, "For kissing you without asking. It just happened."

Running a finger gently down her cheek, "You never have to ask to do that. Promise me, whenever you feel the need to kiss me, just do it. Don't care where I am or what I'm doing, just grab me and lay it on me."

She smiled up at him, "Even if it's the middle of some exam?"

"I'll take the fail."

"What about if ..." she never made it any further because his lips were on hers then, smiling as they kissed her again.

•••

Elizabeth decided it was high time she find out exactly where her son was and the ringing of his phone caused them to jump apart, as if she'd actually been there in the room with them. Making what had to be the most frustrated face Emily had ever seen, he answered, "Yeah? Sorry, hello?"

The conversation didn't take long and he hung up a minute later, ending with, "Yeah, I'll be leaving in a few minutes. I'll tell her. Bye."

"Tell me what?"

"That she thinks you're beautiful and that I should kiss you more often. Possibly all the time."

Her voice caught in her throat out of both embarrassment and giddiness, "Of course."

"Well, that and she wanted to make sure your mom got home all right and if she wasn't, that you were welcome to come back with me."

Happiness dropping a notch at the prospect of more lies, "Thank her for me."

"You sure you don't want to come back? We could just say she had to go back to the hospital for another shift?"

Shaking her head, "I'll be fine. And anyways, I've got plenty to do here. I've got a lot of homework and a bunch of new books to read."

Once he pulled his coat back on, he felt in the pocket and came up with a forgotten gift for her, "Hell, I meant to give you this when we first got here." Holding the unopened cell phone to her, "I bought it at Wal-Mart for you and I didn't want to give it to you with your other gifts, thought it might make people wonder. Anyways, it's cheap, but at least you'll be able to call if you need something and you pay for the minutes as you go once you use the 30 minutes it comes with." Worried that she might be mad about his intrusion into her life, "I'd just … I'd feel really bad if something happened to you and you couldn't call me … us … damn it." After hanging his head for a moment, he tilted it sideways to look at her, "I've been worried about you being here by yourself."

Not yet taking the package, "I've been fine here by myself for a while now."

"But what if you have this sudden and inexplicable urge to call and warn me about some plot twist in the books? How will you get a hold of me? Hmm?"

With a reluctant hand and a widening smile, she took the phone, "Well, I can't stand in the way of literary discussion now, can I?"

"Never." Seeing that she was going to keep it, he grinned, then motioned her towards the kitchen, "Now go open it so I can get the number from you."

Once that was done, he gave her another kiss, after which she hugged him tightly, whispering 'thank you' in his ear before following him downstairs and locking both locks on the door after he left. Back upstairs, she went to the window to watch him trudge through the drifts back to his noisy, warm, people-filled, wonderful-smelling, happy house.

Sitting down and pulling out the books Dex had retrieved from her locker for her the day after she'd walked out, she cracked open the history text.

She couldn't concentrate, however, and after a few minutes, she realized why.
For the first time ever …

… she missed somebody.

Eight somebodies to be exact.

It was an overwhelming feeling and she had absolutely no idea what to do with it.

For the first time ever, she was lonely.

■■■

It seemed that everybody at the Callaghan household was feeling it as well.

Sam asked more than once, "When's Emily coming back?"

Tucker wanted to know if he could go over there and have a snowball fight with her because, "'She's got the best aim ever … even if she is a girl.'"

Even Elizabeth commented on it, "Is it wrong that I'm slightly desperate for a conversation with a 16-year-old girl?"

Jack had to laugh at this one, "It's okay, Mom. I know you wish you could trade Dave in for a girl but you just have to face facts, it's all Dad's fault we're boys. I think you should go yell at him."

She cuffed her son playfully on the back of the head, "Just go shovel the walk with Tim and be quiet."

"Yes mother."

The next day, things got back to normal. The snow still fell lightly, but Will had to go back to work, as did Tim and Jack, but there was still New Year's to look forward to.

Emily had said yes to the New Year's invite, but Dex, now somewhere in Texas with his family, updating Jack and Emily daily with uproarious emails of his extended family's antics, said he wished he could be there, but the entire Grenden clan was holding him hostage.

Chapter 13

Since she didn't have to work that day, Emily showed up around two on New Year's Eve, armed with the story of her mom working again.

"That's too bad. I was hoping she might be able to make it."

The lying twisted her up inside but not having much of a choice, "It's hard to turn down overtime."

Patting her on the back, "I know. My dad missed a fair amount of holidays as well, but with eight of us and my mom not working, it was either that or starve."

"There were eight of you?"

Elizabeth nodded, "Yup. Which is probably the reason I had my own bunch."

"Was Will from a big family, too?"

"Nope. Just him and his younger brother. His mom died when they were young so it was always just the two of them and his father."

Emily watched as Elizabeth's lips tightened involuntarily at the mention of Will's dad and she realized, yet again, that Will may understand her more than anyone else in the world, but still, she steered the subject away quickly, "Is it all right that I'm here this early?"

Elizabeth's face returned to its natural smile, "Of course. Most of the boys are gone actually. Dave, Nate and Tucker went over to a friend's house for awhile so it's just you, me and Sam." With a twinkle in her eye, "He's been waiting to see you."

"Really?"

"He's in the living room."

She went into the kitchen and the minute she called out his name, he shot into the room, wrapping himself around her legs, "Do you want to color?"

Laughing, "Of course. Just let me put my coat away and I'll be back."

Returning to the hall to hang up her coat, she made her way into the living room. Lying down on the floor, she began coloring, causing Sam to sigh happily as they both delved into that lovely, shiny new box of 128 crayons.

•••

Once everyone arrived home, Emily nudged Jack as they worked their way around the kitchen, making tacos for themselves from the giant spread on the counters, "Where's Tim?"

"Sarah's having a party for a bunch of her friends. I guess he's there for the night. Something about Mom told him to get drunk and stay there."

Elizabeth was reaching between the two of them for some cheese and she swatted him quickly on the arm, "Good lord, I did not tell him to get drunk." Turning to Emily as her son grinned at her, "Her parents called and said that they'd be having some champagne at midnight and they prefer it if any one who drinks some has permission to stay for the night. I gave it because I don't need my son wrapping himself around a tree or worse, having someone else's drunken kid wrapping him around a tree." Turning to Emily, "Speaking of which, I know there's no alcohol but you're welcome to stay if it gets too late. Your mom's working until tomorrow morning, isn't she? I can call her if you'd like?"

Elizabeth could have swore Emily hesitated ever so slightly before answering, "Yeah, um, it's usually really bad tonight so everybody stays around, but I'll call her later. They know me over there."

"Okay then. The couch is yours if you want it."

Already turning to continue her taco preparation, "Thanks."

...

Dave noticed Emily's third trip to the kitchen, "Hey, you finally made thirds."

"I finally learned the trick."

Dave grinned at her and they both echoed each other, "Don't fill the plate so much."

She smiled back, "Y'all could have told me."

"It was more fun to see how long it would take you to figure it out."

Suddenly half a taco shell leapt right off Jack's plate and flew through the air at his little brother. Will managed to intervene before anything else took flight and turning to both his grinning sons, "Not tonight. I can't handle trying to get ground up cheese out of the carpet. Remember what the old floor looked like?"

Jack made a face and lowered his plate, "Sorry."

Dave apologized as well and all continued, with Emily asking quietly, "What happened to the old carpet?"

Apparently she didn't ask quiet enough because Will, who was sitting behind her up on the couch, couldn't help but chuckle, "Oh lord, it was disgusting. We were all eating in the dining room of our old place, which was really just the other half of the living room. Somehow, both Elizabeth and I left for the kitchen at the same time, which we know better than to do. By the time we heard the commotion and got back from the kitchen, food was flying everywhere. Stuck to the cupboards and ceiling. And, of course, since the boys were younger, none had really good aim, so most of it overshot its intended target and flew into the living room and all over in there as well." Emily grimaced at this as he continued, "And it was one of those nights we were all eating leftovers so the food ranged from pudding

- 131 -

to nachos to mashed potatoes and gravy, spaghetti, hot dogs …" Remembering vividly the entire incident, he shut his eyes, "Everybody went to bed early that night. No allowances for weeks …"

"So it destroyed the carpet I take it?"

"Some of those stains never came out, especially the ketchup and spaghetti sauce. It looked like we'd held ritual slaughter in the living room on a regular basis."

Trying so hard not to smile at the images flying around in her head, "I'm sorry."

Will saw her lips quivering and he laughed outright, "It's okay. It's kind of funny now, but, at the time, I wanted to kill them all and I don't think any judge in the world would have convicted me."

"Did you ever find out who started it?"

"Amazingly enough, no. Not one of them caved, not even Tucker, who was only three."

Studying his face for a second, "You kind of admire that, don't you?"

Answering her with only a wink, "So, anyone need anything to drink?"

■■■

After dinner, both the puzzles and the board games came out and the hours flew by.

More food was eaten, desserts were devoured, friendly arguments were settled and finally midnight approached. The kids became positively ecstatic when Will called everyone into the kitchen and began passing out pans and pots and lids and spoons.

"What in the world are we about to do?" Emily asked, slightly unnerved by the whole affair.

Jack just bumped her shoulder, a huge grin plastered on his face, "At midnight, we bang the hell out of the pots on the front porch, then we run back inside and pretend we have no idea where the noise came from." They all crowded onto the front porch and Will, official timekeeper, called the countdown out loud along with the TV. At exactly midnight, the nine of them on the porch let it rip. Emily had never heard her ears ring like this before as she banged away with the rest of the troops. Suddenly, almost as soon as it began, it ended and she was caught up in the rush of people all trying to get back in the front door at once.

The laughter carried through the house for a good two minutes as the family hugged and toasted each other with plastic glasses of milk, water, juice and other things.

Once that was finished, Jack, deciding now would be a perfectly appropriate time to let his family see, turned Emily around and kissed her, full on the lips in front of a chorus of "eew, gross" from his younger brothers and, from his parents, well, not much because they were already kissing and didn't seem to care.

And to his utter glee, she wrapped her arms around him and gave him a nice, long kiss right back.

...

The younger kids gave up around twelve-thirty and Will and Elizabeth said goodnight about a half-hour after that, leaving Jack and Emily in the living room.

Fishing his iPod from his pocket, he held up something he'd purchased the day before, "Here you go."

"What are they?"

"It's a set of earphones but they're split so two people can listen at the same time instead of having to use only one ear each."

Snuggling up against him on the couch, "What're we listening to tonight?"

Scrolling through to find his latest playlist endeavor for her, he slid his arm around her shoulder and settled back into the cushions, Just listen."

...

Somehow, during the night, they'd slid around and were now curled up into each other on the thankfully deep couch. Her head buried in his chest, he had his arm around her waist and his feet entwined with hers.

Will didn't have the heart to wake them up, so he silently poured himself a cup of coffee he'd set on the timer the night before and drank it sitting in the front room while reading his book.

Elizabeth found him there about an hour and a half later, dozing with his book closed on his lap. He woke up when Elizabeth came in the room though, "Morning. What are you doing in here? Don't you usually watch the news?"

Stretching his arms above his head, "Jack and Emily are still asleep in there, so I figured I'd see how much further I could get in this," holding up his book.

"Wait. Both are asleep in there?"

Will nodded, "Yeah, on the couch." He stood and, putting his finger to his lips, he led her into the living room, and whispered, "They looked too comfortable to wake up."

As she took her husband's hand and walked him back to the front room, "That's my problem with it. They look a little too comfortable. Like it's happened before."

He let go a second later and headed towards the window, spending a few moments in silence before replying, "She needs this, El."

Coming to stand next to him, "What do you mean, she needs this? She needs to be asleep next to our 16-year-old son?"

Turning away from the window, he sat down on the window seat and nodded, "Yes."

"How does that work? Because last time I checked, it wasn't the best thing in the world to leave a 16-year-old boy with his girlfriend, regardless of what either may need." She would have said more, but the sadness around his eyes made her stop. Instead she moved between his knees, resting her arms around his shoulders and, kissing him on the forehead, she took in a slow breath, "Can I ask what you know that I don't?"

Linking his hands behind her waist, "Can I ask that you trust me with what I know?"

With her index finger, she traced around the small wrinkles in his forehead and across the delicate skin near his still sad eyes, willing to let the subject drop for the moment, "Of course. I just wish it didn't make you so sad."

■■■

Jack woke up just after his mom and dad went back upstairs. Realizing his hand was yet again on Emily's hip, he dared not move for fear she'd jump up again.

Instead, he spent the next ten minutes just breathing her in, feeling her heartbeat next to his and knowing with utter certainty that he wanted to wake up like this every day for the rest of his life.

■■■

She woke up to an eyeful of blue thermal shirt and it made her grin involuntarily. Loving the feeling of being so close to him, she hated to move but when your nose itches, your nose itches. Moving her hand to scratch, she bumped the bottom of his chin and he laughed, whispering, "If you're trying to hit me, that was a damn feeble attempt."

Sliding back slightly, she moved her head to look at him, then slid up so she was eye-level, "Sorry. My nose itched."

"You're not allergic to me, are you?"

"I think it's just breathing in shirt fuzzies for the last six hours." Smiling at him, "Not that I'm complaining."

Rubbing her back through her shirt, he felt her tense for a moment, then relax again, "How'd you sleep?"

"Perfect."

He moved his head forward a bit and kissed her lightly, "Good morning."

Kissing him back, "We've gotta stop waking up like this or someone's gonna get the sneaking suspicion that I just might be your girlfriend." The look on his face was priceless and she couldn't help but laugh, "I am your girlfriend now, aren't I?"

His body began tingling from head to toe, "Well, actually, you said you would love to be sometime in the future, but you didn't nail down a concrete date."

Moving closer and giving him a longer kiss, "I'd say there's nothing like using the first of the year as a concrete date."

Removing his lips from hers for just long enough to answer, "Agreed." He pulled her closer and sliding his tongue into her mouth, he grinned as he felt her tongue connect with his own.

•••

They were forced to separate and hit opposite ends of the couch when they heard a toilet flush upstairs. Emily gave him one last quick kiss before heading into the bathroom and Jack remained on the couch for obvious reasons, that apparently Emily had not felt, which he was extremely grateful for.

And by the time she returned, he was relaxed and watching the Weather Channel. "Snow's coming again."

Before she could reply, Tucker walked in, "Morning. More snow's coming?"

"Yeah. Another 8 inches or so tonight and tomorrow."

"Why don't we get all this when school's open?"

Getting up, Jack ruffled his younger brother's hair, "Because if Mom had to put up with all of us any longer than necessary, her head would explode."

"True."

Jack pulled at the arm of her t-shirt, "You hungry?"

"Starving."

"I'm gonna go see who else is up and find out if we're making breakfast or if it's fend for ourselves day."

Emily stood and followed him, stopping by the sink for something to drink and to wait for further cooking instruction. A minute later, Jack came back downstairs, followed by several pair of pounding feet. Amused at the noise that seemed to be perpetually filling the house, she asked over her shoulder, "Are we cooking?"

He crouched next to her and dug out the electric frying pan, "Yup. Pancakes all around."

···

Emily playfully waved away all assistance but Jack's during the pancake making, telling Elizabeth, "You've cooked enough in the past week, let me do it this time."

And so she did, making wave after wave of light, fluffy pancakes to which she'd added a touch of vanilla and some sugar. She got countless compliments from everyone, adoring looks from Sam and, for the first time, praise from Tucker, who leaned over and whispered loudly to Dave, "She cooks the best pancakes and she can throw. I didn't know girls could do both."

Emily leaned in between them when she heard this and stealing a bite of Tucker's pancake, "I can also fix a bicycle, mow a lawn, repair an oven and stop a leaky faucet."

Dave even looked impressed now, "Wow."

"Pretty good for a girl, huh?"

The rest of the morning flew by and Emily realized she had best get home before someone began to ask questions. Will had promised to take all the boys to the movies for the afternoon, so Jack didn't walk her home. He did, however, give her a lingering kiss on the porch before she left, "I'll come by when I get home if it's not too late, all right."

She nodded back, her stomach happily fluttering at his touch, "Bye."

Waving, he watched her head down the street.

Chapter 14

Several weeks later, near the end of January, Emily was getting ready for school when she began to feel dizzy and light-headed. Her ears were ringing and thinking that laying down might be a good idea, she discovered it wasn't such a hot plan after all.

The world tilted and as she hit the floor only a few feet from her bed, she vaguely wished that Elizabeth was there with her.

...

Figuring the only person who'd be ringing her doorbell at eight-thirty in the morning would be the mailman, Elizabeth gasped in surprise to find a shivering Emily on the porch without a coat and dripping with sweat.

Immediately pulling her inside, "Emily? Why aren't you at school?" Feeling her head and realizing she was burning up, "More to the point, why aren't you at home?"

Giving her a glassy stare and a confused look, "What?"

Already jamming her feet in her boots and pulling coats out of the closet for both of them, she wrapped Emily in one, and turned her towards the door, "I'm gonna get you home okay? Then we'll call your mom and go from there."

Emily tried to shake her head, "No, no home."

Ignoring the protest and gently pushing her towards the car, "It's all right honey."

Finally managing to get her in the seat, Elizabeth drove them the few blocks over and, getting out, "Do you know if you have your keys?"

Emily's head was rolling around at this point and she was turning a lurid shade of green. Pretty much in no condition to answer, Elizabeth felt in the pockets of Emily's jeans and came up with the key. Using the only one on the ring, she let them in and half-carried her up the stairs.

Finally getting into the house, Emily's stomach began to lurch and, moving fast, Elizabeth did the only thing she had time for … she got out of the way.

Once the puking had stopped, Elizabeth led her over to the bed and sat her down, leaning her against the wall, "Stay here for a minute, okay? I'm gonna go get you a pan." She kept asking questions as if Emily were in some condition to answer them, more to keep her awake than anything else. Grabbing a pot from under the sink, she went back to the bed and set it down.

Next she examined the situation. Emily was soaked with sweat, shivering from the fever and the cold and covered in a fair amount of her breakfast. She made this priority one and crouched down in front of Emily, trying to get her to focus, "Em, I'm gonna help you get changed okay? Which are your clothes?"

Looking around the room for the first time, she took in exactly what Jack had a month earlier: the single bed, the one chair, the fact that the only door in the place led to the bathroom, which she could see into from where she was. The pieces of the puzzle fell into place so perfectly she felt stupid for not seeing it sooner.

Turning back to Emily and stroking her damp hair, "Honey, your mom doesn't live here, does she?"

Emily, in no condition to think of a lie, or to really even think at all, shook her head, "No."

"Does anyone live here but you?"

Shaking her head, she began to gag again. Elizabeth had the pan under her head immediately and held her hair as the next round began and ended.

At this point, Elizabeth pushed all the crowded thoughts from her mind and focused in on the once again shivering girl. First, she switched out the pot for a clean one, then found a t-shirt in one of the crates against the wall. "Honey, I'm gonna help you get changed, okay? We need to get you into some dry clothes."

Pushing against her hands, she tried to wiggle away, "No."

"Emily, you can't stay in what you have on."

With another feeble attempt, she brushed Elizabeth's arms away and tried to get up, "No."

Contributing this to the fever, she tried again, this time using her 'Mom' voice, as the boys called it, "Put your arms up."

By now, the fight was completely gone and Emily obeyed, putting her arms in the air so Elizabeth could pull off the thermal shirt she was wearing. She found the t-shirt underneath soaked and pulled it off as well.

What she saw next made her stop. Emily sat there, slightly slumped over in just her jeans and her bra, with an angry pink scar running diagonal across her chest.

It had to be a good 12 inches long and Elizabeth, for the life of her, couldn't come up with any idea where it might have come from.

But as Emily's eyes rolled back in her head, she again had to ignore her own thoughts for the moment. Getting the shirt on, Elizabeth gently laid the girl down, working on the button of her jeans. Finally sliding those off, she wiggled a pair of old sweat pants up her slim hips and, rolling her onto her side, pulled the covers over her.

The next priority was cleaning the floor and, pulling open the closet doors, she located the washer and dryer, as well as a mop and bucket. Putting them to good use, she had the floor mopped quickly and she then dumped Emily's clothes, along with several towels she'd used on the floor, into the washing machine. She didn't start it however, because, inevitably, there'd be more dirty items before the night was through.

A noise brought her back to the side of the bed and this time, Emily didn't even really wake up as she leaned into the pot. Deciding to just sit beside her for awhile, Elizabeth ran a cool hand over Emily's flaming hot cheeks, and pushing the sweaty hair from her forehead, "I'm sorry."

···

Jack listened to the bell ring and kept an expectant eye out for Emily. He'd had to meet with some kids from his history class and hadn't stopped by her house that morning, so he didn't know she was sick. Dex noticed her absence as well, leaning towards Jack before math class began, "Where's Emily? She sick?"

Shrugging, "I hope not. Maybe some teacher's got her?"

And so began 45-minutes where Jack didn't hear a word the teacher said. He stared at the door the entire time, which the teacher busted him for, "Since when is the door more interesting than me, Mr. Callaghan?"

It took a poke from Dex to bring him out of the fog, "What?"

"X is up here, Mr. Callaghan, not in the hall."

Embarrassed and still more than a little worried, "Sorry."

Jack caught Tim as he walked by between classes, "Hey, Tim, was Emily in class today?"

Shaking his head, "Nope. And when I asked, Ms. Tassleman didn't know."

Dex crossed the hallway, lunch in hand, "What'dya thinking?"

"I'm thinking I'll never make it to her place and back in time for my next class, especially in the snow."

Knocking him on the back, "She's a big girl. She can take care of herself for a few hours."

Jack could only hope he was right.

A little before one that afternoon, Elizabeth headed into the bathroom, settling on the edge of the tub while she pulled out her phone to call Will. She would have liked to have talked to him earlier, but knowing his meeting was scheduled to run until around noon, she waited until now to call.

"Afternoon, wife, how goes it?"

In a quiet voice, "Not so great. Do you have a few minutes?"

Getting up to close his office door, he sat back down at his desk, "Why are you whispering? What's wrong?"

"I'm whispering because I don't want to wake up Emily."

With a quick glance at the clock to confirm he hadn't accidentally stayed at work after hours, "Why isn't she in school? She okay?"

"She showed up on our porch this morning looking worse than you did after you had those bad clams. She's been throwing up every 45 minutes since around nine."

Will's stomach clenched involuntarily at the memory, "Where's her mom?"

Resting her forehead on her hand, propped up by her elbow on her knee, "This is where I'll need to know if you have a few minutes to talk."

Now he was just plain nervous, "Yeah, yeah, I've got at least twenty until Bill gets here. What happened?"

"I bought Emily back to her house this morning and when I got her upstairs … I just … I don't know how we didn't figure it out. I mean, she never talked about her mother, but what kid …" Her eyes filled with tears suddenly and, swiping them away, "She's by herself, Will. I asked her if her mom lived here and she said no. Now, I thought it might be the fever talking or something, but looking around, there's no way a second person is staying here." Letting this hover between them in silence for a moment, "Who would leave their child to fend for themselves? How could she just walk away from her own daughter?"

Will, attempting to digest this news, "What do we do?"

Given Elizabeth had been screaming this question at herself for the last five hours and remained clueless, "I have absolutely no idea. I was hoping maybe you'd be able to spout some words of wisdom and make everything better."

"All I got right now is just … stay with her, I guess. I'll be home as soon as I can but it probably won't be until after five. Do Tim or Jack work today? Could one of them watch everybody until I get there?"

"I don't know. I'll ask Jack when he gets here."

Even though he was alone in his office, Will looked up in surprise, "How do you know Jack'll be there?"

This was the other train of thought that had been keeping her occupied, "He knows, hon, he has to. I can't think of one conceivable way that he couldn't know. That means he'll be here right after school because she wasn't in class today and he's probably worried about her."

Wishing he could be there with her instead of twenty minutes away trapped in meetings, "We can't punish him."

Hearing Emily begin to move around the corner, "I know." She stood up, "I have to go though, Em's time is about up."

"I'm sorry you have to deal with this."

"I'm more sorry that she does." After telling him 'I love you' and saying good-bye, she went back to the living room, settling on the floor with the pot ready in her hand.

···

Jack toughed it through the day, but as soon as the last bell rang, he was out of that school like a shot. Running all the way to Emily's house, he stopped to catch his breath before knocking on the door. Since no one answered, he argued with himself, then got out the lock-box key to let himself in. Walking up the stairs, he nearly fell back down them when his mom appeared on the landing above him, "Jack?"

"Mom? What are you doing here?"

Pointing back into the house, "Emily showed up at our door this morning sick, so I brought her back here. But now I need you to go home and watch your brothers until Dad gets there."

Panic coursed through him and he groped for some kind of believable lie, "I can stay here if you like and wait until her mom gets home …"

Elizabeth gave him a warm, but sad smile, "It's okay, Jack."

"Mom?"

"Jack, it's okay … I know. Go on home, all right. She'll be fine."

"But …"

"I'll talk to you later."

He stood still at the bottom of the stairs, looking up at her, until, "I hated to lie to you."

"I know. We're okay, I swear. Just go watch the kids for me, please. Dad said he'll be home around five-thirty."

Nodding, he zipped his coat back up, "I love her, Mom, I didn't see any way around not telling you."

Now, normally she would have been angry for the deception, but Elizabeth just smiled at the confidence with which he made his confession, "I know." She then looked over her shoulder at Emily moving restlessly on the bed, "I'm probably here for the night, so make sure to help Dad out, okay?"

As he opened the door, "Will do."

Emily's stomach calmed down around four in the afternoon and she fell into a sound sleep, her restless movements finally quieting. Elizabeth had been tinkering around the house most of the day, straightening shelves, scrubbing the fridge, napping at times. After making herself dinner, she also cooked some Jell-O and noodles for Emily when she finally woke up.

Settling on the couch, she spied a crate full of old sketchbooks that she had somehow missed earlier. Without thinking, she pulled them over to the couch and began thumbing through, immediately sucked in.

The images doodled across the pages were magnificent. Castles and animals and gardens and reflections and buildings and any number of other objects. One whole book was filled with nothing but intricate flowers and leaves. Another held only clear glass cups and bowls. A third was nothing but hands, all in various positions.

And the last ten or eleven drawings in this particular book, she'd have recognized anywhere. They were her two oldest sons. The wide scar on the back on the first few hands told her those were Tim's, but the rest had curved in pinky fingers and a faithfully rendered fisherman's bracelet, making them uniquely Jack's. She stared at these for a long time, picturing him sitting patiently for her, watching her work. Tracing the edges of his fingers, the delicate lines and shading, she could only shake her head in amazement, wishing for a moment that she could create something that perfect.

Finally moving onto the next book, she eventually made it through the collection. Once she'd put the crate back in its spot, she looked back towards the sleeping girl, leg hanging off the side of the mattress, arm flung across the pillow next to her. How had she managed to take care of herself so well? She was well fed; she had clothes to wear and a place to live. She worked, she went to school, she was an artist and, as stated at breakfast a few weeks back, knew how to fix a washing machine. Where had this girl come from and what had brought her here?

The questions were now so thick in her mind, she began pacing back and forth across the apartment, walking out her anxiety until she calmed down enough to focus on the Sudoku book she'd found on the coffee table.

Knowing the numbers would keep her from dwelling on the situation, she settled on the couch again, pencil in hand and phone at her side.

...

Will called after he got home and got everybody eating. Going to sit at the top of the stairs instead of in the bathroom, Elizabeth told him everything again, this time asking, "Is this what you were talking about before, when you asked me to trust you?"

"No. It's something else, but I can't really get into it right now. Everybody's here."

Elizabeth nodded, even though he couldn't see her, "Well, I'll let you get back to it."

"Are you okay?"

"Just sad. And slightly stir crazy, but I think I'll go to sleep soon."

"You know, I can have Jack come by with a few things, some pajamas, your book, something ..."

Considering for a moment, "Pajamas, my toothbrush and my book would be nice. I just don't want anybody getting sick."

"Well, I can have him leave the bag on the front porch?"

She hesitated for a moment, then, "If you wouldn't mind, that'd be nice."

Grinning on his end of the line, "Which books?"

...

After Jack dropped the knapsack off, Elizabeth brought it back upstairs and immediately changed into her pajama pants and t-shirt. Brushing her teeth, she returned to the couch and dug in to see what else got packed.

Her husband and boys, as usual, didn't disappoint. There were the two books she'd asked for, along with the puzzle book she'd been working on.

Nate had included his handheld NintendoDS and her favorite game. Tim had slipped in his portable DVD player, charger and a couple of movies and Jack had put in his iPod, with a note stuck to it, 'Have Emily listen to playlist Em3 … she knows how to do it.'

Even Sam had packed in a few colored pictures and magnets, so Elizabeth immediately hung them on Emily's refrigerator, thinking she'd enjoy them once she felt better. Back on the couch, wrapped in a blanket she'd found in what she figured was the linen crate, she opened her book, wondering if she'd be able to sleep at all.

···

It took a few hours of reading and some game playing before her eyes began to burn and, a little after ten o'clock, she finally gave in, turning off the kitchen light before lying down, the room now only lit by the glow of the blue nightlight in the corner and the soft green glow from the bathroom.

···

Jack lay in his bed, his heart aching and sleep eluding him. He had no idea what tomorrow would bring. He just wished he could be there next to Emily, to hold her and tell her things would be okay. He just wanted to touch her and listen to her tell him things would be okay back.

Will lay awake down the hall, wondering just how much they knew and scared about what they didn't.

Jack wound up down on the couch a little after midnight and it didn't take long until Will joined him without a word. Slipping his arm over his son's shoulders, together they sat watching the Discovery Channel in silence, until finally their thoughts calmed and both slept.

And the world was quiet.

Chapter 15

Emily began stirring just before midnight, waking up slowly, not sure of where she was, what time it was or even what day. Sitting up, she felt every muscle in her body scream from what she vaguely recalled as hours of vomiting. Once her eyes had adjusted to the darkness, she saw a figure lying on the couch. "Jack?"

Elizabeth sat up almost immediately, "Em? You all right?"

Still more than half-asleep, she asked again, "Jack?"

"No hon, it's Elizabeth." Getting off the couch, she came over and sat on the mattress, "Do you remember me being here?"

Racking her brain, which also hurt, "Not really." It was also in this split second that she realized Elizabeth was in her house, "Did my mom come home from work yet?"

"Emily …"

"No, she said she'd be …" trailing off when she caught the look on Elizabeth's face, "I mean, she told me …"

Putting a hand on Emily's cheek, "Please, you don't have to lie anymore."

The tears she'd been holding in since her first lie to Elizabeth welled up and spilled over in a torrent. Curling into a ball, she rested her head on Elizabeth's lap and sobbed like a small child.

She calmed a while later and, sitting back up, began apologizing profusely, for everything she hadn't said in the last six months and for the river of snot leaking out her nose. Standing unsteadily, she pointed towards the bathroom, "I'll be back in a second."

"Take your time."

While Emily was occupied, Elizabeth stripped the bed and put the other set of clean sheets on. Once that was back in order, she walked to the bathroom door and knocked lightly, "Are you hungry?"

Coming out of the bathroom just then, Emily smoothed back the hair she'd just put in a long braid that fell down her back, "I don't know. I might be."

With a smile, "Well, I made you some Jell-O and some pasta. I didn't know which would sit best for you."

"You cooked?"

"Yeah, I've been here for a good 15 hours or so. I got hungry a few times."

Glancing over at the clock radio by the mattress, "It's almost midnight?"

With a nod, Elizabeth headed towards the fridge, "Why don't you sit down and you can start with some Jell-O and move on from there."

Between the trips to the couch, the crying and the puking, Emily was more than ready to shut her eyes again, which she did, until Elizabeth showed up with a bowl of strawberry Jell-O, causing her stomach to growl. Taking the spoon, "Maybe I'm hungrier than I thought."

Elizabeth sat down next to her and watched in silence as she slowly swallowed the entire serving. "More?"

Shaking her head, "No, I don't want to push it."

"Well, then, would you like to go back to sleep? You look completely beat."

Instead, she rolled her head to the right to face her, "Why haven't you asked?"

"Because I think you'll tell me when you're ready."

"What if I was ready now?"

Elizabeth took in her sunken eyes and pale skin, her limp body and her chapped lips, then asked cautiously, "How long have you been alone?"

The minute Emily heard the question however, her heart froze and she just sat there, eyes shut. She sat for so long in fact, that Elizabeth thought she had fallen asleep and was about to cover her with the blanket, when, "I've been on my own since February 29, three years ago. I moved in here March 24 of the same year."

"You've been on your own since you were 13?" She didn't even try to keep the shock from her voice, "Oh my god."

Giving her a detached look, she stood and reached for the bottom of her shirt and, hesitating, pulled it over her head. Elizabeth watched her swallow hard before she slowly turned around, "Would you have stayed any longer?"

Even in the dim glow of the night lights, Elizabeth could see the criss-crossing pattern of scars and burns. She had honestly thought nothing was worse than the ones her husband had, but his paled in comparison.

Emily stood there shivering in fear as she heard Elizabeth get up from the couch and stop behind her. Gently reaching around her, Elizabeth coaxed her arms in the air and slipped the shirt back over her head. Smoothing the back down, she then wrapped her arms around the girl, trying desperately to hug away her past.

After a few moments, Emily stepped forward out of Elizabeth's grip and turned, "You're the first person to see me like that."

"Jack?"

Emily shook her head, "No." A lone tear escaped and her voice cracked, "I've been too afraid to tell him."

"Do you think he won't like you after?"

"How could he?"

"He still loves his dad."

She finally looked Elizabeth in the eye, "I'm damaged goods though. Will will always be his dad but I'll be the girl who …" She couldn't get any further with the statement and she shut her mouth up tight, a sob caught in her throat. Elizabeth moved towards her once again but Emily skirted backwards, "No."

"Emily …"

Suddenly the words came tumbling out, "I'll always be the girl who got traded out in exchange for a bag of heroin and a fifth."

Her stomach already turning, "What?"

Yelling in no more than a whisper, "My father gave me to his friend in order to get what he wanted!" She dropped to the mattress and curled, her arms wrapped around her knees. Putting her head on her arms, the world disappeared and she was back in that dingy living room.

···

(February 29, 3 years earlier)

"No."

"You gonna say no to me? No way in hell do you say no to me!"

She knew it was coming and prayed it would be over fast. But as with any terror in the world, it seemed to drag on for days, everything moving in slow motion, the pain shaking her to her core.

Hoping he wouldn't actually carry out what he said, she laid quietly on the floor, blood soaking the shirt he had made her take off, then threw back on top of her when he was finished, her back and chest bruised and bleeding.

Sometimes, if she pretended to pass out, he'd drag her to her room and leave her there. She usually did end up falling asleep at some point, but only after she'd arranged herself so her feet were against the slightly open door. That way, if he tried to come back in, the pressure on her bare feet would wake her up.

This time was different, however. She heard him laughing above her somewhere. Heard the chortling she knew never led to good things.

Grabbing her by the back of the hair, he pulled her to her feet and shoved her forward into her room and kept shoving, until she stumbled and fell on the bed. "Stay here."

The stinging of the newest layer of cuts on her back didn't really allow her to move much anyway so she remained there, face down on her blanket, praying with all her might that someone, anyone would come and save her.

As the front door opened, she thought that maybe, maybe, maybe, it was the help she'd been silently screaming for.

The footsteps came closer and she heard the bedroom door creak open, "Just turn her over and remember, regardless, I get what's mine."

The man with him snorted a laugh, "I ain't gonna be disappointed. Never had one this young before."

Out of the corner of her eye, she saw her father settle into the chair in the corner, his gun sitting clearly on his knee, "I'll keep her in line."

···

It was over almost before it had begun and both left the room, talking about whatever, her father busily weighing the bag in his hand, satisfied that it should last him quite a while.

Once she heard the front door shut, she stood, beyond pain, beyond embarrassment, beyond anger … she felt nothing and realized for the first time that she was nothing.

Blindly fumbling into the bathroom, she cleaned up as best she could, then returned to her room. Ignoring the bloody sheets, both from her back and from what had just happened, she silently shut the door and moved to the other side of the bed. Prying up a floorboard with her nails, she pulled out the Ziploc bags she had stored there.

Money. Money she had been lifting from her father's wallet, drawers, nightstand, coat pockets, dirty clothes, for years. A dollar here, a lone five there, on the rare occasion, a ten, but that was always pushing it. Most of the time she left the tens alone because he might remember a bill that large. But a twenty?!? Oh she prayed she'd never find a twenty, or anything higher really, because she didn't know if she'd have the strength not to take it.

The man was pure evil in her opinion, but his one saving grace, if she was generous enough to call it that, was that he always carried change in his pants pockets, which tended to fall out when he collapsed in a drunken, drug-addled haze on either the couch or the floor. She only saved the quarters though, knowing that leaving some behind would keep his suspicions of her away.

She hid her collections under a loose board in her room, one that ran beside a joist in the floor and had not been nailed down properly when the house was built. She'd found it on accident one day when she was nine, lying on the floor and trying to ignore the burning fire in her ribs from his shoes. She absently picked at the seams in the floor and discovered one of the boards moved.

It was the next day that she began her collection. She didn't have any idea at the time why she began collecting the money, but something told her that she had found the hidden spot for a reason and she had better put it to good use.

Now it made sense. Not bothering to count either the paper or coin money, she shoved both bags into her backpack, along with a pair of jeans, some socks that didn't match, two shirts, the penknife she'd taken from a gas station some years before and a small, wool blanket she had found in the neighbors' trash one early morning.

Getting dressed in her remaining pair of jeans and her last semi-clean t-shirt, she shoved her feet in her shoes. Going into the living room, she set her bag by the door and started towards the kitchen.

Now, the thing was, she could have sworn she was alone. He always made noise, never having learned how to move quietly. She could, for the most part, always tell where he was in the house. Not this time however, as she walked smack into him standing silently at the counter.

He'd already started a fresh line and combined with the giant gulps of whiskey he was swallowing, she could already see that he was way beyond buzzed. Turning towards her, he grabbed her faster than she could turn away, "Who said you could come in here?"

Not giving her any time to answer, he had her twisted around and leaned back over the counter, "Next time, act like you enjoy it ..." he fumbled around and digging in the drawer, came up with a paring knife. Pushing her shirt up, "Nasty business, but I never asked for you anyway. I might as well get some use out of you."

He dragged the knife from her collar bone diagonally down her chest, at first not pushing, then finding some perverse pleasure in it, forcing the knife down just a bit to puncture the skin.

She bit her lip to keep from crying out and, as he slowly carved the line, she felt a hot anger building in her stomach. It moved through her body like fire and, before she knew what she was doing, she kicked him hard.

He stumbled back and she rammed him with all her might in the stomach, sending him flying backwards and sideways. He tripped over one of the kitchen chairs and disappeared down the basement stairs.

She stood, terrified at what had just happened, then, as her mind began to turn, she walked over to the door and saw him piled at the bottom of the steps, his body contorted at severe angles.

As she slowly pulled the door shut, the shaft of light from the top of the stairs shrank, until the only thing illuminated were the two fingers of his left hand.

The door clicked shut a moment later, plunging him into complete darkness and for the first time, showing her the light.

■■■

She told Elizabeth this in jagged sentences with long pauses sprinkled throughout. After mentioning she left him there, then took her bag and walked out the door, she was silent.

By the end, Elizabeth was sitting beside Emily, tears running down her cheeks and, reaching out, wrapped her arms around the still rocking girl.

At her touch, Emily seemed to emerge from her fog and, rolling towards Elizabeth, she wedged her body as close as humanly possible to her, letting the remains of her history pour out.

...

Early the next morning, Emily's coughing woke them both up. Sitting up with a groan, she took one look at Elizabeth and realized it hadn't been a dream. A cold sweat broke out on her forehead and when Elizabeth touched her arm, "Honey, are you okay? Are you gonna be sick again?" Emily jerked away and stood, ignoring the sharp muscle pains in her stomach and chest. Not sure what to make of her, Elizabeth sat up quietly and tried again, "Are you okay?"

Emily stood there, playing with the frayed hem of her t-shirt, "I shouldn't have said anything, I shouldn't have told you anything. You should have shut the door in my face and told me to get off your porch."

"Emily!"

"No, I should have never talked to Jack. I never should have let him help me," her voice was already hoarse from having thrown up so many times and, on top of that, she was on the verge of tears, "I shouldn't have come over ... I shouldn't have let my guard down ... I shouldn't have ..." By now, she was pacing back and forth, "I shouldn't have dragged any of you into this ... I should have told him to go away."

"Could you really have done that?"

Stopping her pacing, she slowly shook her head, "I don't know."

"Then don't worry about it." Coming over to give her a hug, "What do you say we have some breakfast and go from there?"

Her stomach growled at the mention of food, "Didn't you say something about pasta?"

■■■

After Emily had finally eaten enough, she sat back on the couch and looked over at Elizabeth, "So, what happens now?"

Looking at her in surprise, "What do you mean?"

"I'm underage, alone and blatantly lying to everyone. Aren't you supposed to turn me in to Social Services or something?"

Elizabeth gave her an odd look, "I'm not going to do anything. I would like to be able to fix a few of the lies, but from what you told me last night, the last thing you need is someone else you can't trust."

A small glimmer of hope began emerging, "You mean, I get to keep my life?"

"If you want it, of course. And now, you have the added bonus of at least one person you can talk to about things." Setting her bowl on the table, "I just ask a few things."

She slipped back into wary, "Yeah?"

"One, that you come over as often as you can for supper and any other meal you choose. Two, you let us know if you need anything. Three, you let me look into this whole emancipation thing --"

Emily stopped her right there, "I've already done that. In most cases, abused kids go to foster care. I won't. I'll leave again before that happens."

Elizabeth nodded, "I'd like to just find out for myself and if that's the case, then we won't go there, promise."

With a sigh of what could be called immense relief, "Okay."

Continuing, "Four, you let me tell at least Will. He may be able to help you more than I ever could. And five, I think you should tell Jack."

Shaking her head, "Not today."

"That's fine, just sometime in the near future. I think he needs to know, more than anyone else."

Emily stood, "Just not today."

Wishing she could make her smile, Elizabeth pulled up next to her, "So, how are you feeling anyway?"

"My body feels better, just sore. My head is pounding so I should probably get some drugs for that." Allowing her lips to curve into a slight smirk, "But my emotional state is several steps below complete and total chaos so, really, I should probably be getting ready for school because I'll fit right in."

"You don't have to go today. I can call you off." Debating it for a few seconds, "I can pretend to be your mom, if you'd like."

Chuckling slightly through her nose, "I already do a pretty good impression, but … oh, crap, I didn't call in yesterday." Shutting her eyes briefly and sighing deeply, "Shit … oh sorry … uh, well, if you stay around for another few minutes, you can witness my first lie of the day."

Elizabeth's hand on her shoulder made her open her eyes back up, "I'm here as long as you need me and probably a lot longer after you wish I'd leave you alone. Go ahead and call right now and tell them both of you were too sick to remember yesterday, but that you'll send a note in tomorrow with Emily."

Feeling the weight of Elizabeth's lie as well as the lightness of finally being honest with her, Emily hugged her, wrapping her arms tightly around her waist, "I both love and hate that you just said that."

"I do, too." Holding her for another few moments, "But you should probably go get a shower while I call home and see how everyone survived a night without me."

Heading towards the bathroom, she turned and looked back at Elizabeth, who was now unearthing her phone from the couch cushions, "Thank you."

With a slow-spreading, warm smile, "You're welcome."

•••

Just after she got out of the shower, Elizabeth knocked on the door, "Emily?"

"Yeah?" She stopped toweling her hair off, "What's up?"

"I called the boys and they told me the schools are closed. We had another snowstorm last night."

Hurriedly getting dressed, she pulled the door open, "Seriously?"

"Yeah. There's another nine inches out there, I think Jack said."

"I swear, we never get this many snow storms this close together." Emily pulled the curtains back and laughed, a sound that Elizabeth wished she could hear more of, "We totally need to look outside more often."

"That we do." Waiting for Emily to turn back in her direction, "So, what would you like to do today?"

With a serious debate going on in her head suddenly, "I could sleep or I could do my homework or ... maybe ... I could come and see everybody?"

Putting her arm around Emily's shoulders, "I think that's exactly what you should do."

Chapter 16

Elizabeth tried digging out the car but a plow had been by, burying any hopes of her driving them back to the house, "You up for a walk?"

Already fighting exhaustion from simply getting her coat and boots on, walking down the stairs and forcing the front door open against a drift of snow, she ignored her sore muscles and nodded, winding her scarf around her neck a third time, "I may need a nap when I get there, though."

Taking it slow, she was desperate for a place to sit down by the time they began trudging up the drive, but Jack was right there to catch her as she dragged herself in the front door. He helped her out of her coat and led her to the couch, "I saw you guys coming when I looked out my window."

Instead of sitting down, she threw her arms around him and hugged him tight, "I missed you."

By now, Jack didn't care who the hell was watching as he held her close, "I missed you, too. Are you feeling better?"

Looking over his shoulder at Elizabeth and Will, who were standing by the closet, watching surreptitiously, "I feel better than I have in years."

Jack turned them both around without letting go and glanced at his parents, "Do we need to talk?"

"Not right now. Go relax. We'll sit down later."

The rest of the kids were wrestling themselves into boots and snow pants in order not to miss out on any of their 'free day' snow. Tim was reenacting one of the scenes from 'A Christmas Story' with Sam and everyone heard him laughing from beneath the layers of scarf as they walked by.

Finally freeing his brother from the wool prison, Tim swatted him on the back, "All done. Go, be free, have fun, nail Dave with at least two snowballs for me." Standing up, he looked over at Emily, "Hey there. Feeling normal yet?"

With a smile, "Kind of. I'm exhausted but nothing a day of sleep won't cure."

"Then why aren't you asleep now?"

Squeezing Jack's hand, "'Cause I wanted to see all of you more than I wanted to nap."

Tim grinned and tugged the end of her braid as he walked by, "Welcome back kid."

...

After lunch, Tim, realizing something was going on and deciding to be the dutifully good son, volunteered to take the boys to the park to sled down the big hill. Elizabeth pulled Emily aside for a minute, "Would you like me to talk to Will or do you want to do it?"

Still raw from the first telling the previous night, "I don't know if I could do it again."

"Then, unless you have some objection, I'd like to do it now? I can't keep this from him."

Nodding her head, "I don't want to either. Not anymore." Tears swam to her eyes for a moment, but she blinked them back, "But I don't want him to know everything, please."

Elizabeth could plainly see the anxiety suddenly cloud her face, "I would rather not keep anything from him if that's alright."

Thinking for a second, realizing how much Elizabeth had already done for her, Emily nodded her head, "Okay."

After running her hand across Emily's shoulders a few times, "Everything is going to be fine. I'm gonna hunt down Will. Why don't you go lie down? You look exhausted."

Her entire body suddenly ached for a soft bed, "A nap sounds really good right about now."

"Jack?"

He popped his head into the front room, "Yeah?"

"When did you change your sheets?"

"This morning."

"Okay." Turning back to Emily, "Go on upstairs to Jack's room. He's got the cleanest bed and if you shut the door, the other kids won't wake you if they come in before you're up."

This conversation, of course, set her to yawning, "Thanks."

Elizabeth then disappeared into the small room that served as Will's office and shut the door behind her. Jack took her hand and led her upstairs. Kicking Tim's dirty socks under his bed, he put his hand on the bedspread, "Underneath or on top?"

Already crawling on, "Top is fine."

Since she kept her eyes open, he sat on the corner of the bed, "Is she telling him now?"

"Yeah."

"Ah, okay." Standing back up, "Well, I'll leave you alone."

"Wait." She propped herself up on her elbow, "Maybe you could stay?"

With a half-smile, he moved to shut the door as instructed, then grabbed his iPod, which his mom had brought back from the apartment, and laying down behind her, "Did you ever listen to your playlist?"

Shaking her head, "I didn't have time. I'm sorry."

"It's okay." Handing one of the earphone sets over her shoulder, "We can listen to it now if you want? Hope you like it."

"I can't imagine I won't."

After rolling to one side of the bed, he settled behind her and she slid back against him. With his arm over her waist, he hit play and laid the player on the bed in front of them, "Let me know if it's too loud."

As the opening notes filled her ears, "It's perfect."

...

Will sat silently as Elizabeth filled him in. He nodded every once in a while, but mostly he just absorbed and digested. By the time she'd finished, he had gone pale.

Then suddenly, he stood and began pounding the cushions of the small couch he had in the corner. He raged on that couch for several seconds before turning back to his wife, his face now a vibrant red color, "If he ever shows up, I'll kill him myself."

"Honey, would you please sit back down? You're starting to scare me a little bit."

Instead, he took to pacing, "She's been on her own for three years? What if he'd come back? What if she'd opened the door and there ..." He couldn't continue as he once again hit the couch several times, then went on, "We can't leave her by herself, El, we can't."

Standing, she reached for him, slipping her arms around his waist, "Well, I already promised her that we weren't going to turn her over to Social Services and I don't think I could bear forcing her to do anything. We can offer to help, but we can't make her do anything she doesn't want to do."

Will finally let go of the fierce fire in his eyes and returned to a somewhat calm, human state, "But I can't just leave her there."

"Will, honey, it's not our choice."

"Then what would you think about …"

...

They talked for a good hour and when they finally came out, the boys still hadn't returned from the sledding hill. Seeing this as a pretty good opportunity, they both headed upstairs to find Emily and by obvious default, Jack.

Elizabeth opened the door and was kind of shocked to see them both sound asleep, curled around each other, two pairs of earphones lying beside them. It probably should have bothered her more to see her 16-year-old son in bed with a girl, but given what she now knew, she just motioned for Will to be quiet as she pulled the door shut.

But of course, the door let out a loud creak that seemed to echo off the walls and Jack picked his head up suddenly, "Tim?"

"No, it's us."

Jack sat up and slid off the bed. Coming over to the door, "I didn't mean to fall asleep. She asked me to stay and I guess I was more tired than I thought."

Will beckoned him out, "Let's just leave her alone for now. We can talk later."

Her voice bought them all into the room though, "It's okay. I'm awake, for the most part."

Elizabeth apologized, "Sorry, I don't think any of us know how to be quiet."

Smiling, "s'okay. I don't mind the noise. It's nice, actually." As she sat up, she realized that all her muscles had yet again stiffened, "Oh, I hurt."

"Hurt?" Jack came back over to her, "What hurts?"

"Mostly my chest and back." Giving him a sheepish smile, "I've never been an easy puker."

"Now there's information I didn't really want to know."

Will put his hand on Jack's shoulder, "Would you mind leaving us alone for awhile?"

Glancing over at Emily, "We both lied, Dad."

Elizabeth jumped in, "I know, but right now, we need to talk to Emily, okay? Nobody's in trouble, all right? Can you just go downstairs and start cleaning the potatoes in the sink for me?"

With a quick look at her, Jack left and pulled the door shut behind him. Emily, still sitting up, refused to look Will in the eye as he sat on the end of the bed. He didn't push it, but he did lean forward a little, "Do you know you're one of the bravest people I know?" Leaving her bangs as a curtain between them, she shook her head, still silent. "Well, you are. And even though I wish you'd told me earlier, I think now that we both know, we might be able to help."

This got her and she looked up, "Help?"

"Yeah. You'll decide everything and we'll respect any decision you make but, we'd like to put a few things on the table, if that's all right?"

Looking over at Elizabeth, who had pulled the desk chair to the side of the bed, "I get final say though, right?"

"Of course. First of all, we don't want to make you do anything. I think you've had enough people controlling you to last a lifetime. Feel free to jump in and tell us to shut up at any time."

A small smile played on her lips, "Okay."

"We'd like you to think about the possibility of moving in here with us. We could either fix up that room above the garage or we could shuffle the boys around, move Tim to the basement ... something like that."

For a moment, Emily forgot how to breathe, but recovered nicely, "Move ... move in ... here?"

"Yeah, I know you did pretty good by yourself these last few years, but now that we know you're on your own, if anything happens to you or you get sick again or something worse, I don't think I, or either of us actually, could live with ourselves." Looking over at his wife, "Before I finally told El about me, I was all on my own and thought I could handle anything, keeping everyone at arm's length. But then something happened. I met her family and her friends and I realized I needed them. I needed people and interaction and friends and a life."

"But I have a good life, Will."

"Yes, you do. But if you think about it, he's dictating your entire existence. You have to keep yourself a secret because of him. He still has that hold on you." Emily continued to stare at him, her face a wrinkle of concentration and thought as he went on, "And even though you're 16, you need to be able to also be a kid. You never got that. You grew up when you were five years old. No one should have to miss out on their entire life because of what one person did." Leaning forward, he tapped her on the bottom of the foot, "I'd like to be able to let you be a kid again. Maybe just for a couple years, but still, let someone else do the worrying for you."

The wall she'd kept up for so many years cracked a little more.

"Em, you don't have to decide now, but for what it's worth, we'd love to have you here."

In a quiet voice, "But I'm not yours."

Elizabeth, who'd been silent until then, "That doesn't mean we don't want you."

Will added to this, "And you and I probably have more in common than I do with the boys. I think we might actually be good for each other; in a weird 'son's girlfriend/boyfriend's abused dad' kind of way."

The wall now had a big, gaping hole in it, "What if I can't answer you now?"

"Then we'll all wait until you can. There's no rush, no hurry. Just know that we'll be here whenever you're ready, yes or no."

"What happens until then?"

"Until then, we get to demand that you call whenever you need us and according to the deal you already made with Elizabeth, you come here as often as you want, you get to eat as much as you want and you can stay over any time. We also get to check up on you with disturbing regularity." Looking at his wife, "And you get to handle Jack at your own speed and your own pace. We'll be quiet about it."

Letting out the breath she didn't know she'd been holding, she nodded, "Thank you."

He waited a second, then spoke again, "I think if I'd ever had a daughter, I'd have wanted you."

With that, he stood and left quietly, leaving them both until Emily got up and went to the door, "Will?"

He turned back from the stairs, "Yeah?"

Not saying anything, she went over to him and hugged him around the waist. Standing like this for awhile, she finally pulled back and looked up at him, "I wish you could have been my dad."

■■■

Jack walked her home after a quiet dinner with just the nine of them.

Well, as quiet as seven kids under 19 can be.

That is to say, after a very loud and boisterous dinner.

Anyhow …

After digging out his mom's car, which was still at Emily's, he turned it on to warm it up a little, then went and stood just inside her front door, "You gonna be okay tonight?"

With a nod, she slipped her bundled up arms around him and settled her cold cheeks on his jacket, "I'll be fine. I think I'm just going to sleep until tomorrow." He hadn't asked at all what was said in the bedroom after he left and she loved him for it. Leaning up a little, she rubbed her cold nose on his, "I'd ask you to come up, but I'm exhausted. I'll see you tomorrow morning though, right? Bright and early?"

Kissing her forehead, then both cheeks and finally the end of her red nose, "I'll be here."

...

Things slipped back into routine: work, school, homework, only this time there was something different.

Emily began smiling again.

She still had to lie to certain people but that had become second-nature to her years ago.

What she relished in was the fact that she could tell the truth to certain people as well.

It was liberating and scary at the same time.

How do you just stop doing something you've been doing for years?

You just begin.

Chapter 17

It took nearly a week before Emily finally felt truly better. Jack had been by the night before and, together, they'd spent their first quiet evening at her house. It was rather unnerving not to have at least four people sharing the couch with them, but as Jack stated, he could easily get used to it.

And now, the next morning, she stretched luxuriously under her mountain of quilts and blankets and marveled at the feeling of not aching. With a grin, she decided that today was going to be a very good day. The sun was pouring in the front window and she could almost imagine it summer and boiling hot outside.

Almost.

She did, however, come back to reality when she slid out from under the covers and was met with the biting cold floor under her feet. Hurrying to get dressed and cleaned up, she was just walking out of the house when Tim's car pulled up to the curb. Hopping in, she couldn't help but smile. Both boys just looked at her, their eyes still cloudy with sleep.

"You realize it's entirely too damn early to be this happy, right?"

She just stuck her tongue out at Tim and, turning to Jack, she handed him the homework he'd left on her table, "You might be needing this today. I found it after you left."

Taking it from her, he leaned in for a quick kiss, "Thanks."

...

The day, afternoon, evening and night were indeed very good. And late that night, after having already dropped off Sarah, Tim just wanted to get home. He debated telling Jack to walk. But, of course, they'd waited while he'd said goodnight to Sarah, so for karma's sake, he made himself not lay on the horn to make them hurry up.

That, and the fact that it was after midnight and he didn't feel like waking the entire neighborhood up.

So he sat …

Until he saw both of them coming back to the car. Once Jack had opened the door, Tim looked over, "What's wrong?"

With his breath hanging in a thick cloud in the cold air, "I think the power's out. The house is cold and the lights aren't working."

Knowing she was alone, Tim made an executive decision, "Then get back in. We'll go home and worry about it in the morning." Looking past Jack at Emily, "You need anything from up there? I've got a flashlight here somewhere."

With a shake of her head, she shivered, "I'm good."

Turning the heat up more, "Then get in here before we all freeze. Why the hell did Delia decide to get married in February? Mom really should have chosen a smarter Goddaughter."

As Jack helped Emily in and pulled the door closed behind him, "Dude, you've been in love with her since you were five years old, so shut up and crank the heat would you?"

"Already cranked. We'll be home in a flash."

...

Once inside, they explained what was up and Elizabeth sent both upstairs so Jack could find her something to wear. Instead of finding the pajamas, however, he twirled her once again into his arms, "Sorry, had to dance with you one more time tonight."

As she laughed, she swung her hips slightly, her dress flaring out at the bottom, "The last four hours weren't enough?"

Bending at the neck, he kissed her once again, "I think I could dance with you forever," and with a wicked grin, "as long as your toes can take being stepped on a few more times."

Returning the kiss, "For giving me one of the best nights I've ever had, I think my toes can handle a bit more."

With a last turn, he let go, "Best night?"

He couldn't help notice the twinkle in her sleepy eyes, "So far, at any rate."

As he pulled out a clean pair of flannels and a shirt for her, "Did I tell you how beautiful you look tonight?"

"Once or twice."

Coming back over, he handed her the clothes, then with one last hug, he not so sneakily reached around and unzipped the back of her dress, "You look beautiful."

And with that, he grinned and left her to change, closing the door quietly behind him, leaving her trying very hard to remember how to breathe.

By the time she'd carefully laid her dress, a rare and beautiful find at the thrift store she frequented, over the end of Jack's bed, pulled her nylons off and worked the pins from her hair, she was yawning uncontrollably. Her body screamed at her to lie down and she did, just for a second.

She was asleep immediately, curled on top of his unmade bed.

...

Elizabeth set up the couch for Emily, then headed to bed herself, leaving Will downstairs with Jack and Tim. After having a fast snack, "Dude, how long does your girlfriend take to change?"

"I was just wondering that myself. Back down in a second." Going upstairs, he knocked quietly on the bedroom door and, opening it slowly, let the smile spread across his face as he saw her asleep. Returning to the kitchen, he told his dad, "Um, she's asleep on my bed."

Will couldn't help shaking his head and smiling, "Okay, Tim, do you mind sleeping down here? If she wakes up, it might be better that she sees Jack."

Tim was already stripping to his boxers and heading into the living room, "That's fine. I've gotta work early anyway." Turning back to his dad, "could you wake me up though? You'll be up early, won't you?"

Nodding, "Five-fifteen as usual."

"How 'bout six-thirty?"

Giving his sons quick hugs, "Six-thirty. G'night."

Left alone, Jack swallowed another granola bar before telling Tim goodnight and going upstairs himself.

And it was there that Jack covered her up with the quilt.

And it was there that he finally told her he loved her. Granted she couldn't hear him or respond because she was asleep but now that he'd said it, felt how the words played on his tongue, he knew he'd be saying it often … and every time, he'd feel it even more.

After watching her for a few minutes, he changed silently, but regardless of how hard he tried to be quiet, Tim's bed creaked when he tried to get in, "Jack?"

Sliding back onto the floor, he came over to her, "Yeah, Tim's down on the couch and I'm sleeping in his bed. Dad figured it wouldn't freak you out as much if you woke up and found me."

Blinking a few times before focusing in on him, "I should really go downstairs so Tim can have his bed."

She punctuated her statement with a jaw-splitting yawn and Jack smiled, "Why don't you just go back to sleep? We've already switched everybody around and, besides, might be kind of fun."

Immediately snuggling back down in the pillow, "If you insist."

Leaning over, he kissed her lightly on the cheek, "I'll always insist."

...

The problem was now she couldn't fall back to sleep; she could only hear Jack breathing about three feet away from her and, with every breath, she felt more and more guilty.

He was lying there, thinking the evening had been perfect, that she had been beautiful and perfect.

It took her nearly twenty minutes to work up the courage to ask him, "You still awake?"

She heard him roll over, presumably so he was now facing her, "Yeah?"

"What if there was more you didn't know?"

"If you tell me it's your birthday again, I'm not getting you anything."

Almost smiling, "Do you think your mom'll get annoyed if we shut the door for a little while?"

Moving, he got up and silently shut the door. Coming to sit next to her on his bed, "I was the last one to come upstairs, so we'll be fine, as long as it's opened before morning."

Emily reached over and turned the bedside lamp on, "Then I need to talk to you." Worry creased his forehead in a heart-meltingly enduring way and she suddenly felt her chest tighten, "And I need to show you something."

Turning away from him, with hands shaking, she slipped the t-shirt over her head. Since she wasn't sleeping in her bra, her back was completely exposed to him,

As were her scars.

In a voice barely above a whisper, she heard him ask, "Who did this to you?"

Managing to say, "My father," she suddenly felt a tentative finger on her back. Surprisingly, she didn't shy away, but held still as he followed each line and jagged, raised edge, tracing the outline of the iron burns, the glass cuts, the poorly stitched pocket knife gouge and finally, the small, slightly puckered hole where he'd punctured her with a screw driver.

His finger lingered here the longest, "I'll kill him, I swear to God."

Still not able to turn and look him in the face, "I think I did that already."

Now, maybe he didn't hear her or maybe he decided to discuss it later on, but regardless, the comment went by and he continued to run his hands over her bare back, "Can you tell me what happened?"

Finding it relatively easy to talk to him without having to see his face, she told him everything. Every last horrid detail because, once she began, she couldn't stop.

And he listened in silence, never interrupting, never questioning, never commenting.

He did however, reach around her shoulders and gently pull the shirt back over her head so he could put his arms around her and hold her tight to him.

He also did this so his tears wouldn't fall against her skin.

He wept silently for her as she whispered her life story to him over the course of the next hour. Just as the clock was switching over to two, she took a deep breath and was quiet.

Without a word, he reached around her and turned off the desk lamp, laying them both down on the mattress in the dark. Moving her hair off her neck with a brush of his nose, he kissed the only scar she hadn't told him about, the one that ran the length of her hairline.

For the first time in that hour, he spoke, "This is the first one I'm going to kiss and make better. Eventually, if you let me, I'll work on the rest but, for now, I'll just focus on this one." Continuing to lay kisses from one end of it to the other, "If that's all right with you?"

She nodded and felt her entire body relax as it never had before. Jack knew everything. And he still wanted her.

He had touched her past and he had stayed.

"I love you, Jack Callaghan."

■■■

He'd moved out of her bed a few hours later, opened the door and crawled under his own covers about 15 minutes before his dad began his morning routine.

That routine was altered a tad when Will popped his head in to see just where Emily and Jack had wound up.

With satisfaction, he saw Emily curled in a ball in the bed she'd started in and Jack, snoring slightly, his foot hanging off the end of his brother's bed, right where he should be.

■■■

She slept for another hour or so, then, waking up, she moved quickly, digging in Jack's drawers until she found the jeans from Christmas and the belt she wore. Pulling them on, as well as an old sweatshirt from his closet, she crept downstairs, dress and shoes in hand. Holding her breath as she tied her boots and slipped her coat on, she prayed she wouldn't wake anyone up. With a sigh of relief at having succeeded, she slowly pulled the front door open and headed out into the pre-dawn morning.

Tim and Will held themselves still in the kitchen until they heard the front door click shut, then, "Why'd she leave?"

Will shook his head, "I don't know, but given how quiet she was being about it, she must have had her reasons."

Shrugging, he took another doughnut as he got up from the table, "Well, at least now I can get in our room without worrying about waking her up."

"What about Jack?"

"Don't care if he wakes up." With a grin, he headed up the stairs.

Tim decided to be quiet, however, and Jack didn't wake up until the rest of the family did, which was a little after nine. Rolling over, ready to wake Emily up, he instead saw the empty bed and sat up, wondering what had happened. It was then that he noticed the paper tucked under the end of the pillow. It only said, "Come by after work. I love you," but it was all Jack needed to smile.

···

He ran into Will as he was coming out of the bathroom a minute later, "Hey Dad."

"Morning. Can I talk to you a minute?"

Ignoring his growling stomach, he nodded, "Am I in trouble?"

Will led him back to his room and motioned for Jack to sit down, "What happened last night after we went to bed?"

"I had a granola bar and came upstairs."

"I mean, what happened after you got up here?"

Jack looked at him warily, "Em woke up and wanted to talk. Why? What happened?"

Slightly relieved, "She just left pretty early this morning. Wasn't sure if something happened last night that made her want to leave."

He looked at Will for a minute before, "She told me. She woke up and she told me and she showed me. I think maybe she didn't want to deal with everyone this morning."

"She told you?"

"Yeah."

"Why wouldn't she want to deal with us this morning?"

Standing back up, "She probably mostly didn't want to deal with me. It's one thing to tell someone something in the dark; it's another to look at them again afterwards in the daytime." Jack showed Will the note she'd left, "But she's okay. I think she just wants to wrap her head around me knowing."

Will regarded him with what one might have considered a hint of awe if they looked close enough, "When did you grow up?"

"'Bout one o'clock this morning. Give or take a few minutes."

With a shake of his head, "And how are you wrapping your own head around it?"

"Ask me again in a few days. I may have an answer for you by then, but right now, I'm hungry and think we should go find us some breakfast."

Knowing when to stop pushing, he started towards the hallway, close at his son's heels, "I think it's fend for yourself morning."

...

He knocked on the door after work that night, his stomach full of butterflies much like the first time he picked her up. He also couldn't help the smile on his face, hoping she'd be glad to see him. He heard her coming down the stairs and, after the pause where he knew she was checking the peephole, the door opened up, revealing Emily, clad in pajamas and smudged with charcoal on her cheeks, "Hi."

Stomping the bit of snow from his boots, "Hi."

They shuffled awkwardly for a moment until a blast of cold air caught the door and sent Emily shivering, reminding her it was indeed winter, "Um, come on in."

"Thanks." Once they'd gotten upstairs, the weirdness descended again, with Jack shedding his coat and gloves, then standing, unsure what to do next. Emily, in turn, began quietly picking up stray art supplies. "Need some help?" After seeing her nod, he knelt down beside her, stacking the scraps of paper, "What're you working on?"

"Not much. I turned in my project on Friday, so I'm just messing around really." They finished in silence and once the last pencil had been put away, Emily sat back on her heels, "I'm sorry."

"For what?"

"For leaving this morning." Hanging her head now, "It was stupid of me. It was wrong to just drop that on you, then disappear."

Scooting closer to her, he tilted her head back up, "It wasn't stupid at all. I'm just glad you left me a note so I knew you weren't mad at me or something."

"You should have been mad at me."

Coming in even closer, "All I wanted to do was kiss you good morning." And his lips met hers, kissing like he had wanted to when he woke up.

And she kissed him back, moving closer to him as his arms slid around her waist.

Now, usually they'd have come up for air, but this time, Emily had absolutely no desire to let go of his lips and he sure wasn't giving up hers. Soon, though, she pulled back enough to mention, "You know, you smell like a deep fryer."

"The perils of working at a diner." Wondering if he was pushing his luck, he asked anyway, "I could always take it off, if it's bothering you."

Already boldly fingering the hem of his shirt, "It might be nice if it was somewhere else."

He laughed at her as he pulled the shirt off, "Can we at least get off the floor though? It's kinda cold."

Pulling him to the couch, she laid her warm hands on his stomach, "Warmer?"

"Much." Returning to her mouth, he reached tentatively for the bottom of her own shirt, "You know, you're covered in charcoal and it's tickling my nose."

"Well, we can't have that now, can we?" She let him pull the shirt off her, but when her head reappeared, he was staring at her chest. Looking down quickly, she realized her scar was completely exposed, the jagged line only broken by the cotton of her bra.

Quickly, she pulled the shirt back down and sat against the arm of the couch, "Sorry."

"I ... I didn't see that one ... last night."

"And you probably shouldn't have seen it now."

Knowing this was a good moment for a little humor, he took advantage of it, "Geez, always fishing for a complement. You know you'd be beautiful covered head to toe in boils and bald. Who cares about a measly little scar?"

They studied each other intently for a moment until the corners of Emily's mouth began to quiver, then the smile emerged. Jack grinned back at her and without another moment, their lips were together again.

It didn't take long for them to be lying on the couch, hands roaming farther than ever before. Emily's began drifting down his stomach and, as her fingers touched the button of his jeans, something began vibrating only inches from her.

Of course, being that she wasn't exactly expecting his pants to be vibrating, she jerked backwards and slid off the couch, landing on the floor with a hard thump.

Jack, in turn, couldn't imagine why his body should be vibrating at a time like this. It took a moment to realize what was happening. Reaching into his pocket, he pulled out the phone, "Hell on wheels, how does she do that?" Answering it, "Yeah? Um, hello?"

■■■

When he hung up a minute later, Emily had already shifted, stationing herself a respectable few feet away on the other end of the couch. She watched him sigh and lean back into the cushions, "Everything all right?"

With shut eyes, he nodded, "I'd just like to know how the hell she knows whenever we're ..." Raising his hands in defeat, "When we're here."

She couldn't help but shrug self-consciously, "She's a mom. I guess they can do that."

Reaching over, he rubbed her stocking feet for a minute before, "I've gotta go. My grandparents called and I need to call them back."

"Fat scarf grandma?"

"Yeah, they call most Saturdays and they like to talk to all of us. Tim usually calls back on his cell, but," scrolling through his stored numbers, "I don't have the number in here."

Standing and holding out her hand to pull him up, "Far be it from me to be the one to stand in the way of talking to Grandma and Grandpa." Holding out his shirt, "Get out."

By now he was chuckling, "You're lucky I love you."

As she gathered up his coat, "I know I am."

Chapter 18

The following Monday, she slid into her seat next to Tim a few minutes before art class began, "Hey."

"Hey."

"So listen, I'm sorry you had to sleep on the couch."

Tim looked over at her, his perpetual half-grin right where it should be, "Are you kidding? For the first time in I don't know how long, I didn't have to listen to people going to the bathroom, snoring, talking in their sleep, having bad dreams," stretching his arms up behind him, "I may have to move down there permanently. I never knew peace and quiet could actually be peaceful and quiet."

"Well, for what it's worth, I didn't mean to fall asleep up there."

Dropping his voice a little, "How 'bout next time, you stay for breakfast and we'll call it even?"

She smiled at him as Ms. Tassleman walked through the door, "All right. Who's first?"

Critiques went quickly and, soon, they were getting their next two week assignment. "You will draw your family. I don't care what you use or what you do it on … as long as it's your family."

Tim, with a loud groan, "Man, there's seven of them. I can guarantee you there's no way I can get all of them to sit still for that long. I don't even think I could get all seven in the same spot, let alone keep them there without hefty bribes."

Ben, another student with a rather large family, thought for a second, then called across the room, "You know, we can interpret how we want. She didn't actually say you have to draw each one."

"So, already trying to work your way around my assignment, hmm?"

Tim turned red, "No, just …"

Ms. Tassleman smiled, "I'm joking. The more you try to work your way around it, the more creative you'll become. I say drive me crazy with interpretation."

"Then you will definitely not be receiving seven portraits."

As she stopped to talk to another student, Tim bumped Emily's arm, "So, feel like helping me figure out a way to cheat?" When she didn't respond, he looked over at her, "Hey, did you hear me?"

She came out of her fog, "What?"

"I asked if you were going to help me figure out a way to cheat."

"Um, sure, yeah, I'll, uh, I'll be around after work. We can think about it then."

Realizing she looked like she'd just swallowed a pound of rocks, "You okay?"

"Uh-huh. Just thinking about the assignment."

The bell rang, and, after grabbing his books, "This should be an easy one. It's just you. You don't have to figure out how NOT to draw seven portraits and still get a passing grade." Heading out the door, he called over his shoulder, "See you tonight."

Still not moving, she gnawed on her bottom lip for a few seconds, "Yeah, an easy one."

For the first time in her life, Emily dutifully ignored an assignment. She sat for hours trying to do the project but something kept standing in her way. The problem, however, was she couldn't figure out what that something was.

Tim though, found the angle he needed at Emily's suggestion and managed to finish a week early. He also began his week-long ribbing session of her, because she had let it slip that she hadn't finished yet.

By the Friday before the assignment was due, Jack finally had to tell him to back off while they were comfortably jammed on the couch, watching sci-fi movies with Nate, Dave and Tucker. Tim had been laying it on fairly thick and, finally, he broke her. Getting up, she left the living room and Jack turned to his brother, fire in his eyes, "Goddammit, you're such a jackass sometimes. Would you just back off already?"

Tim, feeling instantly horrible, followed him in to the kitchen and found Emily standing at the sink, "Em, I'm sorry. I guess I forgot you're not used to … well, I'm sorry."

She just shook her head, "I'm just annoyed with myself I guess, for not finishing yet." Turning to Jack, "Walk me home? Maybe I can make a dent in it tonight," aiming a forgiving smirk in Tim's direction, "seeing that if Tim can do it, I certainly ought to be able to."

•••

Later that evening she sat, stared and thought until her brain hurt. The night passed slowly and watching the sun come up, she knew what she had to do and she knew who she wanted to go with her. Since it was Saturday, she knew Jack probably wouldn't be up yet, but she got dressed and walked over anyway.

Tapping lightly on the door, she was surprised to have Jack answer. Still in his pajamas, he rubbed his head and yawned, "I was just coming down to get something to drink and I heard you knock." Standing aside, he motioned for her to come in, "Is anything wrong?"

"Do you have to work today?"

Caught completely off-guard, "I'm supposed to, but I can call off if I have to." He looked at her more closely, "You okay?"

"Would you maybe like to take a road trip with me?"

Now he was really awake and extremely curious, "A road trip?"

She nodded, "I need to go someplace and I think I need to go now."

Expertly moving her aside so they could avoid being trampled as the four younger kids came down the steps in a stampede, each passing and yelling hello as they made their way to the kitchen, then to the TV, "Where do you need to go and why do you think you need to go now?"

She shook her head, "I just need to do this. If you can't go, I can take the bus, it's okay."

He made his decision, "Let me call work, then ask if I can get one of the cars."

In that instant, both Elizabeth and Will came down the steps, "Em, morning."

"Morning."

Jack turned to them, "Do you think it might be all right if I borrowed the car for the day?"

"Don't you work?"

Emily spoke up, "He does, but I asked if he'd take me somewhere. It's about a five hour drive."

Will looked at her in surprise, "Where're you going?"

Biting her lip, she looked him square in the eye, "I need to go home."

∎∎∎

They were in the car about an hour later, Jack driving, Emily in the passenger seat and a bag of munchies and sandwiches in a cooler in the back.

They had a GPS, Jack's iPod and their cell phones.

It would have been a blast had they had nothing to think about but each other.

But of course, they did not.

"Do you really want to go back? I thought things were getting better. Why do you want to mess with that?"

She sat silent for so long that Jack figured he had pissed her off somehow and was about to start apologizing when she finally answered, "Remember when I was over last week and Tim and I were trying to figure out how he'd represent all of you for our assignment. He didn't think he'd be able to actually do portraits of all you, so he wanted to draw one thing that represented each of you instead. He came up with items that fit all of you perfectly and he's actually really excited about how it turned out."

Jack, confused, "But how does that have anything to do with where we're going?"

"I don't think Tim ever thought about what kind of problem I'd have with the homework. He mentioned off-hand when we got the assignment about how I was lucky 'cause I really only had to draw myself."

"What an ass."

Touching Jack's leg, "No, that's the thing. I think he figured I'd be happy that my only family was me. He knows my father hit me and my mom died years ago, before I ever really knew her, so in his mind, I was okay with this assignment."

"He's still an ass."

Swatting him lightly, "Would you stop saying that please?"

With a nod, "Okay, but that still doesn't explain why we're going here."

"I sat up all last night and I realized that even if I could be, I didn't want to be the only one in my family picture. But the problem is, I need something I think I left behind. At least I hope I did."

"What's that?"

Staring out the window, "My mother."

Chapter 19

It took them a little longer than expected to get there and as they approached, her stomach began to twist. By the time they saw the exit sign for Daley, her leg was jiggling and she was chewing on her bottom lip. Seeing this, Jack slid his hand over and rested it gently on the bouncing leg, "Hey, we can always just stop for some pancakes, then go home."

The bouncing stopped, "Pancakes sound perfect, but after, okay?"

The GPS bought them to a fairly nice neighborhood, but told them that the exact address did not exist. Figuring she was remembering wrong, "Just drive down the street and I'll tell you when to stop." After a minute or two, she pointed to the curb where she wanted him to park, "Right there is fine."

Stopping, he turned the car off, "You okay?" She didn't answer at first, given she was staring past him at the house across the street. She stared so long that Jack tapped her thigh lightly, "Hello??"

It still took her a second to come back to him, "Sorry, um, that's where I lived."

He'd been expecting some run-down, slightly gross neighborhood with uncut lawns and dilapidated cars on the grass. This place looked like your average neighborhood, maybe even a little nicer. There were a couple kids out playing in the semi-spring like air, tossing snowballs from the few small drifts that remained. It all reminded him of his own house, which made him shudder. For a split second he wondered if the same thing that happened to Emily could be happening to one of the families on his street.

Shaking off that unnerving thought, "Did it always look like this?"

She nodded, "For the most part. He didn't let me out much."

Realizing something, "Wait, you went to school, didn't you?"

"Not as much as I should have and the last two years, I didn't go at all."

"Didn't someone notice you weren't there?"

"No. He called and told them we had to move and asked if he could come pick up my school records. He waltzed in, got the papers, left and came home. He thought there was too much chance that I'd talk." Watching as a taller man came around from the back of the house and headed towards the car, "But that's not important right now."

Jack turned his head as the man crossed the street carefully and put his hand up in greeting. Rolling down the window, Jack called a friendly, "Hi."

The man's voice was pleasant enough, but there was a cautious edge to it, "Hello. Can I help you with something? My wife noticed you out here and thought maybe you were lost?"

Emily undid her seatbelt and climbed out of the passenger door. Coming around to the street side of the car, she put her hand out and he shook it, "My name's Emily Ward. I used to live here, a while back."

Jack was out of the car by now as well, "I'm Jack. We, um, just drove in from Cavendish ... Pennsylvania."

The man nodded, "Bit of a long drive."

"About 5 hours or so."

"Well, I'm Tom and I didn't mean to sound mean. It's just my wife's a little skittish of a couple of teenagers staring in her windows."

Emily went red, "I'm so sorry. We didn't mean to scare her."
Smiling, "Would you like to come in for a second? Show her you're not some serial killing stalkers; have a look at the house?"

She nodded, "If you wouldn't mind?"

"Not at all. Follow me."

They crossed the street and went through the now open front door. Emily stood silent as she looked around the radically changed house. Things were neat and tidy, the carpet and paint were new, the furniture was actually whole. She'd never seen the house this perfect before.

Tom's wife, Gretchen, shook hands with them both and let go of the panic from her face, "Would you like to show Jack around?"

Emily shook her head, her chest tight, "No, thanks. This house has more than a few bad memories for me." Both Tom and Gretchen now looked slightly embarrassed as people usually do when the situation catches them by surprise and Emily caught the look. Smiling reassuringly at them, "I really just wanted to ask you a question."

"Okay."

"Did you find anything under the floorboards in the back bedroom? The one on the right?"

Looking at each other, they both shook their heads in unison, "No. Should we have?"

"I left in a hurry and I'm hoping I left something behind. Would you mind if I took a look?"

At such an odd request, the couple didn't really see a way to say no, nor did they want to, "Um, sure. Mind if we come along?"

"Of course not. It is your house after all." Emily waited while they led her down the hall and Jack, who was bringing up the rear, could almost see her harden up as she squared her shoulders and tightened her jaw.

The room was, of course, nothing like she'd left it. Ignoring the bed, which happened to be in the same place as hers, she immediately knelt down and, asking for Jack's keys, she gently pried up the floor board to reveal an old plastic box wedged in tight. Putting her hand in, she shut her eyes and felt for something she'd been missing for years.

A lone tear squeezed itself out as her fingers found what she'd been looking for. Pulling out the picture, she sat back on her heels and stared. In her zeal to get out of the house three years earlier, she hadn't thought to check whether she had grabbed the picture. She had just assumed it was in one of the Ziploc bags with the money but, once she looked, it wasn't.

She knew she couldn't go back to get it and had resigned herself to that fact. But it was that stupid family assignment that made her begin to churn out her plan. And finally, finally, she had back what she missed most in the world.

Her mom.

It had been the only picture she'd ever found in the house. She was in it, two years old at most and her mom was smiling because her world must have been perfect at that point. She knew her father could never have been like he was while she was alive. He told her as much, saying it was Emily who had messed everything up, that things had been perfect before she was born.

Standing up, she cradled the picture, "We'll get out of your hair now. Thank you for letting us in."

Tom looked befuddled at the apparent treasure hidden in the floor, "Was there anything else you wanted?"

With an enormous smile, "Nope. I've got everything now." And with that, she put the floorboard back in place and, thanking them, took Jack by the hand and headed out the front door.

Tom turned to his wife after waving good-bye to the pair, "I'm glad she made it."

Gretchen agreed, "Who knew she'd ever come back? Remember the story the neighbors told us? I honestly figured she was dead somewhere."

"Well, I'm very happy to see that she's not." With a smile, he shut the door and returned to the kitchen to help his wife with the dishes.

···

Jack drove them away but only a few miles, then pulled into the parking lot of a local diner. "You could have told me that's what we were here for, you know?"

Still staring at the picture, "I know. I'm sorry. I just thought that if I talked about it, I'd jinx it. What if they hadn't offered to let us look around, what if the picture hadn't been there, what if ...?"

He stopped her with a kiss, "But everything worked out exactly how you deserved it to." Lingering on her lips for another second, he pulled back, "so, you think maybe I can look?"

She held out the picture but kept her fingers firmly gripping it, not about to let go just yet. Studying it closely, he looked from it, to her and back again, "Do you have any idea that you're the spitting image of your mom?"

Nodding, "I didn't know it until now and I'm so glad I am. I don't think I could handle looking like him."

Running a finger along her jaw line gently, "Well, you'd be beautiful no matter who you looked like."

They sat for another minute in the lot before he asked her quietly, "Did you want to get those pancakes now? I'm starved and conveniently, there's a diner right here."

Emily shook her head, "If it's all right with you, can we maybe hit the next town? I really don't want to stay in this place any longer than we absolutely have to."

With a nod, he turned the car back on and pulled onto the road, "Will do. Next stop, ten minutes."

Chapter 20

While they were plowing their way through stacks of pancakes, the snow started.

It was light at first, soon switching to really big flakes then turning heavier. By then, they were back in the car and trying to navigate their way home. Listening to the news, they heard about the blizzard that seemingly came out of nowhere and had plans to dump at least a foot of snow on them. Temperatures were dropping and wind chills were already in the teens.

It was going downhill fast, so to speak. After visibility completely disappeared and the wind began nudging the cars on the freeway back and forth, Jack took the first exit he found. Slipping his way down the exit ramp and muttering about the asinine amount of snow this damn state seemed to receive, he pulled into a gas station, dialing home once he came to a stop, "Mom?"

"Jack? I tried to call, but it said you were out of area. Has it started snowing yet?"

"Mom, I can't see more than a foot in front of me and the wind's trying to blow us into on-coming traffic."

"Then stay put, find someplace to sleep and wait it out. I don't need the two of you dead on the side of the road somewhere."

Jack was kind of surprised at the ease with which she told him not to come home, "Are you sure?"

"Honey, I don't think I could take it if something happened because I told you to come home." He could almost see her twirling the old-fashion phone cord on her fingers, "Just call me back when you find a place to stay and let me know where you are. Okay?"

Nodding, he smiled when he realized she couldn't see him shaking his head, "Okay. I'll call back in a little while. Love you."

"Love you too, honey. Did you get done what you went for?"

Watching Emily still gripping the picture, "Yeah, we did."

"Good."

...

Once they slid their way to a hotel, Jack registered with his emergency credit card, which he had never actually used until now and felt rather scared at the prospect for some reason. He could just imagine the look on his parents faces if they saw a hotel charge to their card that they didn't already know about.

Heading to their room, Jack let them in and, shutting the door, turned to survey the place. There were two double beds, a TV, bathroom, a typical hotel room, at least in comparison to the two he had stayed at in the past. As he had explained to Emily as they were registering, "With eight people, you never stay in hotels. It's either camping or relatives floors."

Emily smiled, "Still beats me."

"True."

The only thing un-typical about the room was the fact that they were both in it, several hundred miles from home.

Luckily, Jack had to disturb the awkwardness by calling his mom again to fill her in. By the time he hung up, Emily had gone back out and brought in the cooler and bag of snacks they hadn't eaten from the car.

Stashing the food in the fridge, "So, hungry?"

"I'm still stuffed from the pancakes." With a yawn, "I am tired though. How 'bout you?"

Emily nodded, "I didn't sleep at all last night."

With a glance at his watch, "It's almost six. We could nap now or just wait until later, watch some TV and go to bed?"

Having the obvious internal debate, the bed won, "Maybe just a little nap?"

He laughed at her and, without embarrassment, "You need someone to keep you warm?"

"Of course. Who else's leg am I gonna shove my freezing feet under?

"Wow, you make this nap sound more and more appealing all the time."

They fell asleep quickly and stayed that way for the next four hours or so until Jack's bladder decided to get the better of him. Sliding out of the warm nest they'd made, he hurried, then slid back behind her, shivering slightly because of the freezing floor in the bathroom.

Cuddling up, he moved his arm back over her waist and, feeling the warm skin there, shifted his hand to her belly. It was about now he realized he wasn't that tired anymore.

Instead, he lay enjoying the closeness of her and surveying her very tempting exposed neck. The temptation won and he began lightly kissing the same scar he had before. Then he moved on.

Slowly, he kissed the exposed nubs of her spine until he ran into the top of her shirt, at which time he turned a little and headed along until he found her ear. She wasn't awake but had shifted a little onto her back, giving him more surface area to work with.

He now had that beautiful jawbone to deal with as well as the perfect curve of her ear. Kissing them both thoroughly, he didn't notice her eyes had opened up and that he was being watched.

He didn't know it until he felt her cheeks pull into a grin. Looking up in surprise, he saw the smile and couldn't help but return it.

"Hi."

"Hi."

Propping himself up on one elbow, "You were too beautiful not to kiss."

"I'm not complaining." Lifting her head slightly off the pillow, she met his lips.

It didn't take long for the kiss to go beyond where they usually stopped. Way beyond. Way, way beyond.

By now, she had rolled towards him and his hand was traveling up and down her back slowly, feeling the ridges of the scars. After a few minutes, without pretense, his hand moved up her side and to the front. Before he realized, his hand was grazing the side of her breast and there it froze, because reality came back into the picture. Breaking the kiss, "I'm sorry."

Emily looked at him, almost amused, "I didn't stop. You did."

"You know that you can though, right? Just say the word and I'll quit, I swear." Her mouth curved into a smile that Jack had no choice but to kiss again, "I love you."

"I love you back."

After another minute, she pulled away, "One second." Sitting up, she pulled her shirts over her head, then as she watched him watching in awe, she pulled off her bra as well.

Lying back down on her back, she laughed as he asked, "Can I?"

With a nod, he shifted down a little and began kissing her now exposed belly button, which he savored for a few moments before slowly working his way upwards. He enjoyed each of her ribs equally before finally reaching the bottom tip of the scar that ran diagonally across her chest.

He gave this scar, as promised, its due time and kissing the length of it, he asked her quietly when he reached the end, "Have I made this one better?"

Her voice, low and slow, "You make everything better." Smiling, he moved back down to her belly button, tongue darting around the edges, shivers racing up her spine and causing her back to arch towards him, "Jack?" Unwilling to leave his spot, he asked in a muffled voice, "Yeah?"

"Have you done this before?"

"Never. Why?"

"Because you're really good at it."

■■■

Nearly an hour later, just as both were beginning to drift off, Emily growled deep in her throat, "Damn it."

His grip tightened momentarily on her hip, "You okay?"

"I just realized I need to go to the bathroom and it's freezing out there." Sitting up, she grabbed the closest piece of clothing, namely Jack's extremely thick and extremely warm long-sleeve thermal shirt. Sliding it over her head, she hurried and was crawling back in bed, shivering, a few minutes later.

Jack took his turn even faster and having pulled his socks, boxers and t-shirt back on, could barely keep his teeth from chattering as he snuggled back up behind her. He had ventured a quick look out the window and left the curtain partly open so she could see the snow. Lifting his head to look over her shoulder, "At this rate, we could be here for days."

"Could be worse, you know."

Finally warming a little, he rested his head and now non-chattering teeth on the pillow behind her, "Couldn't have been better either." Burying his nose in the back of her neck, he shut his eyes, not tired but not really wanting to be awake either.

She lay there in the dark for quite awhile, before quietly asking, "Why'd it take you almost three weeks to stop and talk to me?"

Grinning into her neck, he whispered, "I had no idea how to talk to someone so beautiful."

"So it was just on accident that you drove your bike past my house that first time?"

"Yup. Decided I didn't want to go home just yet, so I kept going down the block and there you were." She was quiet for so long after this that Jack wasn't sure if she fell asleep, so he whispered, "You still awake?"

She nodded, "Just thinking about how much had to happen to get us here."

With a final snuggle, he shut his eyes, "Entirely too much."

"G'night Jack."

"G'night Em."

Chapter 21

The following morning, Jack woke slowly, opening his eyes to find himself only a few inches from a still sleeping Emily. Memories of the night still foremost on his mind, he grinned, his body warming as he reached out to run his finger across her forehead.

"Are you trying to wake me up?"

Her mumbled voice amused him, "Naw, just like touching you."

Even though her eyes were still shut, her cheeks pinked while her hand slid across the distance between them, coming to a stop when she found a bare piece of skin, namely the upper part of his arm. Stroking it lightly, "You should do it more often."

"You are dangerously close to tickling territory, young lady."

Finally opening her eyes, she saw his twinkling mischievously back at her, "Really?"

His fingers flew too fast for her to stop them and, soon, she was giggling uncontrollably, her neck vulnerable as she curled in a ball to protect her sides. About to call 'uncle' so she could take a breath, Jack stopped suddenly when his phone began ringing from the corner where he'd been charging it. Looking down at her in surprise, "How the hell does my mom do that? Can she see through the damn phone?"

As both struggled to untangle themselves from the sheets, "How do you know it's your mom?"

"Because we're alone in a hotel room 120 miles from home, who else could it possibly be?" Finally working his way off the bed, he picked up the phone and with a self-satisfied grimace, he held it up towards her before hitting re-dial, "Told you."

"Hey Mom."

"Morning. How'd it go last night?"

He suddenly forgot how to breathe for a second, then, "Fine. We got in, ate some of the food, watched TV then went to sleep. Woke up a little while ago."

"Any idea when you'll be heading out?"

Moving towards the window to look out, he saw a good foot of snow over everything, but he also saw the revolving lights of the plows working on the freeway that criss-crossed the view, "Um, well, there's about a foot out there and the plows are working, but I have no idea when we'll be able to leave."

On her end, Elizabeth was looking out the front window at roughly the same amount of snow covering their street, "Well, call when you leave, okay?

Watching as Emily pulled her own clothes on, he momentarily forgot about his mother completely until, from somewhere very far away, he heard her voice in his ear, "What?"

"I said, drive safe and let me know when you leave? Are you okay?"

"Um, yeah, sorry, just hungry I guess. We'll call."

Pretty sure the distraction was in the form of a 16-year-old girl with whom he'd just spent the night, she forced down her imagination and worry, "Okay. Love you."

"Love you too, Ma." Hanging up, he turned to see Emily, half in her jeans, sitting on the edge of the bed, grinning at him, "What?"

"Just enjoying the socks." Jack looked down at his stocking feet, then moved in front of the full-length mirror hanging off the back of the bathroom door. Standing for a moment, he beckoned for her to join him. Shucking the jeans back to the floor, she came over, stopping beside him, "You called?"

Laying his arm loosely over her shoulder, "Just wanted to see how good we look together."

Emily squeezed him tightly around the chest, "I think we look awfully good."

"Even with the socks and boxers?"

"Especially with the socks and boxers."

●●●

They managed to leave around two that afternoon and, limping their way slowly home, finally pulled to a stop in front of Emily's house around ten that night. Giving her a good, long kiss goodnight at the front door, Jack held her close, "I'm gonna be lonely tonight."

"You've got seven other people with you. I highly doubt you'll be lonely."

"But none of them are you."

Kissing him again, "I'll see you in the morning."

●●●

Driving home, he made it into the house and was just knocking the snow off his boots when the family piled into the front room and hallway. All kinds of questions were flying at him and, for the first time ever, he found it to be too loud. He held up his hand, "Just a second."

Only Elizabeth ignored this and pulled him into a hug, "I'm glad you're okay. Did you drop Emily off already?"

With a nod, "Yeah. She got in fine and I'm here and I'm starving."

Will bustled most of the boys upstairs to bed while Jack followed his mom to the kitchen. Pulling out a few bowls, she quickly filled a plate and slid it into the microwave, "Thirsty?"

"Yeah."

Handing him a full glass, then setting the gallon of milk in front of him, "So, what happened?"

He nearly choked on the milk halfway down his throat, "Not much. I'd rather you let her explain if you don't mind."

Elizabeth nodded, "Fair enough." Getting up to grab the now warm dinner from the microwave, she set it in front of him, suddenly feeling awkward, "So, do you think they'll cancel school?"

Jack just looked at her with tired eyes, desperately hoping to head off whatever was ahead, "Do you think we could talk tomorrow? Em'll be here after school for awhile and she'll tell you then, okay?"

Knowing a dismissal when she heard it, she got up and leaning over to kiss the top of his head, she tousled his hair, "Okay. I'm going to head to bed then. I didn't get much sleep last night."

"We were all safe and holed up someplace warm, Ma. Why were you worried?"

Hugging him good night, "I always worry."

...

Will came through the kitchen a few minutes later just as Jack was putting his dish in the dishwasher and filling it up with detergent, "So, how'd it go yesterday?"

Jack kept his sigh to himself, wishing he could just crawl into bed and dream, "It was fine. Like I told Mom, Em'll be here tomorrow and she would rather tell you herself."

Looking at his son closely, "I meant for you. I know she's got a lot to deal with, but so do you. I just wondered how you were holding up."

Turning and leaning on the counter, he crossed his arms and couldn't help but grin at his dad, "I'm holding up just fine."

"I'm glad she found you."

"So am I." Will turned to go, but Jack stopped him, "You okay?"

With a smile at his son, "Yeah, glad you two made it home in one piece. See you in the morning."

With that, Jack was once again alone in the kitchen and he seriously considered sneaking out to Emily's, but fought the urge and headed upstairs instead.

...

Walking into his bedroom, he found Tim sprawled on his bed, finishing up what looked like history homework. Once Jack shut the door behind him, Tim shoved the book back in his backpack and sat up, "So, alive I see?"

"Yeah, sorry to disappoint you."

Tim shook his head and stood, heading over to turn off the light, "You know, it would have been nice. I could have had my own room, a bit more elbow room at the table."

Jack stripped down and crawled into bed, "You love me and you know it."

Settling under his own blankets, "Maybe, occasionally."

They both lay there for a few minutes until, "Tim?"

"Yeah?"

"Remember when I asked you if you loved Sarah?"

"Uh-huh."

"Have you slept with her yet?"

Tim, who had almost been expecting the question eventually, answered his brother honestly, "No. We've come awfully close, but we both kind of decided we weren't quite ready yet." Settling with his arms behind his head, he grinned at the ceiling, "But I've got all the time in the world." As almost an afterthought, he jokingly asked, "How about you and Em? Ever gonna get there or are you waiting for your third date?" The silence in the room was deafening and Tim slowly sat up as the silence continued to hang above them, "Jack?" By now he was out of bed and standing over his brother, who was staring thoughtfully at the ceiling, "Jack Andrew Callaghan, I asked you a question?" Jack stared past his brother for another second or two before locking eyes with him. Tim's opened even wider as he backed up and sat down on his bed again, whispering, "Holy shit."

"You can't say anything, Tim."

Sitting there, still dumbfounded, he couldn't help but repeat his previous, "Holy shit," followed by, "yesterday?"

"Really late last night."

Tim stared at his younger brother, "Did you plan it?"

Rolling to his side, "No. Of course not. It just happened. We were there and just, suddenly, everything was perfect."

"I don't know whether to yell at you, be jealous of you, kick your ass or ask how it was?"

"First off, don't yell at me, okay? There'll be enough of that if Mom and Dad find out. Jealousy is your issue. I really don't want to get a boot in the ass and," closing his eyes for a second, "it was better than you could ever imagine."

Given he was now wide awake, Tim slid back and leaned against the wall, "At the risk of sounding like Dad, I gotta ask, where did you find a condom in a hotel room in the middle of nowhere in the snow at midnight?"

Deciding at this point that honesty was the best policy, "We didn't."

"Oh hell, are you kidding me?"

"No. The thought never even occurred to me until the ride home today. When I mentioned it, Em said she just finished, so it should be fine but ..."

"Dumbass. What were you thinking?"

"Apparently not the right thing."

Tim reached down and rummaged through his backpack for a second, then tossed something across the way. "Here moron, don't leave home without 'em. Ever again."

Jack fingered the two condoms that had landed on his pillow, "What kind of odds are we playing?"

"The odds of you ending up a father? I have no idea, but the odds that Dad's gonna kill you are pretty damn good."

Groaning into his pillow, "How could I have been so stupid?"

Suddenly realizing he didn't need to continue his lecture, "Hey, we're all stupid at times. But hopefully God'll see that Mom and Dad are a little too young to be grandparents at the moment."

"I've been pleading with him about that for the last seven hours."

Tim almost felt sorry for his brother and he switched subjects, kind of, "So, um, how do I look at her tomorrow?"

"Like you always have."

"But I now know that you've seen her naked and ... oh god ... you were naked with her."

"Tim!"

"What? You have and you were. And I now know this. And now, when I see her tomorrow, all I'm going to think about is her naked and you, as disgusting of an individual as you are, naked with her and I'm gonna have to throw up somewhere and ten to one, it's gonna tip her off."

Jack finally laughed for the first time, "Good night, Tim."

"Hey?"

"Yeah?"

"You do love her, don't you?"

Without hesitating, "More than life itself."

Another few minutes passed, then Tim, his voice barely making it over to Jack's bed, "Were you scared?"

"To death ... then ... just ... I mean, then everything was fine." Finally able to think about what had happened as a whole rather than a jumble of moments in his mind, "It was like it was supposed to happen that way and any other time or place would have been completely wrong. Like the whole universe conspired to get us to just that moment and then ... let us go."

Even across the dark room, Tim could clearly hear the debate going on in Jack's mind, "And I'd stop thinking about sneaking over there, little brother. The universe might not be so generous tonight."

Jack smiled, "Neither would Mom or Dad if they caught me." Relaxing under his thick comforter, even his feet warm by now, "G'night, Tim."

"'Night."

...

After Jack had dropped her off, Emily made her way upstairs. Walking into the living room, she headed immediately for the kitchen. After digging up something to calm the growling in her stomach, she stood there, munching her apple and looked around.

Jack had said he'd be lonely without her and, in reality, her heart was already aching to see him again. Her sleepiness gone, she saw the room for what seemed to be the first time. It was quiet and small and sparse and hers ... and empty.

Confusion set in next ... and she did the only thing she could ever do when there was suddenly too much on her mind. She pulled out her paper and her pencils.

Chapter 22

It was just after six the next morning when her mind quieted and she made the final finishing touches on her assignment. She had just been doodling, but around midnight she switched to the family project for class and, letting herself go, she watched her hand draw what she truly felt inside.

It was the strangest thing. Once she'd decided to draw exactly what she was feeling, the project came easy to her.

She also managed to forget what had happened the previous night with Jack. She knew that if that entered into things, she would forever doubt the decision she fought so hard to make.

And it was done.

Startled, she looked up as she heard a knock on the downstairs door. With a sudden grin, she figured it had to be Jack and ran down the steps. Pulling the door open, she could barely get out a gasp before she received a solid punch to the face.

•••

Jack had woken up and, after tossing and turning for awhile, finally decided he'd had enough waiting. Getting up, he dressed silently, crept downstairs, greeted his dad at the kitchen table and immediately began pulling on his coat and boots.

"Going over to Emily's?"

"Yeah." With a sheepish grin, "I'm awake so I figured, why not?"

Will stared at him for a moment, then, "Please be careful, Jack. Very careful. You're too young and too much has happened to her for you to treat this as a flippant thing."

Jack nodded, "I just," looking down at the floor and shuffling his still untied boots, "I just need to see her." Meeting his dad's eyes, "I just want to tell her I love her. That's all."

A quick smile spread across his dad's face, "Then why are you standing here with me? You've got a girl waiting on you."

With his own grin, he hurried out the door, walking swiftly down the street. Will went back to his paper, worrying as every father does.

...

The first thing Jack noticed was the set of footprints leading to the door. They weren't his or hers from last night and Dex would have come from the other direction. Beads of cold sweat broke out on his forehead as he knocked on the door.

When no one answered, he tried the handle and the door opened easily. Now in sheer, full-on panic mode, he hauled up the stairs and skidded to a halt in the living room. Some guy was straddling Emily on the floor, swinging his fists at her.

It took hearing the thud of her head hitting the floor in reaction to the man's fist to get him moving.

And move he did. Yanking his coat off, he flew across the room, tackling as Tim had taught him, knocking the man completely off Emily and together, they landed in a heap. Jack took advantage of his surprise attack by hitting hard and hitting fast.

Being a strong, solidly built 16-year-old, Jack held his own, but the man he fought had three years of pent-up rage and nothing to lose. As Emily watched from across the room, somewhere in the back of her sluggish mind, she knew this couldn't possibly end well.

It didn't take too long before they'd worked their way back towards the door and with one final, desperate, no-holds barred blow to the man's face, Jack then raised his leg and shoved the man cleanly through the door.

He watched from the top of the stairs, in what seemed like slow motion, as the man stumbled and pitched down them. In his statement later, he would also describe the gunshot-like sounds he heard when several of the man's bones cracked on the sharp-edged wooden steps.

Hesitating and breathing long, jagged breaths, Jack watched, then cautiously made his way downstairs. He couldn't see the man breathing and, tentatively putting his fingers to the man's neck, he felt around for a pulse, but couldn't find one.

Backing up the steps, never taking his eyes off the crumpled figure lying on the landing, he sat on the top stair and pulled out his phone, ignoring the blood pouring from his nose and the gaping split in his lower lip and chin.

●●●

Once he hung up from his fairly calm conversation with 911, he turned to see Emily attempting to sit up across the room. Not willing to leave his spot, wanting to be able to see if the man made any kind of move, he called over to her, "You okay?"

She groaned and put her head back down on the floor, her face already swollen to a nearly unrecognizable state. Then he saw her nod slightly as she curled into a ball, clutching her sides.

He let out a sigh of relief and dialed his own house, "Hello?"

"Dad, I need you to come over right now."

"Jack?"

"Now, Dad." Hanging up, he sat equidistant from the person he loved with all his heart and the one he hated most of all, the one he could only assume was her father, and waited.

●●●

The police, ambulance and Will and Elizabeth all showed up at the same time. For the next hour, everything was in chaos: Will sitting by his son, listening to the story as he told it to the police, Steven Ward being loaded into an ambulance, Emily being wheeled out to a second truck and Jack, desperate to go with her, demanding that Elizabeth go instead.

She did and Jack managed to calm himself down again in order to re-tell the story for the third time to someone else. "The only thing I knew is that I had to get him away from her. The rest is a blur. I hit him, he hit me, we worked our way to the door and I shoved him out. I was just hoping to be able to lock the door. It never occurred to me he'd fall down, much less," waving his blood-covered and trembling hands around, "this."

The officer watched as Jack began shaking more and turn an almost gray color. Deciding to wrap things up for now, "Okay. First, I think you need to be going to the hospital yourself. I'll follow behind and we can continue this there and then I'll need to wait for Emily's side of things." Helping Jack to his extremely unsteady feet, "Second, I'll have my guys finish things here and they'll lock up when they leave. Do you have a key?"

Jack swung his head slowly around, the fog closing in, "Um, yeah. Her keys should be by the door."

The officer pocketed them as they moved to leave, "All right. Now, third, do you think you can make it down the stairs and to the car or do you want me to get another truck out here for you?"

Will took a look at his son and shook his head, "I can get him down." And with that, the policeman watched Will, who was slightly shorter and smaller than the boy, put an arm around his waist and practically carry him down the stairs, past the cluster of officers and out to the waiting squad car.

...

Tim had been awake when Jack called and, suddenly, finding himself in charge, he now had the job of getting everyone fed, cleaned, dressed and to school without raising suspicions of where his parents were and why the hell he was actually in charge in the first place. He found it easiest to go with the vague and boring, "They went somewhere and told me to get you guys to school on time." When Dave opened his mouth to ask more, Tim just glared at him, "Dude, just go get ready, all right?"

Dave wasn't buying it, but didn't really need Tim pissed at him, so he shrugged and did as asked. The other boys didn't even question, each carrying on with their normal routines.

Tim's route luckily didn't take them past Emily's house, so Tim still had absolutely no idea what was happening when he arrived at school ten minutes after the first bell. Taking his tardy notice without a word, he spent the next two hours not hearing a damn thing said in his classes, using class exchange to dial and re-dial his dad's phone, the ringing going unanswered. Finally, after his third useless class, as he was pulling his coat back on to go outside to his car to continue calling until someone finally decided to answer, he got a text message from his dad, "J and E at Oak Grove Hosp. R okay. Call later."

Ducking into the art room, he found Ms. Tassleman getting ready for class, "Tim? You're about an hour early."

"Do you know where Oak Grove Hospital is?"

Her smile immediately faded, "Yeah. Why?"

"My dad just sent me a message that my brother and Emily are there, but I have no idea where it is."

She quickly gave him directions and also demanded that he call when he knew anything. Nodding to the teacher, he high-tailed it out of the school and started across town.

...

Elizabeth watched them take care of Emily, standing quietly in the corner out of the way trying not to bother them, lest they throw her back into the hall. She answered what questions she could and hated herself every time she could only shake her head with an, "I don't know, I'm sorry."

Eventually they wheeled Emily out of the room and one of the nurses stayed behind to fill Elizabeth in, "First she's going to get a head CT to make sure there's no brain swelling, then they'll be x-raying her ribs and chest, her face and her arm. After that, she'll be back down here."

Visibly paling at the thought of everything, she nodded, "Anything else?"

"Not at the moment but if you'd like to wait down the hall, I'll find you when she comes back."

"Would it be possible for you find out if my son was brought in? Jack Callaghan. He stopped the man who did this to her, but I left him talking to the police at her house. He wanted me here with her."

The nurse nodded, "I'll find out right now for you."

Elizabeth went into the hall and ran smack into Will. Telling the nurse to never mind, "Is Jack here?"

"Yeah. We just got in. I told him I was going to find you." Taking her hand, he walked her to the other end of the hall, "We're down here."

...

Jack woke up slowly, blinking his eyes several times before he focused in on his parents, "Where's Emily?"

Elizabeth ran her fingers lightly through his hair, "She's still getting her cast on."

He struggled to sit up but Will held his shoulders, "Slow down. We've got a few things to tell you before you go storming down the hall, tearing the place apart looking for her."

Letting his head fall back on the pillow, he felt jolts of pain through his face, "Uugghh."

"Yeah. Don't do that. You've got a broken nose, you cracked your cheekbone and two of your teeth are gone."

His tongue involuntarily began running around the inside of his mouth and he quickly found the gaping hole on the lower left side. More pain and he decided not to do that again. He also realized why his voice sounded muffled when he went to lick his lips and found stitches running down his chin. He couldn't feel anything there, so he figured he must still be numbed up from the sewing. "I had all my teeth when I got here."

"They had to pull them out. They were mostly in pieces anyway. The only thing holding them in was the swelling of your jaw."

He groaned again, "What happened to him?"

Elizabeth and Will exchanged a look, then, "He didn't make it. They worked on him but I guess it was hopeless from the start."

"I didn't mean for that to happen. I swear."

Elizabeth bent and hugged him, "I know, honey. No one blames you."

He would have said more but the nurse came in and after asking a few questions about how he was feeling, she smiled, "If you're feeling good enough, you can go whenever you're ready. And your friend should be in her own room in a little while. You can go see her then, if you'd like."

Jack smiled back as best he could, considering it felt as if he was tearing his face in two, "Thanks."

...

About an hour later, he was finally discharged and Will walked him out to the waiting room, where Tim jumped from his seat the minute he saw them coming. Going up to his brother, he nearly hugged him, but Jack just backed away quickly, "Pain. Severe pain."

Tim opted then for leaning in to examine the injuries before locking eyes with him, "What the hell happened?"

Jack shook his head, "Ask Dad. I just need to sit down."

Will filled him in quickly and Tim let out a low whistle, "Damn, will she ever get a break?"

"About that. I have a question or two for you. " Turning to include Jack as well, "Both of you actually."

Tim looked at his dad, quizzically, "All right. What is it?"

Chapter 23

Elizabeth was sitting next to the bed when Emily began waking up. She'd had better drugs than Jack and it took her longer to realize where she was. Without even opening her eyes, "Jack?"

"No honey, it's me, Elizabeth."

Forcing her eyes to open, she rolled them in the direction of the sound and she slurred her words, both from the swelling and from the medication, "Where's Jack? Is he all right?"

"Yeah. He's waiting to be discharged so he can come see you. He ordered me to sit here and stay with you until he got here himself."

Already more lucid, "Why can't I move my arm?"

"You've got a cast up to almost your shoulder because you broke both your hand and your elbow along with your cheekbone, nose and four ribs. And you have stitches in the back of your head so I wouldn't move that any time soon either."

"I should have looked to see who it was."

Elizabeth reached in and gently wiped the tears sliding down her face, "It doesn't matter now. Everything's gonna be fine. He won't bother you again."

"Is he dead?" Elizabeth just nodded and watched as Emily shut her eyes again, "Jack didn't do it on purpose. I saw."

"I know."

"I shouldn't have opened the door. I thought it was Jack coming over." Her eyes overflowed again, "I thought it was Jack."

Elizabeth leaned down and hugged her the best she could, "It's okay. Shhhh, it's okay."

...

By the time Jack made it to Emily's room, she'd already spoken to the detective and made her full statement. The policeman was just leaving as Jack slowly made his way through the door. Nodding to Jack, "You saved her life."

After nodding back, he walked immediately over to her and holding the bed railing, kissed her, stitches be damned. Leaving her lips, he kissed her forehead as well before standing back up. Twining his fingers with her good hand, "I love you."

"I love you, too."

Still not realizing there were other people in the room with them, "So, think you might want to come live with us now?"

Emily nodded as best she could, "If you still want me?"

Bending towards her once more, he whispered into her lips as he kissed her again, "I'll always want you."

Tim broke the moment from the doorway, "Good lord, not even stitches can stop them."

Jack straightened up and looked surprised when he saw his mom and dad standing there, "Sorry, what?"

Tim just grinned and came over, knocking Emily's foot gently through the blanket as he walked by, "Nothing little brother. Just making fun of you, that's all."

Emily looked at the bunch of them, all standing around, "You really don't mind me moving in?"

Will nodded, "I told the police you'd be moved in in the next few days. I talked to the Social Services people and to one of the lawyers I know and we ought to have the guardianship papers within the next few weeks and as of sometime tomorrow, Tim's gonna move into the basement. We thought maybe Sam could go in with Jack and you can have Sam's old room. It's small but it'll be all yours and I think we'd prefer to have you upstairs for a while instead of by yourself downstairs."

Another stray tear ran down her face, "I'd like that."

...

They all stayed a little longer, then, as Emily's eyes began to flutter closed, Elizabeth shooed them all away. Jack tried to avoid his mother's herding but was unsuccessful, "I'll stay with her for now. Why don't you go home, get some sleep," looking over at Will, "and your dad just might bring you back later, but for now, go."

Jack wouldn't move until he got an answer, "Does she have to stay the night?"

"Yeah. The doctor wants to watch her for awhile. She's got a mild concussion."

"I'll come back tonight and stay with her then."

Emily, who was still just a shade above asleep, "I'll be fine, Jack."

"I'll be back tonight."

"She'll be fine by herself. There're plenty of people here to keep an eye on her."

Jack looked her straight in the eye, "I'm not leaving her alone. If I have to, I'll sneak out of the house, walk here and sit next to her until she can go home."

Seeing the fire in her son's eyes, she almost smiled, "Okay, how's this? You stay for a few hours," looking over at Tim, who nodded, "with Tim while we go home, get the kids, sort of explain what's gonna happen and whatnot, then I'll come back here to stay the night." She could already see the wheels in Jack's head turning so she cut him off, "But you need a good night's sleep, in your own bed so you will be going home after that, understood?"

Looking from his mom to Emily, he pulled a chair over to the bed, "Okay."

Elizabeth kissed the three of them before her and Will headed out the door, "I'll be back in a few hours."

•••

Emily fell asleep a few minutes later and Tim looked over at his brother, "So, do you think I can use the phone in here. I'm supposed to call Ms. Tassleman and let her know what's going on, then I've gotta call Sarah. And Dex has already left me two messages."

Jack gave him a lopsided, still slightly numb smile, "You probably have to go down to the lobby for that."

"I also figure you might want to be alone with her for a bit, am I right?"

"Thanks,"

Getting up, "Just glad you're okay. I don't know what I would have done if you weren't."

"I like you too, Tim."

As soon as they were alone, Jack gently laid his head down on the pillow next to hers, making sure it was his non-broken side. Even though she was asleep, she moved her head closer and he was asleep before long, wishing with all his might that he could have some kind of do-over for the day.

•••

Tim made his calls and reassured everyone that the pair was fine. He didn't give too many details and it took him a good ten minutes to convince Dex not to come down that very second. Instead, he told him to wait until tomorrow, when they took her home.

Dex was not happy with this, but he obeyed, sure as shooting, he was gonna be at the front door when she came home.

Returning to the room, Tim found them both asleep and opted to sit quietly, alternating between watching them and reading the paperback he'd stuffed in his pocket to read in the waiting room. Eventually, even he took a nap and only woke when the nurse came in. He sat up quickly and realized too late that he'd been drooling on his coat. Looking up, embarrassed, the nurse just smiled, "Honey, that's nothing. Trust me."

Jack woke as well when the nurse switched Emily's IV and, moving too fast, he groaned, "Oh hell."

The nurse came over and helped him sit up, "That's not the best position to be sleeping in."

"I'm realizing that."

As the nurse stood over him, a sympathetic look on her face, "Where you really need to be is in bed."

Keeping his tone light, "Not leaving until my mom gets back. That was the deal and I'm not moving."

Elizabeth's voice came through the door, "I'm back. Go home."

Jack looked up and, for a split-second, was extremely angry at her because now he had no choice but to leave. The anger was short lived however, once his face began throbbing. Standing slowly, he gave Emily another kiss, "See you in the morning."

···

With lots of Tylenol in his system, Jack slept the next 14 hours away in a thankfully dreamless sleep.

Emily wasn't so lucky and at 2:30am, she had had enough. Sliding her legs slowly over the edge of the bed, she waited for the wave of dizziness to pass before she put her feet on the floor and shuffled out through the door to the nurses' station.

The only nurse there looked up in surprise, "Are you all right?"

"Um, could you tell me please if the morgue is open?"

Now the nurse was just confused, "The morgue? No honey, it's closed at night. Would you like some help back to bed?"

"Are you sure there's not a way to see someone down there?"

By this time, the nurse had come around the desk, "Honey, do you feel okay?"

Suddenly realizing she must sound like a complete raving lunatic, "I'm sorry, I just ... I need to make sure someone is really down there."

Elizabeth had been about to panic when she looked in the hallway and saw Emily. Coming over to her, "Em, what's wrong? Why didn't you wake me up?"

"I need to see if he's really down there." She was not above begging at this point, "I need to know if it's okay to close my eyes."

···

About ten minutes later, they were traveling downstairs and the nurse let them in, "Give me a minute to find out where he is, then I'll bring you in okay?"

She nodded and Elizabeth looked over at her, "You sure?"

Nodding again, "I have to. I didn't check last time and look what happened. I need to see for myself."

"Okay." They stood in silence until the nurse called them in and, without thinking, Emily reached for Elizabeth's hand. Curling her fingers around, she took a deep breath and walked through the door.

...

They returned to Emily's room an hour or so later, after having taken a slow walk around their floor a few times once they got back. Emily climbed exhausted, ribs aching, back into bed and fell asleep, still gripping Elizabeth's hand.

Elizabeth couldn't help but think of Jack, who used to do the same thing when he was small and had a nightmare. He'd come get her and pull her back to his room and make her hold his hand until he fell asleep. He never told her what the dreams were about, but her hand seemed to make them go away.

Chapter 24

Tuesday morning, Jack woke around nine o'clock to the sounds of banging and swearing. Not sure what was happening, he just knew he wanted to smile but his face wouldn't let him. Putting his hand to his chin, he felt the bandages and remembered.

Boy, did he remember.

Slowly he worked his body out of bed, muscles screaming and stitches pulling in his mouth. Shuffling out of the room and into the bathroom, he finished, then began the long trek downstairs.

The noise got louder with each step and when he finally reached the first floor, he saw his dad wince slightly at what had to be his face, which is not real comforting when you haven't looked in a mirror yet.

His words coming out slurred and muffled, "That bad, huh?"

Will came over to him and began examining his face, "I've seen you look better."

He let Will poke around for a minute before backing off, "So, um, what's the noise and why are you home? It's Tuesday."

"Well, I'm home because we had a few things to do around here and I'll be going in to work in a little while. Tim stayed home to keep an eye on you and to finish up after I leave."

"What's he finishing?"

Will turned him around and walked him into his study, which was now bare save for a mattress. "Tim's gonna finish up in here, then probably go over to Em's place and pack up a few things. If you're up to it, he'll need some help."

More than a little confused, "Wait? I thought she was gonna be in Sam's room?"

"She is. Tim's going to be in here and my study's now in the basement."

"Why isn't Tim in the basement? I'm confused."

Smiling secretively at his son, "I don't think Tim is a real big fan of the basement and when he hesitated, I figured this would be the best way to go."

"Ahh."

"Just don't make too much fun of him, okay?"

Jack nodded as best he could to keep the throbbing to a minimum, "I won't."

"Thanks. So … hungry?"

"Yeah, I just don't know how I'm supposed to eat."

"Your mom made mountains of Jell-o for you, there's a vat of soup in the fridge and she's got a stash of applesauce in the cupboard."

Already working his way to the kitchen, "I really need to tell her I love her more often."

Will grinned as he headed back to the basement, "She'd like that."

●●●

Will left an hour or so later and Tim came back upstairs, "So, feel like going over to Emily's yet and getting some of her stuff or should I keep going on mine and Sam's things?"

With his latest round of Tylenol finally kicking in, "Maybe Em's while I'm still up for it?"

Tim stood up to grab both their coats, "Dad took my car, so we've got the van. Let's see if we can get most of it in one shot."

Jack shrugged his on, then gingerly pulled his hat over what he realized was still blood-stiffened hair, "Um Tim, can you do something for me first?"

Stopping mid-glove pull, "Maybe."

"Do you think you can help me wash my hair? I can't take a shower yet with the stitches and I don't think I can lean over the sink very well to do it myself."

Looking at him with his problem-solving, 'chew the inside of my cheek while I think' expression, "Okay, go clean off the kitchen counter and lay down on your back with your head at the sink. I'll go grab the shampoo and a towel."

It took Jack a second to get the visual, then he grinned as best he could. This should be interesting.

It went much smoother than either of them thought it would. With Jack's head hanging in the sink, Tim washed and rinsed with the faucet hose. In a few minutes they were done and Tim dried his head, helping him to sit up. While Jack waited for his dizziness to pass, he eyed Tim from under the towel, "You know, this'll make a great story to tell at school."

"If you ever so much as breathe a word about me washing your hair, so help me, I'll get out the pictures of you in Mom's shoes."

Sliding off the counter, "Come on, girls would love to hear how gently you massage the scalp and how well you condition."

He received a well-deserved kick in the rear for this, albeit a light one, and they moved back down the hall to get their coats on again. Tim's phone rang just as they were heading out the door, "Hello?"

He listened for a minute, then said good-bye, "That was Mom. She's on her way home to clean up and have some breakfast. They're keeping Emily until tomorrow because of the concussion, so Mom's gonna hang out here for a while, then head back."

"I want to see her."

Tim smiled, "Yeah, Emily knows you too well. She told Mom to tell you that you're supposed to stay at home and feel better. She'll be fine and she'll see you later."

With an exasperated sigh, "I don't want her there alone."

"She's okay, Jack. She said so herself."

Anger racing to the surface, he couldn't help but shout, "I left her alone Tim. I left her there alone in her apartment and look what happened."

Finally understanding, he walked over to his brother, "There's no way you could have known. She's been alone for the last three years."

For the first time ever, he started to cry in front of his brother, "But if I'd been there, she wouldn't have answered the door. It was unlocked. He didn't break in. She opened the door. She thought it was me."

And in another first, Tim pulled his brother into a hug, "You saved her. You went to her and you saved her. If you hadn't shown up, way worse things would have happened. You couldn't have prevented this, but you did stop it. I don't think she could have asked for a better hero." They stayed silent for a minute before Jack stepped back and Tim stuffed his hands in his pockets, "So, let's just not tell anyone about this whole morning. Fair enough?"

"The girls would love it though, I'm telling you."

"Sarah already knows how fabulously sensitive I am, we don't need word getting out."

...

Jack sat while he packed her things into the crates on the wall, trying in vain to ignore the dried blood stains on the wood floor from Emily's head. He did his job quickly, the panic and the anger building together slowly. Tim got the job of hauling everything out to the van and after the first four or five trips he sat down for a breather. Looking over to the same stain Jack was avoiding, "Is that from him or you?"

With teeth clenched as tightly as his mouth would allow without too much pain, "Her."

Swallowing hard, "Did he really … he didn't … you got here before anything really bad happened, didn't you?" Knowing exactly what he was trying not to say, Jack just nodded and moved to pack her loose books into another of the crates. Tim sat for another minute before standing up and, hefting the book filled bin, "Back in a minute."

Another six trips down the stairs and almost everything was out of the apartment save the food and furniture. It hadn't been too hard to do given how little she actually had. The last things to go were her art supplies, and Tim stopped as he uncovered what Emily had been working on just before opening the door to her father. A nearly life-size drawing of seven sets of feet lined up on a table, sneakers untied and socks with holes in them; six sets of boys' feet and one lone girl's squished in the center.

He laughed as he remembered that day. They'd all been in a particularly odd mood and had piled onto the couch with Emily and Jack. Sam had wiggled between them and suddenly, all the feet were together on the table. Will had laughed and found the camera for them, amused by the whole image.

It had to be their art assignment for class and it made him warm inside to know that Emily thought of them as her family. Showing it to Jack, "Hey, look at this."

Taking in the picture, "I'd forgotten that day." After sorting through the pile of supplies, he found a copy of the picture, along with the one of her mom, "I thought she'd be doing her mom, not us."

Tim, who had heard the story of their trip in the last hour, had a flash of what might be called insightfulness, "Maybe she had to find her mom to ask if it was alright that we're her family now?"

Jack stared at both images for a minute before sliding the pictures into one of Emily's books for safe keeping and, handing Tim the finished drawing, "I'm glad she found the answer she did."

...

Soon Jack was pulling the door shut behind them with a satisfied bang. Breathing as deep as his bruised body would let him, the cold rush of air made him woozy and the world spun, "Tim?"

Making a grab for Jack's arm, he caught him before he hit the ground. Helping Jack to the van, Tim got him into the front seat, "You okay?"

Jack nodded, "Yeah, just ... I think I need to lay down again."

"You sure you're okay? You look awfully pale, even for you."

Jack nodded, "I just need to get out of here."

By the time Tim and Elizabeth finished unloading the car and carrying the crates up to what was now Emily's room, they were exhausted. Elizabeth went to take a short nap in her room while Jack, already on his bed, watched through half-closed eyes as Tim came into their room. Dropping down on his own bed, the two brothers slept for the second to last time in the same room.

...

Shortly after Elizabeth left to go home, one of the nurses came in and helped Emily wash up a little. The cast was cumbersome, her broken ribs made her wince with every move and her face ached, even with the mild painkiller she'd been given, but soon, she was as clean as she was going to get and feeling better than she had all day. The nurse left her alone after that, returning only once to bring the pad of paper and pencil Emily had quietly asked if she could borrow.

And then, she slowly and carefully began teaching her left hand how to draw.

The next few hours passed quickly and, by lunch time, she'd begun to feel somewhat happy with her progress. Even if her lines would probably never be perfectly straight, she could do it and that made her smile.

About to stretch out for a nap, she heard the door open and, looking up, she wasn't as shocked as she ought to be to see Dex crouched down and holding his finger to his lips, "Shhhh."

Whispering back, "I can have visitors."

"But I'm supposed to be with an adult, so I snuck in. Ninja moves all the way down the hall." Standing upright, his back cracking as he did so, "Damn, you do not look good right now."

Wincing her way to a half-smile, "I figured as much, but thanks for pointing it out."

"That's what I'm here for."

Feeling better already, "What are you doing here, anyways? Shouldn't you be in Government right about now?"

"Government is too boring to stay for, especially today."

"Why today?"

"It's Tuesday. Tuesday's never a good day in Government."

About to comment, Emily stopped when the nurse came in, "How are you doing, Emily? Feeling any better?" She hesitated when she caught sight of Dex, who had gone rigid, then continued, "Who's your friend and why isn't he blinking?"

"I'm pretty sure he thinks that if he doesn't move, you won't be able to see him and tell him to leave."

The nurse turned to him, "And why aren't you in school, young man?"

His eyes darted to Emily, "She can see me, can't she?"

"Yes, Dex, she can."

Coming back to life, "Damn it. One day, that's gonna work." Giving the woman his most charming smile, "I have decided that my friend is more important than Government class and if you had Mr. Dillons you would completely agree with me and let me stay here for awhile out of pure sympathy."

She couldn't help it. She liked him instantly and nodding her head as she winked, "You were never here."

"Thanks, ma'am."

As she left, she pointed at him but looked at Emily, "I'd keep him if I were you."

"I plan on it." Holding up two fingers on her left hand, waving them in his direction, "You're gonna have at least this many detentions waiting for you when you get back, you know that, right?"

"Naw. I'll talk to Phil. We'll get it straightened out."

Emily just shook her head, "Phil's gonna run out of patience with you one day."

"Then I'll just kick him in the shins and run like hell." Coming over from his corner, he stopped at her mattress, "But enough about Phil because I have this total urge to hug you right now. Do you mind?"

"Of course not ... just ... gently, please."

"Tim and Elizabeth warned me about all your broken," waving his hand at her aimlessly, "stuff ... so yell if I hurt anything." Giving her a good hearty squeeze as lightly as possible, he then pulled a chair over, sitting down and propping his boots up on the frame of the bed. Next, he tilted his head slightly, his temple and cheek settling against his splayed fingers as he studied her for a long, quiet minute, which she dare not interrupt. He broke the heavy silence with a simple statement, "I never got to the conclusion that your father was the biggest asshole in history. I figured out most of the rest, but that … that threw me a little bit."

Emily could only stare at him, "What?"

"I knew you were alone, well, you were either alone or your mother was practicing to be on an episode of 'Hoarders', one or the other." Giving her a scrunched up set of eyebrows in response to her dumbfounded look, "You realize I never ask about your parents? I don't hassle you about letting me come over? That I believe the weird ass shit you tell me without question? Example, if your mom worked all the hours you tell people she does, you would live in a way better house and be able to buy clothes in an actual store." He continued, seeing that she was digesting his insights better than expected, "There are hundreds of odd things that you do which, to the normal individual, would be inconsequential to their idea of you, but as you discovered very early on, I am not your normal, average, every day individual."

Swallowing hard, "No, definitely not."

Glad she was still listening without trying to argue, "But to me, each and every one of those 'oddities' added up to something bigger. And here's the real shocker that may quite literally knock you off your bed."

Somehow feeling just a little better inside, "What?"

"The real shocker is, from the very beginning, I cared about you and not about all the extraneous shit. I believed you had your reasons and I respected them because somehow, for all your lies, you were the most sincere and awesome person I had ever met. I never once felt that you were lying to me because you wanted to; you seemed to be driven to do it with an all-consuming reluctant necessity. There was purpose behind your lying and you had absolutely no way around doing it."

Taking in all the past tenses on his side of the conversation, she breathed in deep, "But what do you think now?"

"I think that I wish I'd been there to help Jack in the fight." Moving forwards, he folded his arms on the mattress and propped his head up with his clasped hands, "And I think that I have never been more scared than when Tim told me you were in the hospital."

In a voice barely above a whisper, she had to repeat it to get the words all the way from her throat to his ears, "You still like me then?"

"God, I love you, idiot girl. Not like Jack does, with that sappy, 'oh, I want to kiss you and feed you popcorn and gaze into your brown eyes for hours' way. I'm pretty sure it's more the girly, pink, frilly 'you are my bestest best BFF friend ever and ever and ever and a few days after that' kind of thing."

"My eyes are green."

He finally gave her a smile as he rubbed his mohawk across her hand, "Smart ass."

Petting him much like she did his family dog, "I love you, too, Dexter Dean Grenden."

Dex enjoyed the ruffling of his hair for a few more moments, then sat back up, "So, before we move onto happier, more proper afternoon conversation, can I ask, with all the lying you had to do to keep me as a friend, why did you keep me in the first place? How come you didn't run the hell away from me? If I were you, I'd have been reduced to thumb sucking and been scared of every person in the world, yet you befriended a dude on the other side of weird. You came to my house and put up with my family and all their craziness which, when you think about it, makes me the most normal one in that house."

"I have an answer for you, if you can believe it."

"I'll believe it." Winking at her, "Just no more lies, okay?"

Emily nodded as best she could, her headache bearing down on her, "Agreed. I liked you because you were so not normal. A 'normal' guy did this to me, my 'normal' school didn't pay enough attention, my 'normal' neighbors never wondered about me or, at least, wondered enough to ask. 'Normal' people are way more frightening to me than purple-haired, pierced ones with parents who used to work in the circus and now run a candy factory and work for Crayola. Annie is a professional fortune-cookie fortune writer who freelances as a tattoo designer. You people are all damn crazy and it's completely damn perfect for me."

"And Jack?"

"Well, he and his family aren't exactly normal either, are they?" He looked at her, smiled, then settled back in his chair, feet back on the bed. Her world made just a little more sense than it did ten minutes earlier, "Is that all you want to ask?"

"For now … or maybe forever. Who knows? What I have come to understand is that I'm keeping you and that I'd like a nap." He gave her a smirk, his eyebrow ring glinting under the diffused light, "I'd probably be asleep at school by now anyways."

Trying to get comfortable without putting pressure on the back of her head and her other various aches and breaks, "How awful is that chair?"

After contemplating for a second, "actually, It's not too bad."

Emily closed her eyes, "Then I say we both get some sleep. My head has reached its explosive pounding point."

"Do you want me to go find somebody?"

She smiled, "Go to sleep, Dex."

"G'night, Em."

"G'night."

...

Dex disappeared about two hours later to get back in time for music and, once Emily woke from her nap, Elizabeth was back, sitting in one of the chairs reading her book.

Elizabeth nodded at the stuffed saxophone next to Emily's head, "Dex?"

Finding that her headache had subsided some, she moved her bed so she was sitting up, "Yeah, he stopped by and must have come back with this after I fell asleep." She picked it up, then looked at Elizabeth, her face serious, "Do you think we can talk the doctor into letting me go home?"

"Honey, they need to keep an eye on you."

"I want to see everybody. I thought … I just … I want to go home."

Elizabeth hated to say it, but, "Sorry. We'll get you out of here as soon as we can in the morning. Promise."

Giving into the fact that she'd be there until tomorrow, Emily began fiddling with the stuffed toy, "Did you know Dex would be coming over?"

"Yeah. He called this morning after I got home. Tim talked to him then he asked me if it would be all right if he came by. I figured you'd want some different company." Smiling at her, "Hope you didn't mind. He sounded fairly desperate to see you."

"Naw. I'm always good with him, but," not sure why she was hesitating, she finally just blurted out, "Dex knew I was alone. He figured it out a long time ago, but never said anything."

This blind-sided her, the shock clearly trying to win out in the myriad of expressions that crossed her face, until she settled on an apologetic half-frown, "I'm sorry. I guess he paid a lot better attention than any of us did. We'll do better from now on."

"Elizabeth …"

"We'll do better."

Ignoring the finality in her voice, Emily made sure she got the last word, "There's no earthly way you could have done any better than this. Please, don't apologize." Having said that, she made an attempt to lighten the mood that had descended, "And are you sure we couldn't sneak out of here? You could carry me out like I'm your really, really big baby?"

"No."

"Stuff me in a cart and roll me out?"

"No."

"Hike me on your back, cover me with your coat and pretend to be a hunchback?"

By now, the frown had disappeared, "No."

"Wanna play some cards?"

"Yes."

...

Jack slept for a few more hours before getting up to eat several bowls of soup, several mounds of Jell-O and several containers of applesauce. Longing to be able to chew properly again, he settled for knocking the spoon on his knee as he sat down and tried to have a normal night with his brothers.

It didn't work and he excused himself after a while. He wandered first to Tim's new room, then upstairs to Emily's, through his own, winding up sitting on the edge of the bathtub, his mind racing along with his heart.

Will found him there a few minutes later, having come upstairs to check on him, "Hey, you okay?"

With sweat running down his face and his hand gripping the wall, he shook his head, "I don't know."

Beside his son instantly, "Does anything hurt? Are you gonna be sick? What's wrong?"

Jack just shook his head again, "I can't be here. I can't ... I ..." He trailed off, "It's too much."

Crouching down, Will put his hand on Jack's clammy, cold arm, "Why don't you go lay down, then you can tell me what's too much."

Faster than lightning, Jack pushed his father away, unbalancing Will and causing him to stumble backwards, nearly falling, "I can't get it out of my head, there's too much noise. He ..." By now, Jack was swaying, dangerously close to tipping onto the floor, "It's too much."

Will righted himself and knelt back in front of his son, putting a firm grip on either arm to keep him from falling, "What's too much Jack? What do you hear? What's the noise?"

Rolling his head towards his dad, "I can hear him breaking." With that, he gagged and Will leaned him quickly over the toilet, where he neatly deposited his dinner.

Once Jack had finished, Will slowly pulled him to the floor and settled him against the wall. Flushing the toilet and shoving the bathroom door closed with his foot, he sat down beside the boy, and knowing the answer, asked quietly anyway, "Who's breaking?"

"I can hear him breaking." Closing his eyes, "It's all I can hear. A cracking noise and then nothing. Not even a scream or a yell. Just ... nothing."

Prodding gently, needing his son to say it out loud, "Jack, who's breaking?"

In a defeated voice that sent shudders through him, Will heard Jack say quietly, "I killed him."

Twisting so he could look at his son directly, "Open your eyes. Now!" Following orders, Jack saw a fire in his dad's eyes that woke him a little from his nightmare, "You didn't kill anyone. He fell. You said you only wanted to get him out the door. He fell himself. You didn't do anything wrong. Do you hear me?"

Barely above a raspy whisper, "What if I did it on purpose, without knowing it?"

"The only thing on your mind was Emily, as it should have been. You didn't do anything wrong. I promise you."

Sliding sideways along the wall, he put his head on his dad's shoulder and, as Jack sobbed, they sat.

Chapter 25

He didn't do well that night, not falling asleep until just before dawn and sleeping through the usual morning hubbub of everyone leaving for school or work. After finally coming downstairs, he was extremely restless and was about to go out for a walk when the front door opened and in walked Emily and his mom.

Normally, he would have walked right up to her, hugged her and confessed just how much he had missed her but instead, he stood awkwardly in the doorway while Elizabeth helped Emily get her coat off over the cast. Once that was done, Emily turned and stopped, staring at Jack while he stared back.

Suddenly, Emily's eyes filled with tears and she walked into his arms, careful of sore spots, but, nonetheless, wrapping herself in his familiar warmth, "I'm sorry."

Kissing the top of her head, "I'm sorry, too."

Elizabeth watched in silence for a minute before reluctantly interrupting with a subtle cough.

"Yeah, Ma?"

"You two hungry at all?"

Jack hoped Emily would say no, but her stomach won out over telepathic messaging, "Starving."

Elizabeth turned to her son, "Did you leave any soup and Jell-O or do I need to make another batch?"

Slapping on a cheery face, "There's some left of both, but between us it'll probably be gone tonight."

"Well, once we get you to the dentist tomorrow morning, we'll find out just when you can get back on solids." Turning to Emily, "As for you, feel up to gumming some pasta or you want to stick to the liquids?"

Her belly growled in response, "I'd love to try the pasta. If I look at more Jell-O, it'll be too soon."

With a laugh, "Tim basically lived on Jell-O for almost a week when he got his wisdom teeth out. He still makes a face every time I make it."

Jack held his half-smile until both had left for the kitchen, then his face returned to what would soon become his everyday, slightly sad countenance. He stood there until Elizabeth popped her head back in, "You coming or you gonna stand there all day?"

With a silent sigh, "Coming."

...

Emily had taken a tour of her new room and fallen asleep there later that afternoon. By the time she woke up, the troops had returned and everyone pretty much settled right into suddenly having a girl in the house, well, another one aside from their mother. She had napkins tossed at her at dinner when she asked for one, she knocked over her glass of water with her cast and when she dropped a forkful of pasta on the floor, Sam scooped everything up in his hand, blew on them and promptly handed them back for her to finish eating.

She fell in love with every one of them all over again.

And it was too busy for anyone to notice how little Jack ate or talked for that matter.

...

After Elizabeth had helped her into her pajamas, she settled in the living room with the rest of the family and made it until nine o'clock or so before she finally had to throw in the towel. Saying goodnight to everyone, she locked eyes with Jack for just a second longer and, as she headed up the stairs, she warmed as she felt him get up to follow her.

Stopping next to her bed, she turned and found Jack standing there, his bruised hands dangling from his belt loops, "Need anything?"

She shook her head, "No. I just wanted to say goodnight."

Still not moving, "G'night."

Suddenly confused with the way he was acting, "Okay. Um, are you going back downstairs?"

"For a few minutes. I need to grab my iPod. It's on the couch."

"Okay, well, I'll see you in the morning then."

Finally he moved towards her, leaning in to give her a quick kiss, "Sorry, I'm just tired I guess."

Reaching out with her good hand, she gently touched his stitches, "You seem more sad than anything."

With a shrug, he turned to go back downstairs, called quietly over his shoulder another goodnight.

...

Emily half woke when everyone else drifted to bed, then, again, around three in the morning when she heard the toilet flush. She had only slept upstairs with everyone once and, even though it seemed she woke to every random mumble and stray snore, she still smiled. She had a lot to get used to and, closing her eyes, she was about to drift off again when she heard footsteps pass her doorway. Figuring it had to be someone on the way to the bathroom, she finally went back to sleep.

...

Living with eight other people was so totally out of Emily's realm of understanding that, by the end of that first weekend, she felt more exhausted than she thought possible. She hadn't been doing much, but just keeping track of so many people's habits, conversations, likes, dislikes, jokes and more that she dropped to her bed by Sunday night thinking there was a good chance she'd be sleeping at least until the following Thursday.

Sam, who should have been too small to worry about such things, stopped by her door before going to bed, climbing carefully onto her mattress to give her an extra long hug. Scooting as close as possible, he whispered in her ear, "You're doing great, Emily. You haven't screamed once and you've been here four whole days. Even Grandma tells us to shut up for ten minutes or her head will explode." Sitting back, he studied her critically, his face wrinkled up and his head tilted, "I'm glad you live here now and you can tell me to leave you alone any time you want to. I won't get mad ... promise."

It both broke her heart and made her smile. The need to scream she'd been feeling quieted the minute Sam told her she was not the only one who felt it and she hugged him back as best she could, her ribs and her clumsy cast dictating how tightly she squeezed, "I think I just need to learn a few things to get up to speed and I'll be fine." Winking over his head at Jack, who'd heard most of the exchange, "And just to let you know, I would never tell you to go away ... Dave, maybe, Jack, probably, Tim, most definitely, but never you."

Sam wiggled and grinned when she gave him two kisses on each cheek then poked him off her bed, "Goodnight, Mister Sam."

"G'night, Emily."

After Sam headed down the hall, Jack leaned a little further into her room before going to make sure his brother had actually gotten into bed and under the covers, "Probably?"

Struggling to stand, she kissed him quickly, "Just kidding."

After kissing her back, "I know. Now go to bed. You look more tired than Dad does after an 18-hour day."

Choosing not to comment on the fact that he looked just as tired, she was out within minutes of putting her head to the pillow and, for the first time in several days, not even waking up when everyone else came upstairs.

She slept through the commotion of getting ready for school, unaware that Elizabeth had taken pity on her and shut her door before the real noise could begin. It was after nine when Emily finally opened her eyes and, getting downstairs a little while later, she found Elizabeth sitting quietly on the living room floor, not doing anything but sitting still in the silence. Emily studied her for a moment, then, as quietly as she could, she sat down cross legged in front of her, shut her eyes and listened to nothing.

It felt nice after the weekend of chaos, but Emily found herself frowning slightly.

By then, Elizabeth had opened her eyes and asked her, "Why so down? Feeling okay?"

"Yeah, I just … I love it here and completely appreciate all that you and Will and everybody else are doing for me, but …" by now, her eyes were smarting, threatening to spill over, "but it gets really loud here sometimes and crazy and I'm enjoying the quiet right now and," her face crumpled at this point, "I'm sorry."

Not being able to help herself, Elizabeth laughed, not a condescending laugh, but a relieved chuckle, "Is that all? Emily, wonderful, beautiful, intelligent girl, why do you think I'm sitting on the floor at nine-thirty on a Monday morning? I crave quiet like Nate craves peanut butter. " Leaning forward a little, "I guess I just figured you were here enough to have gotten used to it, so I didn't pay attention and I'm sorry for that."

All she could do was nod, then, "Sam said his grandma never makes it as long as I have without telling everyone to shut up for ten minutes."

Elizabeth hugged her tightly, "Sam is very correct. There were eight of us kids growing up and she started the ten minute thing even before my youngest brothers were born. She waits the full ten minutes while everyone sits there in silence, then she tells them to 'commence with your insanity' and begins tickling everyone she can reach which, really, just makes it louder because everyone knows it's coming and tries to be the first to escape."

Already feeling better about things, "Would everyone really sit there for that long?"

Nodding, "It was especially funny when my dad got caught with us. He would sit there, fidgeting whenever Mom wasn't looking and, since we couldn't laugh, this made us want to laugh more. When she turned around though, he would straighten up, looking at us like we were being awful while he was perfection on a chair."

Finally, she laughed, "I really need to meet these people."

Elizabeth stood, pulling Emily up carefully beside her, "If not before, you'll definitely see them at Tim's graduation party, but, for now, how about you come in the kitchen with me, get some breakfast while I make my grocery list and reassure you that it's okay to disappear into your room for awhile or go for walks or just hang out alone in the backyard? I don't want you to feel obligated to be with us all the time." After seeing Emily nod, "You went from one of one to one of nine overnight, but it's okay to still be the person you were before all of this, and I, for one, don't want you to change. I love you for you."

"You are totally making me cry again."

Handing her a bowl of cereal with a watery smile, "I'm about to as well so here, eat your breakfast."

Things got easier for Emily after that and, soon enough, she was disappearing upstairs or losing herself in a book on the back porch, bundled up against the spring chill in the air. She never, however, told anyone to go away if they interrupted her, happy in the knowledge that they cared enough to come find her in the first place.

In the week since she'd moved in, she also discovered, very quickly, to lock the door to the bathroom. Luckily she was only brushing her teeth when Tim busted through the door. Enjoying the deep shade of red he turned and the fumbling apologies he made as he backed quickly out the door, she couldn't stop him fast enough from running smack into Jack, who didn't look pleased when Tim knocked him into the hallway wall.

Emily was returning to school today and couldn't keep the fluttering in her stomach down, so the Tim distraction was just what she needed and she told him as much.

Still red, "Glad to be of service."

With a smile, she continued to her room and finished getting ready, leaving only the button on her pants undone because, given the cast position, she still hadn't mastered the art of getting completely dressed. Snagging Jack as he walked back past her room, "Can you close this for me?"

Thinking it was just her bag or something, he came in. The problem was she was now standing there in front of him, holding her shirt up slightly and with the top of her jeans open. "Um, your pants?"

"Yeah. I can't make my fingers work the stupid button just yet. I've been living in pajama pants for a week now."

Hesitating, he sat down on the bed, "Come here."

She went to stand in front of him, still holding her shirt, "I just hope I don't have to go to the bathroom today or else you're gonna be doing this in the hallway."

He didn't hear her because her bellybutton had him entranced. Reaching up slightly, he twisted the button and closed it quickly, then, scooting forward a bit, he settled his hands on her hips. Without a word, he kissed the exposed skin of her belly. Sliding his hands up under her shirt, he would have continued had his mom not called up the stairs, "Em, do you need any help or are you all set?"

Praying her voice was steady, "I'm fine. I'll be down in a minute." Missing the feel of his hands on her skin given he'd pulled them off of her immediately, "Um, we should probably get going or else we'll be late."

He leaned forward, resting his head on her now t-shirt covered stomach, "I miss you."

"I'm right here."

As he shook his head, he closed his eyes, "You're the only thing that seems real sometimes and I haven't been able to touch you in a week. There's always somebody around and ..." he trailed off, "I just want to touch you. To know you're still okay."

Pulling him up, she ran her fingers over his shadowed eyes and the still healing line where his stitches had been taken out the day before, "I'm real, Jack. I promise." Slowly, she pressed her lips to his and slipped her tongue into his mouth, which he opened gladly.

Elizabeth was just about to come upstairs to get them when the pair came down, Jack's arms full of both his and Emily's things. "Sorry, Mom, had to get her stuff for her."

She dutifully ignored the smile on her son's face, something she hadn't seen all week.

This was the last real smile anyone saw for quite awhile and Emily was not the only one to realize it.

Chapter 26

School went much better than she expected. She had kept up with the homework and, even with her left hand, was able to take readable notes and get through her exams with time to spare.

She and Jack also sneaked moments whenever possible, usually in the art room or in the back hall by the band room. Jack lived for these minutes because there wasn't much other reason to go to school at this point. He studied, he did the homework, he tried to pay attention in class, but running on about two hours of sleep a night was a rather sufficient killer to his memory and his attention-span.

He took the tests and, confident he knew the information when he walked in the door, found himself unable to answer anything in-depth. He could squeak by with the multiple choice, but short answer and essays were killing him. Since the teachers knew what had happened, they allowed him leniency, but still, within six weeks or so, he was near failing everything.

He had no idea how to tell his parents what was wrong; he could barely look at them, let alone talk to them with this much guilt looming. So, he went to school under the pretense of learning, but really, he only lived for the times he had Emily close to him. These were the only times he could let the horrible feelings inside him go, because she was standing there, whole and perfect and alive and beautiful.

...

Will watched him. Watched him get lost in thought, sitting over his plate at dinner staring at his pile of cooling mashed potatoes until Emily nudged him lightly on the arm. Watched him eat breakfast with shadowed eyes and his face free of any pillow marks, indicating he, yet again, didn't seem to have laid down the night before. Watched him trudge off to school, backpack heavy on his shoulders and Emily's hand firmly in his. Watched him do things that were out of the ordinary for his second son, but not for someone who had done something extraordinarily out of the ordinary.

Since the night he'd bought Jack home from the hospital and wound up holding his sobbing son on the bathroom floor, Will had been watching. Jack caught him more than once, to which he'd offer up a half-smile, "Geez, Dad, take a picture. It'd last longer."

"Just wanted to know how you were doing? Looks like you haven't slept much lately."

His dark blue eyes flashed momentarily before settling back down, "Yeah, but I can manage."

"Bad dreams?"

With a shrug, he gave the answer he assumed his dad wanted to hear, "Some, but I'm fine. I come down and watch TV for awhile and end up falling asleep on the couch." Then, mustering up what he thought was a full-on, happy Jack grin, "But what I could really go for is a vacation. Got any of those lying around?"

"Jack."

"Dad, I'm fine. I'm tired, but I'm fine. School is school and work is work and I need to eat more vegetables and clean my room and write term papers and buy some new shoes and go to the movies and bake hundreds of cookies. I'm a kid and I'm fine."

Will accepted this for the moment, seeing a glimmer of his boy's humor and deciding maybe he really did just need some time, "Okay, okay. Remember though, your mom and I need to know if you need anything, all right? Be it new shoes or somebody to scream at."

Getting up and hugging Will tightly, Jack simply wished that everyone would leave him alone.

●●●

Will gave it until mid-April and, seeing that Jack didn't look much worse for wear but definitely did not look better, moved to his second source of information. Finding Tim alone was easier than he'd expected. One day, in the garage, Will watched Jack pedal out of the driveway on his way to work then turned to Tim, "Do you have a minute?"

Continuing his digging for a screwdriver in one of the various toolboxes, "I've got about two hours worth of them. What's up?"

"How's Jack doing?"

Tim banged his head on the table he was under and stood up rubbing the back of his skull, "What do you mean?"

With a raised eyebrow, he saw through Tim easily, "You know exactly what I mean and by the way you smacked your head down there, I'd say you are sitting on information I want and you think I shouldn't get."

"Dad ..."

"What happened?"

"Nothing big, okay? He just ... he got into it with some guy a couple days ago, but it never went beyond some yelling in the hall. Nobody got into trouble and it was over before it started."

"Tim ..."

"I'm keeping an eye on him." Leaning against the fender of the van, "Look, he's Jack. Everything always works out for him, haven't you figured that out by now?" With a shake of his head, "He'll come out smelling better than the fucking rose parade. He just has to slog through a few piles of shit to get there."

Will wanted to call his son out for swearing but mostly he just hoped Tim was right.

●●●

Elizabeth took a different approach, coming up behind Jack one night while he sat at the kitchen table, homework spread out and eyes unblinking.

Wrapping her arms around his neck, she surveyed the work in front of him then kissed him lightly on the cheek, whispering into his ear, "Mama always loves Jack. Don't forget that, okay?"

He came so close to crumbling at those words that when he opened his mouth, a barely coherent, "I won't," met her ears.

She waited another minute, but when he stayed quiet, she squeezed him, "You'll be fine, I promise," then continued upstairs to bed.

•••

Emily didn't wake up when the footsteps passed her door, she'd never fallen asleep, given the look that Jack had on his face when she'd said good-night. He'd been laying on his bed, his earphones firmly jammed in his ears and his iPod resting on his chest. He only opened his eyes when he felt her sit down on the edge of the bed, "Hey you."

"Hey."

Lying in silence, he continued to look at her until she reached up, tracing once again the now healed scar on his chin, "You were awfully quiet tonight."

With a shrug, "Just tired."

"Real tired or leave me alone tired?"

Kissing her newly de-casted fingertips, "Real tired. Too much homework, not enough time."

Knowing full well he hadn't cracked one of his books or even opened his backpack, "Jack ..."

"God, I'm just tired." He let go of her hand swiftly, "I just need some sleep, okay? I'll be fine."

"Well, um, I'll go then." Getting up, she moved towards the door, "G'night."

Hearing him rolling over, he didn't call goodnight back and she went quietly to her room, wishing he would just tell someone what was wrong or she would have to.

•••

When his footsteps passed by around one in the morning, she gave him a good 20 minutes before following. Creeping down the stairs, she found him curled on the couch, staring at the Weather Channel. Without looking, "I'm sorry if I woke you up."

She took that as an invitation to sit down, "You didn't. I was already up."

Finally looking at her, his eyes glassy, "Why?"

"I'm worried about you." Pulling her legs up and tucking her feet under Jack's thigh, "You need to talk to somebody. You can't keep doing this."

"What? It's just a little insomnia."

"It's May now, Jack. A 'little' insomnia shouldn't last two months. Trust me." He looked at her sharply and she continued, "I've been hearing you from the beginning. At first I just figured somebody had a really overactive bladder and I would fall back to sleep, but then I noticed no one ever came back."

Tossing the remote down suddenly, he stood, his face glowing in the flicker of the TV, she could see the anger, "I'm fine. I just wish everyone would shut up and trust me. I'll work it out. I just need a way to work it out." With that, he brushed past her, leaving her to stare at the international weather maps, completely dumbfounded.

Tim came into the living room, rubbing his head, making the hair stand on end, "Em?"

Turning towards him, "Did we wake you up? I'm sorry."

He sat down next to her, yawning, "I just heard talking. Was Jack down here with you or have you gone schizophrenic on us?"

Normally, she would have smiled, but not tonight, "Yeah, um, I seem to have said the wrong thing to him."

"Pissed him off?"

Nodding, "Pretty much."

"What'd you say?" Not answering, she just stared forward until she felt Tim's hand on her arm, patting her gently, "he'll be fine in the morning."

Without thought, she scooted over a little and rested her head on his shoulder, "I don't think he will."

Deciding to be honest with her, "Actually, I don't think he will be, either. He hasn't slept in awhile, has he?"

Emily knew late-night honesty should flow in both directions, "Not really. I hear him coming down about one or so. I usually leave him alone and hope he falls asleep on the couch but," shrugging, "I'm pretty sure he stays up until just before Will comes down."

"Do you think we should tell Mom and Dad? I mean, I think this messed him up way more than any of us realizes."

"Or he realizes and just doesn't want to admit it."

"Well, we are a stubborn bunch."

"No kidding."

Not sure if he should continue, he bit the bullet, "Um, both Mom and Dad have asked me how he's doing. I haven't really said anything though, just told them I'd keep an eye out." Sighing and absently leaning his head against hers, "Some of the teachers are wondering, too."

"I haven't heard anything."

Tim chuckled through his nose, patting her knee again in amusement, "Like they'd ever ask the girlfriend. Besides, I don't think anyone wants to pile anything else on you." Leaving his hand there, he raised a finger in the air,

"But it occurs to me that I never asked how you're doing? I mean, granted, that asshole is dead and gone now but still, it's not like you had a great last day with him."

Not sure how she felt with Tim's continued invasion of her space, she pushed it to the back of her mind, realizing she was invading his just as much with her head on his shoulder, "I'm doing a lot better than Jack. I still have my share of nightmares, but they're nothing like they could be. I think going down to the morgue and seeing him there helped a lot."

"You went down to the morgue? Are you kidding me? How did that not freak you out more?"

"Like I told Elizabeth, last time I didn't check to make sure he was dead. This time I had to. And since then, I've been pretty okay."

"You're a lot damn braver than me." Propping his legs on the coffee table and sliding down into the couch, he moved his elbow forward, letting his hand dangle from the end of her bent knee, "So, should we just keep a good eye on Jack and go from there or do we have an intervention of A&E style proportions?"

She'd been asking herself this same question over and over for the last month, "He didn't turn me in when he found out about me, when he realized I was alone. I just … something tells me I need to push him about it, but I don't think I can. I think I'm gonna have to wait and see what happens."

Tim finished the thought, "Unless we realize we haven't got that choice anymore."

"Exactly."

"I agree." Picking up the remote with his other hand, "Feel like watching bad TV for a little while with me?" Feeling her nod against him, "Cool."

After about 20 minutes, she heard Tim snore lightly and, sitting up, she shook his shoulder, "Tim, go to bed."

Opening his eyes immediately, he shut them just as fast, "Huh?"

"Go to bed."

Without further argument, he stood and stumbled his way to his room, leaving Emily to turn the TV off before she headed upstairs. Fighting the urge to go to Jack's room, she instead crawled under her own covers and turned on her side, hoping sleep would come quickly.

...

Things came to a head, however, one Friday evening a few weeks later.

Around six that night, just after Jack and Emily had finished doing the dinner dishes, Tim came into the kitchen and asked to borrow Jack's set of car keys. A simple request from one brother to another and the response should have been an easy one. Instead, Jack, after another sleepless night, another rapidly escalating eye-pounding headache and feeling that it was about damn time for Tim to keep track of his keys, had had enough. Turning from the stove, he dug up his keys from his pocket, then whipped them at Tim. The metal ring missing the intended target of Tim's chest, instead going higher, catching him in the chin, "Make some fucking copies and don't ask me again."

Instant anger had Tim automatically move towards Jack, but he only got two steps in before Jack registered what he'd done and, stepping backwards, knocked Emily, who was behind him, first against the corner of the counter, then down to the linoleum.

Jack could only look at her, then, without a word, he bolted from the house, the back door banging behind him. Both Tim and Emily stared at one another for a moment before Tim, holding his throbbing lip in one hand, extended the other towards her, slowly pulling her up, "You okay?"

Tears jumped to her eyes, "Yeah, I just wish the edges were rounded."

He'd never done it before, but without thinking about it, he pulled her into a hug, "He needs to talk to Mom and Dad."

It was strange contact to her, but she gladly accepted it, hugging him back, "I know. I'll talk to him when he gets back or I'll tell Will and Elizabeth myself."

Stepping back out of the hug, he took her face in his hands and aiming it towards him, he leaned in a bit, "Good … now, do you think my lip's gonna swell up? Tell me the truth, I can take it."

Emily forgot he wasn't a six year old Sam and, with a teary smile, kissed her fingertips, then touched the spot where he did indeed have a red indent and the makings of a small bruise, "It'll heal before you get married."

For a single, split second, he looked like he just might do something else, but then he straightened up, his hands falling to his sides, "Works for me."

Reaching around, she rubbed her back where the corner had dug in, "Are you gonna be mad at him?"

He wanted to, he really did, but looking at Emily with her paled skin and still watery eyes, biting her lip absentmindedly, he gave her a half-smile and mashed down his annoyance, "Naw, I was the idiot who lost my keys in the first place. I probably deserved to be smacked with them."

"Not really," locking eyes for a few moments, Emily broke the look, "but thanks."

Picking up the forgotten keys, "I'll see you later, okay?"

With a nod, "Do you think he'll be gone long?"

"No idea." As he shrugged, "He'll be back when he's ready."

With that, Tim left her standing in the kitchen, alone for just long enough to swipe the last bit of wetness from her cheeks before Elizabeth came in, several boys in tow, "You sure you and Jack don't want to go to the library with us?"

"Um, yeah, I've got plenty to read and Jack rode his bike over to Dex's house, something about video game coma. He asked me to tell you."

"Oh … well, all right then. We'll be back in about an hour."

The rest of the evening passed quietly, Emily leaving Jack a voice mail filling him in on his supposed evening at Dex's. She wasn't sure he'd get the message, but it was about all she could do, so she left it at that. Lying in bed later that night, she first heard Tim come in, then, just before midnight, she heard the faint spinning of gears that signaled Jack was home as well.

...

After the kitchen incident and knocking Emily down, Jack, flying away from the house on his bike, pedaled blindly for a few minutes, until it occurred to him he needed a destination. Luckily, the first destination seemed to be Dex's house, which he'd unconsciously been headed towards in the first place. Hoping his friend would be home, Jack parked his bike against the garage and knocked on the side door. It took a few minutes, but Dex pulled it open, rubbing his apparently just dyed chartreuse mohawk vigorously with a towel, "Dude."

Bypassing the customary 'dude' back, "Can I hide out here for awhile? My house is getting crowded."

He ushered him in, still scrubbing his hair dry, "Getting? I'm surprised you people don't bust out the seams of that place on a daily basis." Any other day, this would have made him laugh and Dex, knowing this, stopped in the middle of the kitchen floor, turning to him, "What did you do?"

"What do you mean?"

Dex had the ability not to question when necessary and, as witnessed through his friendship with Emily, could bite his tongue when called for, but this, in his mind, was not one of those times. Tossing the wet towel over one of the kitchen chairs, "What did you do to warrant needing a place to hide? I don't harbor fugitives unless I feel justified, so spill it." Jack wondered if he had the energy to work up annoyance at the order, but Dex saw it coming and cocked an eyebrow as he leaned against the kitchen counter, "And don't get all pissy. It's a legitimate question and given you've interrupted my evening off in an empty house, I think I deserve what I demand," and, just for kicks, he added, "please and thank you."
In a sudden rush of jumbled thoughts starting at his own house this morning and ending with the thoughts he'd been trying to ignore for the past six weeks, he felt his throat begin closing. It was a frightening

sensation, even though this was not the first time he'd felt it in recent days.

Dex watched his friend go from normal to scary as all hell in under three seconds and he nearly freaked out himself, but being the strong, fairly composed individual that he was (yet holding on by a mere thread of sanity as he would later admit), he could only squeak out, "What the hell?" before digging his cell phone from his pocket, ready and willing to call 911. Jack, however, could still think clear enough to know what the phone meant. Croaking out a 'no' as he pointed at the phone, he watched through his now tunneling vision as Dex tossed it forgotten on the kitchen counter.

After that, things progressed quickly. His lungs began screaming for air and the panic set in, strong enough to make his last attack look like child's play. One hand was clawing at his throat, looking for any way to get air into his body, the other flailing around for something to grab onto.

Vaguely, he felt hands on his upper arms and saw a fast-fading Dex swim close into his vision.

He couldn't concentrate on anything else, however, but the fact that air was not moving to his lungs, supplying his brain or keeping him from passing out on the floor. Trying to think relaxing thoughts or any thought at all at this point seemed ludicrous and, about to give into the darkness graying his vision, he heard a voice screaming in his ear. It must have been screaming because the blood pounding in his ears was deafening at this point and screaming had to be the only way Dex could be heard.

And then a small bubble of fresh air slipped down his throat. He had no idea how it got in through the vice squeezing his windpipe, but he welcomed it, using its minute amount of sustenance to force his brain to begin playing his Mario Brothers video game in his mind. Using every ounce of willpower to forget the visions that had set him off in the first place, he played through the first level of the game, focusing only on what move came next.

Dex was sure his friend was dying on his kitchen floor. As he got a firm hold on Jack's panicked movements, he asked over and over what was wrong, what he could do, what was happening, "Calm down! Jack! Jack," sure that if Jack did indeed ever get back to normal, he'd at least be deaf in his left ear from the screaming he was doing at him.

For some reason, this thought relaxed him just enough to make him stop yelling, bringing his tone back to just below ear-drum puncturing, "Son of a bitch, if you die in my kitchen, I'm gonna be so pissed I'll find a way to come haunt you in the afterlife. I eat grilled cheese sandwiches in here, for God's sake!" He had absolutely no idea where the grilled cheese part came from, but he didn't care, realizing that just after he said it, Jack began to get some color back in his cheeks.

Jack, as he continued to play the video game in his head, suddenly heard mention of grilled cheese sandwiches. Instantly, he also realized he was moving air again. A very tiny amount, mind you, but honest to God air was rushing into his lungs. He stopped his chest scraping, bringing his floating limbs back under control, feeling for the first time the steel grip of Dex, who was an inch from him, if that, looking whiter than even the crayons in Sam's coloring box. Reaching up, he put his hands on his friend's upper arms, steadying his jelly-like legs, "Grilled cheese?"

Dex gave him a bone crushing hug, then shoved him backwards, "Don't do that shit again, do you fucking hear me?" Stumbling backward, Jack ran into the wall, gladly leaning on it, something firm and steady in his wavering world. Dex glared at him for another few seconds, then his eyes got glassy, the tears pooling but never falling, "Please don't do that again."

Taking in a few more deep breaths and nearly singing praise after each one, he gasped out, "It's not like I ... do it on purpose."

After Dex pulled out a kitchen chair and dropped into it, "What the hell happened? And if you tell me you don't know, then you're an asshole, plain and simple."

Jack moved slowly to one of the other kitchen chairs, settling in before dropping his head to the table, enjoying the cold feeling of the wood against his cheek and the faint, sweet smell of 15 years of spilled syrup, "I looked them up and I think I'm having panic attacks ... but I've never had one this bad before." Knowing there was no turning back now, he took a few more deep breaths to try to slow his still racing heart, "I'm more fucked up than you can imagine."

First, Dex blew his nose on a napkin, then handed another to Jack, "You're getting snot all over the table, dude." Once Jack had cleaned up a little, head remaining down however, "And you are not more fucked up than I can imagine. You have no idea the capacity for my imagination, so it's best to just not go there at all." Crossing his arms on the tabletop, he rested his chin, now nearly eye level with Jack, "But something's wrong, man, really wrong and if you don't tell somebody, I'm gonna have to and I hate ratting on people. I mean, seriously hate it."

"You'd rat me out?"

"Damn rightly hell yeah. Especially since both you and Emily seem bent on giving me a heart attack or a stroke or something, scaring the shit out of me every chance you get." Narrowing his eyes at his friend, who paid attention carefully, "I function better as the crazy sidekick, but in rare and necessary cases, I will play my part as the psycho-shrink of our messed up little gang so," tilting his head to one side, "unless you think you'll do that again," waving absently behind him into the kitchen, "talk."

And he did, half his brain keeping him breathing and the other half dumping mental baggage on his best friend.

...

Tracking Jack's progress from front door to kitchen sink to bathroom and, finally, quietly up the stairs, she was about to get up when she saw his shadow fill her doorway. Not saying a word, he came next to the bed, then, lifting the covers some, slid in beside her. "I apologized to Tim a minute ago and now it's your turn." Wrapping his arm around her waist, he whispered, "I'm sorry."

"It's okay. Where did you go?"

"I ended up at Dex's so you weren't really lying after all. He told me to stop being a dumbass and get some help because otherwise you were gonna wake up and realize I was, and I quote, 'not worthy of all the Emily awesomeness and Dexter sidekickness'." Running one of his stocking feet up against her bare one, "And no, it's not okay. I should have stayed and apologized to both of you. Instead I leave you on the floor and run away like some stupid kid." His face scrunched up tight, "Why don't you hate me yet?"

"I don't think I could ever hate you." As she ran her fingers over his cheeks and nose, his face lost some of its pinched look and he opened his eyes again, "I don't think I'd even know how to begin to hate you." With a deep breath, "But I do need you to talk to someone. Please?"

As he nodded, her lips met his, her hand sliding under his shirt and up his chest. His hand did the same and, soon, her tank top was on the floor and Jack was nudging the door shut with his toe. Kissing turned to groping, which turned quickly to frantic clothing removal. It was right before they were completely naked, however, that Jack suddenly stopped, "You hear something?"

Emily froze and whispered, "No."

Listening hard, both heard Sam call out for his mother. With a mumbled, "Shit," Jack was off her quick as lightning and redressed in seconds. Pulling the door open, he sprinted down the hall and back into his room just as his parent's bedroom door opened.

Emily immediately laid down and pulled the covers up tight, waiting until the hallway was clear to try to reassemble her clothes under the covers. Once she was dressed, she went down the hallway and looked in. Will was just tucking Sam back in and Jack, sitting on his bed, looked incredibly guilty.

Will, once he'd kissed Sam goodnight, motioned for Jack to follow him. Passing Emily, he made the same gesture and they both trailed after him back to Emily's room.

Once there, Will turned to them both, "Sam said he had a nightmare and when he woke up you weren't there. He thought whatever he'd dreamt about had gotten you." Giving his son a critical look, "It's almost one. Why are you still dressed? Where were you?"

With the barest of glances at Emily, "I needed to talk, so I came in here to see if Em was awake."

Studying them both intently, Will took a deep breath, "What was so important that you needed to talk to her this late?"

"Can we do this in the morning, Dad? Please?"

"Jack."

The anger suddenly bubbled up from nowhere, "I'll talk to you tomorrow, okay? Can't I just hang out with my girlfriend once in awhile? It's not like we're ever alone in this place."

Will, who wasn't as shocked by his son's outburst as he should have been, stood speechless for a moment before, "Tomorrow. You talk to me tomorrow, but you apologize right now."

"Why?"

"Because I'm this close to grabbing you by the ear and carting you downstairs for a nice long talk that won't go anywhere near as smooth and quiet as this one."

Emily put her hand on Jack's arm and her touch calmed him immediately. Shutting his eyes, "I'm sorry. I just ... I really do need to talk to you ... just not now. Please?"

Having a sudden and vivid flashback to the conversation in the bathroom a few months earlier, "Okay. Just get to bed now and I'll find you in the morning."

Will stood waiting for Jack to leave the room ahead of him, but instead of walking towards the door, he turned towards Emily, putting his hands on the sides of her head and kissing her lightly, "I love you. Things'll be better tomorrow."

Nodding as she moved her hands to his face, she traced his eyebrows slowly, "I love you, too."

With that, Jack turned and brushed past his dad, heading quietly down the hall, back into his room.

Chapter 27

Emily was up and dressed with the sun. She finished the last of her weekend homework and had already put the final touches on her project for art class. Her growling stomach sent her downstairs and the makeshift breakfast she made only fueled her restlessness.

She could hear Tim moving in his room and, not in the mood for people, she went outside quietly and found Jack sitting on the back patio, "Hey. What're you doing out here?"

"I've been out here since the sun came up. Didn't sleep much last night."

Sitting next to him, she wrapped her arms around her pulled up knees, "Do you know what you're gonna say to your dad?"

Shaking his head, "Not a clue. How do you tell your dad that you're failing out of school, you've been lying for months and oh, by the way, even though you didn't mean it, you feel this tremendously horrible weight of having killed someone?"

"Just like that." Leaning towards him, she bumped his shoulder, "Everything's gonna be fine, remember?"

Turning his head, he kissed her ear and whispered, "Will you stay with me?"

"Of course."

With that, they sat in quiet until a voice drifted over from the open doorwall, "Jack?"

Without looking in his direction, "Yeah, Dad?"

"Ready to talk?"

Nodding, he finally met his dad's gaze, "Is out here okay?"

Elizabeth was there with him, "Let me just warn the kids to keep the door shut."

Will came out, but kept silent, waiting for Elizabeth before saying anything. Jack, in those few moments, turned to Emily, "Regardless of what me and my stupid brain have been acting like these last few months, I'd do it all over again. Don't ever forget that."

Her heart ached for him as she kissed first the tip of his nose, then his chin, finally landing on his lower lip for just a second, "You saved me. I will most definitely never forget that."

Both his parents and Emily kept quiet, listening intently and nodding occasionally, taking Jack's confessions in stride … until, "And yesterday, I think I had a panic attack at Dex's house. Actually, I've been having smaller ones for a while, but yesterday's scared the hell out of both of us and Dex made me promise to tell you about them."

Will and Elizabeth exchanged a look that no one could have missed and Emily, who hadn't known either, "Why didn't you tell me?"

"I figured I could get through them and eventually they would stop, but that last one," shaking his head and feeling his throat constrict at the thought, he took a few deep breaths, "I think I'm gonna need some help with that."

Emily squeezed his hand in hers and Will scooted forward in his chair, elbows on knees, "I had attacks like that for years, from when I met your mom up until about the time Dave was born."

It was Jack's turn to look surprised, "Seriously? How did you get through them? Why did they stop?"

"Slow down." Will sent a small smile his way, "Your mom used to make me tell her the contents of the refrigerator, shelf by shelf, to get my mind off my fears." Nudging his wife with his shoulder, "And it was tough going there for a while, but your mom finally figured out why I was having them."

Jack mirrored his father, elbows on knees, "What was it?"

"I feared that one day I'd end up beating her or any of you kids senseless, like my father did. Deep down, I knew I'd never do that, but deep down understanding sometimes doesn't win over sheer and completely absurd panic. My fears would get the better of me, usually when I was annoyed with one of you guys or if your mom and I had a fight, and, to put it bluntly, all hell would break loose."

"So I'm gonna have to wait ten years before I can not feel like I'm having a heart attack? 'Cause that's not comforting … not at all."

This time it was Elizabeth who leaned forward, putting her hand lightly on her son's knee, "Before, neither your dad nor I had decent insurance, but we do now. So, no, you will not have to suffer for the next ten years. We'll find you someone to talk to and go from there, all right?"

Jack nodded, then, involuntary tears flooded his eyes, dropping down his cheeks and off his chin before he could swipe them away, "I'm sorry." His voice cracked, "I didn't mean to let it get this far."

Tears in her own eyes, Elizabeth stood, then crouched in front of her son, gesturing him to lean forward for a hug, "We all let things go too far from time to time." By now, she was talking into the top of his head, "But now, we can help you and, honey, that's the most important thing in the world."

Once Elizabeth let him go, squeezing him tightly before sitting back down beside her husband, Will asked, "Is there anything else? Anything at all?"

Already exhausted from his confession, Jack shook his head, "Not that I can think of at the moment." Rubbing the last of his tears away, "But who knows what the hell will pop up next." Simultaneously shaking his head and making a 'blarhhh' sound, "For right now, though, I'm hungry."

"Aren't you always?" Elizabeth stood up first, pulling Will up beside her, "We'll talk more later, okay, but I think you've had enough for now and the boys are probably destroying my kitchen as we speak trying to make the tallest stack of pancakes or seeing how high the flames can get when you light the batter of fire."

Will smiled, "I'd bet at least a foot."

"We'll be in in a minute." Jack watched them return to the house before he shifted his gaze to Emily, "What's wrong?"

Coming out of her cloudy look, "What do you mean?"

"I mean, what's wrong? You're suddenly too quiet, even for you." His stomach tightened, "Are you mad I didn't tell you about my panicking?"

Pulling him forward by the collar of his shirt, she rested her forehead against his, "I'm not mad. I'm just completely confused why you love me enough to not be mad at me for causing this mess in the first place."

He gave her an honest-to-God, Jack-bright grin, "I am so totally keeping you forever."

...

After breakfast, Jack carried one last pancake taco with him as he made his way out to the furthest hammock, Emily in hand. Sharing it with her as they walked, he finished the last bite just as they reached their destination, "So, feel like relaxing in the hammock?"

Feeling like she hadn't slept for a week, she nodded, "Yes, please."

"Good 'cause I'm gonna fall down in about 15 seconds." Helping her in, he wrapped his arms around her, snuggling her under his chin, "Wake me tomorrow."

They heard the screen door open and, within seconds, the yard was filled with the four younger boys racing around, happy for warm weather, soccer balls and paper airplanes. They seemed to keep it down to a dull roar, however, and with a last kiss to Jack's cheek, both slept.

Tim wandered out soon after the other boys, eating the last pancake as he sat down on the picnic table, sketch pad in hand, determined to kill at least an hour or two before having to go to graduation rehearsal later on. It didn't take long before the back gate opened and he grinned, knowing it was Sarah coming through.

Settling herself beside him, she looked from the drawing to the hammock and back to the drawing, "Will you ever love me the way Jack loves her?"

Digging in his pocket, he pulled out something and handed it to her, "I think this about covers it."

Returning to the drawing, he watched out of the corner of his eye as the look of confusion turned to amazement, "What is this?"

"It's my acceptance letter to Randolph. I decided it might be a good idea if I stayed around here to go to school. And, you know, it'll be easier to ask you to marry me eventually if I'm only a few miles from you as opposed to several thousand."

The surprised look on her face was priceless, "You … you want to marry me?"

Still drawing as if nothing had changed between them in the last eight seconds, "Figured I might as well, seeing how I fell in love with you the moment I saw you. One should never fight fate."

Her hand turned his face away from the paper, "Well, I'll be sure to answer my phone that day."

"But will you answer my question?"

As she leaned in to kiss him, "This should about cover it."

...

Hanging up the phone, Elizabeth turned towards Will, grinning, "They'll be here in time for Tim's graduation party."

He hugged her tightly from behind, "So, do we tell them everything now or do we wait?"

Elizabeth looked out the window at the backyard full of her children, all seven of them. "We've had enough chaos for one day. We'll wait until tomorrow to raise some hell." Still smiling, "Do you think they'll be okay?"

Resting his chin on her shoulder as he followed her gaze, "I think they'll be just fine."

For updates on Jack and Emily and other Orange Books

Like us on Facebook

www.facebook.com/orangepublishing